Bulldog Drummond

Sapper was the pen name of Herman Cyril McNeile, chosen because he served for some years with the Royal Engineers, who are popularly known as 'sappers'. His most famous character – the formidable Bulldog Drummond – inspired a hugely popular series, and several films, making Sapper one of the most popular novelists of his generation. For more information, turn to the Case Notes section at the end of the book.

Robert Giddings is a literary critic and broadcaster who regularly writes for publications including the *Tribune* and the *Dickensian*. He is the author of *A Student's Guide to Charles Dickens*, and co-author with Keith Selby of *The Classic Serial on Television and Radio*.

Other titles in the Crime Classics series:

Bulldog Drummond

The Adventures of a
Demobilised Officer
Who Found Peace Dull

Sapper

Atlantic Books
LONDON

First published in Great Britain in 1920.

This paperback Crime Classics edition published by Atlantic Books in 2008.

Case Notes copyright © Robert Giddings, 2008

10 9 8 7 6 5 4 3 2 1

A CIP catalogue record for this book is available from the British Library.

978 1 84354 851 5

Series Consultant: Robert Giddings

Designed by Lucie Ewin

Printed in Great Britain by Clays Ltd, St Ives plc

Atlantic Books
An imprint of Grove Atlantic Ltd
Ormond House
26–27 Boswell Street
London WC1N 3JZ

www.atlantic-books.co.uk

Bulldog Drummond

The Adventures of a
Demobilised Officer
Who Found Peace Dull

Contents

Prologue

IN the month of December, 1918, and on the very day that a British Cavalry Division marched into Cologne, with flags flying and bands playing as the conquerors of a beaten nation, the manager of the Hôtel Nationale in Berne received a letter. Its contents appeared to puzzle him somewhat, for having read it twice he rang the bell on his desk to summon his secretary. Almost immediately the door opened, and a young French girl came into the room.

'Monsieur rang?' She stood in front of the manager's desk, awaiting instructions.

'Have we ever had staying in the hotel a man called le Comte de Guy?' He leaned back in his chair and looked at her through his pince-nez.

The secretary thought for a moment and then shook her head.

'Not as far as I can remember,' she said.

'Do we know anything about him? Has he ever fed here, or taken a private room?'

Again the secretary shook her head.

'Not that I know of.'

The manager handed her the letter, and waited in silence until she had read it.

'It seems on the face of it a peculiar request from an unknown man,' he remarked as she laid it down.

'A dinner of four covers; no expense to be spared. Wines specified, and if not in the hotel to be obtained. A private room at half-past seven sharp. Guests to ask for room X.'

The secretary nodded in agreement.

'It can hardly be a hoax,' she remarked after a short silence.

'No.' The manager tapped his teeth with his pen thoughtfully. 'But if by any chance it was, it would prove an expensive one for us. I wish I could think who this Comte de Guy is.'

'He sounds like a Frenchman,' she answered. Then after a pause: 'I suppose you'll have to take it seriously?'

'I must.' He took off his pince-nez and laid them on the desk in front of him. 'Would you send the *maître d'hôtel* to me at once?'

Whatever may have been the manager's misgivings, they were certainly not shared by the head waiter as he left the office after receiving his instructions. War and short rations had not been conducive to any particularly lucrative business in his sphere; and the whole sound of the proposed entertainment seemed to him to contain considerable promise. Moreover, he was a man who loved his work, and a free hand over preparing a dinner was a joy in itself. Undoubtedly he personally would meet the three guests and the mysterious Comte de Guy; he personally would see that they had nothing to complain of in the matter of the service at dinner. . .

And so at about twenty minutes past seven the *maître d'hôtel* was hovering round the hall-porter, the manager was hovering round the *maître d'hôtel,* and the secretary was hovering round both. At five-and-twenty minutes past, the first guest arrived. . .

He was a peculiar-looking man, in a big fur coat, reminding one irresistibly of a cod-fish.

'I wish to be taken to Room X.' The French secretary stiffened involuntarily as the *maître d'hôtel* stepped obsequiously forward. Cosmopolitan as the hotel was, even now she could never hear German spoken without an inward shudder of disgust.

'A Boche,' she murmured in disgust to the manager as the first arrival disappeared through the swing doors at the end of the lounge. It is to be regretted that that worthy man was more occupied in shaking himself by the hand, at the proof that the letter was *bona fide,* than in any meditation on the guest's nationality.

Almost immediately afterwards the second and third members of the party arrived. They did not come together, and what seemed peculiar to the manager was that they were evidently strangers to one another.

The leading one – a tall gaunt man with a ragged beard and a pair of piercing eyes – asked in a nasal and by no means an inaudible tone for Room X. As he spoke a little fat man who was standing just behind him started perceptibly, and shot a bird-like glance at the speaker.

Then in execrable French he too asked for Room X.

'He's not French,' said the secretary excitedly to the manager as the ill-assorted pair were led out of the lounge by the head waiter. 'That last one was another Boche.'

The manager thoughtfully twirled his pince-nez between his fingers.

'Two Germans and an American.' He looked a little apprehensive. 'Let us hope the dinner will appease everybody. Otherwise—'

But whatever fears he might have entertained with regard to the furniture in Room X, they were not destined to be uttered. Even as he spoke the door again swung open, and a man with a thick white scarf around his neck, so pulled up as almost completely to cover his face, came in. A soft hat was pulled down well over his ears, and all that the manager could swear to as regards the new-comer's appearance was a pair of deep-set, steel-grey eyes which seemed to bore through him.

'You got my letter this morning?'

'*M'sieur le Comte de Guy?*' The manager bowed deferentially and rubbed his hands together. 'Everything is ready, and your three guests have arrived.'

'Good. I will go to the room at once.'

The *maître d'hôtel* stepped forward to relieve him of his coat, but the Count waved him away.

3

'I will remove it later,' he remarked shortly. 'Take me to the room.'

As he followed his guide his eyes swept round the lounge. Save for two or three elderly women of doubtful nationality, and a man in the American Red Cross, the place was deserted; and as he passed through the swing doors he turned to the head waiter.

'Business good?' he asked.

No – business decidedly was not good. The waiter was voluble. Business had never been so poor in the memory of man. . . But it was to be hoped that the dinner would be to Monsieur le Comte's liking. . . He personally had superintended it. . . Also the wines.

'If everything is to my satisfaction you will not regret it,' said the Count tersely. 'But remember one thing. After the coffee has been brought in, I do not wish to be disturbed under any circumstances whatever.' The head waiter paused as he came to a door, and the Count repeated the last few words.

'Under no circumstances whatever.'

'*Mais certainement, Monsieur le Comte. . .* I, personally, will see to it. . .'

As he spoke he flung open the door and the Count entered. It cannot be said that the atmosphere of the room was congenial. The three occupants were regarding one another in hostile silence, and as the Count entered, they, with one accord, transferred their suspicious glances to him.

For a moment he stood motionless, while he looked at each one in turn. Then he stepped forward. . .

'Good evening, gentlemen' – he still spoke in French – 'I am honoured at your presence.' He turned to the head waiter. 'Let dinner be served in five minutes exactly.'

With a bow the man left the room, and the door closed.'

'During that five minutes, gentlemen, I propose to introduce myself to you, and you to one another.' As he spoke he divested himself of his coat and hat. 'The business which I

4

wish to discuss we will postpone, with your permission, till after the coffee, when we shall be undisturbed.'

In silence the three guests waited while he unwound the thick white muffler; then, with undisguised curiosity, they studied their host. In appearance he was striking. He had a short dark beard, and in profile his face was aquiline and stern. The eyes, which had so impressed the manager, seemed now to be a cold grey-blue; the thick brown hair, flecked slightly with grey, was brushed back from a broad forehead. His hands were large and white; not effeminate, but capable and determined: the hands of a man who knew what he wanted, knew how to get it and got it. To even the most superficial observer the giver of the feast was a man of power: a man capable of forming instant decisions and of carrying them through. . .

And if so much was obvious to the superficial observer, it was more than obvious to the three men who stood by the fire watching him. They were what they were simply owing to the fact that they were not superficial servers of humanity; and each one of them, as he watched his host, realized that he was in the presence of a great man. It was enough: great men do not send fool invitations to dinner to men of international repute. It mattered not what form his greatness took – there was money in greatness, big money. And money was their life. . .

The count advanced first to the American.

'Mr Hocking, I believe,' he remarked in English, holding out his hand. 'I am glad you managed to come.'

The American shook the proffered hand, while the two Germans looked at him with sudden interest. As the man at the head of the great American cotton trust, worth more in millions than he could count, he was entitled to their respect. . .

'That's me, Count,' returned the millionaire in his nasal twang. 'I am interested to know to what I am indebted for this invitation.'

5

'All in good time, Mr Hocking,' smiled the host. 'I have hopes that the dinner will fill in that time satisfactorily.'

He turned to the taller of the two Germans, who without his coat seemed more like a cod-fish than ever.

'Herr Steinemann, is it not?' This time he spoke in German.

The man whose interest in German coal was hardly less well known than Hocking's in cotton, bowed stiffly.

'And Herr von Gratz?' The Count turned to the last member of the party and shook hands. Though less well known than either of the other two in the realms of international finance, von Gratz's name in the steel trade of Central Europe was one to conjure with.

'Well, gentlemen,' said the Count, 'before we sit down to dinner, I may perhaps be permitted to say a few words of introduction. The nations of the world have recently been engaged in a performance of unrivalled stupidity. As far as one can tell that performance is now over. The last thing I wish to do is to discuss the war – except in so far as it concerns our meeting here to-night. Mr Hocking is an American, you two gentlemen are Germans. I' – the Count smiled slightly – 'have no nationality. Or rather, shall I say, I have every nationality. Completely cosmopolitan. . . Gentlemen, the war was waged by idiots, and when idiots get busy on a large scale, it is time for clever men to step in. . . That is the *raison d'être* for this little dinner. . . I claim that we four men are sufficiently international to be able to disregard any stupid and petty feelings about this country and that country, and to regard the world outlook at the present moment from one point of view and one point of view only – our own.'

The gaunt American gave a hoarse chuckle.

'It will be my object after dinner,' continued the Count, 'to try and prove to you that we have a common point of view. Until then – shall we merely concentrate on a pious hope that the Hôtel Nationale will not poison us with their food?'

'I guess,' remarked the American, 'that you've got a pretty healthy command of languages, Count.'

'I speak four fluently – French, German, English, and Spanish,' returned the other. 'In addition, I can make myself understood in Russia, Japan, China, the Balkan States, and – America.'

His smile, as he spoke, robbed the words of any suspicion of offence. The next moment the head waiter opened the door, and the four men sat down to dine.

It must be admitted that the average hostess, desirous of making a dinner a success, would have been filled with secret dismay at the general atmosphere in the room. The American, in accumulating his millions, had also accumulated a digestion of such an exotic and tender character, that dry rusks and Vichy water were the limit of his capacity.

Herr Steinemann was of the common order of German, to whom food is sacred. He ate and drank enormously, and evidently considered that nothing further was required of him.

Von Gratz did his best to keep his end up, but as he was apparently in a chronic condition of fear that the gaunt American would assault him with violence, he cannot be said to have contributed much to the gaiety of the meal.

And so to the host must be given the credit that the dinner was a success. Without appearing to monopolise the conversation he talked ceaselessly and well. More – he talked brilliantly. There seemed to be no corner of the globe with which he had not a nodding acquaintance at least; while with most places he was as familiar as a Londoner with Piccadilly Circus. But to even the most brilliant of conversationalists the strain of talking to a hypochondriacal American and two Germans – one greedy and the other frightened – is considerable; and the Count heaved an inward sigh of relief when the coffee had been handed round and the door closed behind the waiter. From now on the topic was an easy one – one where no effort on his part would be necessary to hold his audience. It was the topic of money – the common bond of his three guests. And yet, as he carefully cut the end of his cigar, and realized that the eyes of the other three were fixed on him expectantly, he knew that the hardest part of the evening was in front of him. Big financiers, in common with all other people, are fonder of having money put into their pockets than of taking it out. And that was the very thing the Count proposed they should do – in large quantities. . .

'Gentlemen,' he remarked, when his cigar was going to his satisfaction, 'we are all men of business. I do not propose therefore to beat about the bush over the matter which I have to put before you, but to come to the point at once. I said before dinner that I considered we were sufficiently big to exclude any small arbitrary national distinctions from our minds. As men whose interests are international, such things are beneath us. I wish now to slightly qualify that remark.' He turned to the American on his right, who with his eyes half closed was thoughtfully picking his teeth. 'At this stage, sir, I address myself particularly to you.'

'Go right ahead,' drawled Mr Hocking.

'I do not wish to touch on the war – or its result; but though the Central Powers have been beaten by America and France and England, I think I can speak for you two gentlemen' – he bowed to the two Germans – 'when I say that it is neither France nor America with whom they desire another round. England is Germany's main enemy; she always has been, she always will be.'

Both Germans grunted assent, and the American's eyes closed a little more.

'I have reason to believe, Mr Hocking, that you personally do not love the English?'

'I guess I don't see what my private feelings have got to do with it. But if it's of any interest to the company, you are correct in your belief.'

'Good.' The Count nodded his head as if satisfied. 'I take it, then, that you would not be averse to seeing England down and out.'

8

'Wal,' remarked the American, 'you can assume anything you feel like. Let's get to the showdown.'

Once again the Count nodded his head; then he turned to the two Germans.

'Now you two gentlemen must admit that your plans have miscarried somewhat. It was no part of your original programme that the British Army should occupy Cologne. . .'

'The war was the act of a fool,' snarled Herr Steinemann. 'In a few years more of peace we should have beaten those swine. . .'

'And now – they have beaten you.' The Count smiled slightly. 'Let us admit that the war was the act of a fool if you like, but as men of business we can only deal with the result. . . the result, gentlemen, as it concerns *us*. Both you gentlemen are sufficiently patriotic to resent the presence of that army at Cologne, I have no doubt. And you, Mr Hocking, have no love on personal grounds for the English. . . But I am not proposing to appeal to financiers of your reputation on such grounds as those to support my scheme. . . It is enough that your personal predilections run with and not against what I am about to put before you – the defeat of England. . . a defeat more utter and complete than if she had lost the war. . .'

His voice sank a little, and instinctively his three listeners drew closer.

'Don't think that I am proposing this through motives of revenge merely. We are business men, and revenge is only worth our while if it pays. This will pay. I can give you no figures, but we are not of the type who deal in thousands, or even hundreds of thousands. There is a force in England which, if it be harnessed and led properly, will result in millions coming to you. . . It is present now in every nation – fettered, inarticulate, un-co-ordinated. . . It is partly the result of the war – the war that the idiots have waged. . . Harness that force, gentlemen, co-ordinate it, and use it for your own ends. . . That is my proposal. Not only will you humble that cursed country to the dirt, but you will taste of power such as few men have tasted before. . .' The Count stood up, his eyes blazing. 'And I – I will do it for you.'

He resumed his seat, and his left hand, slipping off the table, beat a tattoo on his knee.

'This is our opportunity – the opportunity of clever men. I have not got the money necessary: you have. . .' He leaned forward in his chair, and glanced at the intent faces of his audience. Then he began to speak. . .

Ten minutes later he pushed back his chair.

'There is my proposal, gentlemen, in a nutshell. Unforeseen developments will doubtless occur; I have spent my life overcoming the unexpected. What is your answer?'

He rose and stood with his back to them by the fire, and for several minutes no one spoke. Each man was busy with his own thoughts, and showed it in his own particular way. The American, his eyes shut, rolled his toothpick backwards and forwards in his mouth slowly and methodically; Steinemann stared at the fire, breathing heavily after the exertion of dinner: von Gratz walked up and down – his hands behind his back – whistling under his breath. Only the Comte de Guy stared unconcernedly at the fire, as if indifferent to the result of their thoughts. In his attitude at that moment he gave a true expression to his attitude on life. Accustomed to play with great stakes, he had just dealt the cards for the most gigantic gamble of his life. . . What matter to the three men, who were looking at the hands he had given them, that only a master criminal could have conceived such a game? The only question which occupied their minds was whether he could carry it through. And on that point they had only their judgment of his personality to rely on.

Suddenly the American removed the toothpick from his mouth, and stretched out his legs.

'There is a question which occurs to me, Count, before I make up my mind on the matter. I guess you've got us sized up to the last button; you know who we are, what we're worth, and all about us. Are you disposed to be a little more communicative about yourself? If we agree to come in on this hand, it's going to cost big money. The handling of that money is with you. Wal – who are you?'

Von Gratz paused in his restless pacing and nodded his head in agreement; even Steinemann, with a great effort, raised his eyes to the Count's face as he turned and faced them. . .

'A very fair question, gentlemen, and yet one which I regret I am unable to answer. I would not insult your intelligence by giving you the fictitious address of – a fictitious Count. Enough that I am a man whose livelihood lies in other people's pockets. As you say, Mr Hocking, it is going to cost big money; but compared to the results the costs will be a flea-bite. . . Do I look – and you are all of you used to judging men – do I look the type who would steal the baby's money-box which lay on the mantelpiece, when the pearls could be had for opening the safe?. . . You will have to trust me, even as I shall have to trust you. . . You will have to trust me not to divert the money which you give me as working expenses into my own pocket. . . I shall have to trust you to pay me when the job is finished. . .'

'And that payment will be – how much?' Steinemann's guttural voice broke the silence.

'One million pounds sterling – to be split up between you in any proportion you may decide, and to be paid within one month of the completion of my work. After that the matter will pass into your hands. . .and may you leave that cursed country grovelling in the dirt. . .' His eyes glowed with a fierce, vindictive fury; and then, as if replacing a mask which had slipped for a moment, the Count was once again the suave, courteous host. He had stated his terms frankly and without haggling: stated them as one big man states them to another of the same kidney, to whom time is money and indecision or beating about the bush anathema.

'Take them or leave them.' So much had he said in effect, if not in actual words, and not one of his audience but was far too used to men and matters to have dreamed of suggesting any compromise. All or nothing: and no doctrine could have appealed more to the three men in whose hands lay the decision. . .

'Perhaps, Count, you would be good enough to leave us for a few minutes.' Von Gratz was speaking. 'The decision is a big one, and. . .'

'Why, certainly, gentlemen.' The Count moved towards the door. 'I will return in ten minutes. By that time you will have decided – one way or the other.'

Once in the lounge he sat down and lit a cigarette. The hotel was deserted save for one fat woman asleep in a chair opposite, and the Count gave himself up to thought. Genius that he was in the reading of men's minds, he felt that he knew the result of that ten minutes' deliberation. . . And then. . . What then?. . . In his imagination he saw his plans growing and spreading, his tentacles reaching into every corner of a great people – until, at last, everything was ready. He saw himself supreme in power, glutted with it – a king, an autocrat, who had only to lift his finger to plunge his kingdom into destruction and annihilation. . . And when he had done it, and the country he hated was in ruins, then he could claim his million and enjoy it as a great man should enjoy a great reward. . . Thus for the space of ten minutes did the Count see visions and dream dreams. That the force he proposed to tamper with was a dangerous force disturbed him not at all: he was a dangerous man. That his scheme would bring ruin, perhaps death, to thousands of innocent men and women, caused him no qualm: he was a supreme egoist. All that appealed to him was that he had seen the opportunity that existed, and that he had the nerve and the brain to turn that opportunity to his own advantage. Only the necessary money was lacking. . .and. . . With a quick movement he pulled out his watch. They had had their ten minutes. . . the matter was settled, the die was cast. . .

He rose and walked across the lounge. At the swing doors was the head waiter, bowing obsequiously. . .

It was to be hoped that the dinner had been to the liking of Monsieur le Comte. . .the wines all that he could wish. . .that he had been comfortable and would return again. . .

'That is improbable.' The Count took out his pocket-book. 'But one never knows; perhaps I shall.' He gave the waiter a note. 'Let my bill be prepared at once, and given to me as I pass through the hall.'

Apparently without a care in the world the Count passed down the passage to his private room, while the head waiter regarded complacently the unusual appearance of an English five-pound note.

For an appreciable moment the Count paused by the door, and a faint smile came to his lips. Then he opened it, and passed into the room. . .

The American was still chewing his toothpick; Steinemann was still breathing hard. Only von Gratz had changed his occupation, and he was sitting at the table smoking a long thin cigar. The Count closed the door, and walked over to the fireplace. . .

'Well, gentlemen,' he said quietly, 'what have you decided?'

It was the American who answered.

'It goes. With one amendment. The money is too big for three of us: there must be a fourth. That will be a quarter of a million each.'

The Count bowed.

'Yep,' said the American shortly. 'These two gentlemen agree with me that it should be another of my countrymen – so that we get equal numbers. The man we have decided on is coming to England in a few weeks – Hiram C. Potts. If you get him in, you can count us in too. If not, the deal's off.'

The Count nodded, and if he felt any annoyance at this unexpected development he showed no sign of it on his face.

'I know Mr Potts,' he answered quietly. 'Your big shipping man, isn't he? I agree to your reservation.'

'Good,' said the American. 'Let's discuss some details.'

Without a trace of emotion on his face the Count drew up a chair to the table. It was only when he sat down that he started to play a tattoo on his knee with his left hand.

Half an hour later he entered his luxurious suite of rooms at the Hotel Magnificent.

A girl, who had been lying by the fire reading a French novel, looked up at the sound of the door. She did not speak, for the look on his face told her all she wanted to know.

He crossed to the sofa and smiled down at her.

'Successful. . .on our own terms. To-morrow, Irma, the Comte de Guy dies, and Carl Peterson and his daughter leave for England. A country gentleman, I think, is Carl Peterson. He might keep hens and possibly pigs.'

The girl on the sofa rose, yawning.

'*Mon Dieu*! What a prospect! Pigs and hens – and in England! How long is it going to take?'

The Count looked thoughtfully into the fire.

'Perhaps a year – perhaps six months. . . It is in the lap of the gods. . .'

Chapter 1

In Which He Takes Tea at the Carlton and Is Surprised

I

CAPTAIN HUGH DRUMMOND, D.S.O., M.C., late of His Majesty's Royal Loamshires, was whistling in his morning bath. Being by nature of a cheerful disposition, the symptom did not surprise his servant, late private of the same famous regiment, who was laying breakfast in an adjoining room.

After a while the whistling ceased, and the musical gurgle of escaping water announced that the concert was over. It was the signal for James Denny – the square-jawed ex-batman – to disappear into the back regions and get from his wife the kidneys and bacon which that most excellent woman had grilled to a turn. But on this particular morning the invariable routine was broken. James Denny seemed preoccupied, distrait.

Once or twice he scratched his head, and stared out of the window with a puzzled frown. And each time, after a brief survey of the other side of Half Moon Street, he turned back again to the breakfast table with a grin.

'What's you looking for, James Denny?' The irate voice of his wife at the door made him turn round guiltily. 'Them kidneys is ready and waiting these five minutes.'

Her eyes fell on the table, and she advanced into the room wiping her hands on her apron.

'Did you ever see such a bunch of letters?' she said.

'Forty-five,' returned her husband grimly, 'and more to come.' He picked up the newspaper lying beside the chair and opened it out.

'Them's the result of that,' he continued cryptically, indicating a paragraph with a square finger, and thrusting the paper under his wife's nose.

'Demobilised officer,' she read slowly, 'finding peace incredibly tedious, would welcome diversion. Legitimate, if possible; but crime, if of a comparatively humorous description, no objection. Excitement essential. Would be prepared to consider permanent job if suitably impressed by applicant for his services. Reply at once Box X10.'

She put down the paper on a chair and stared first at her husband and then at the rows of letters neatly arranged on the table.

'I calls it wicked,' she announced at length. 'Fair flying in the face of Providence. Crime, Denny – crime. Don't you get 'aving nothing to do with such mad pranks, my man, or you and me will be having words.' She shook an admonitory finger at him, and retired slowly to the kitchen. In the days of his youth, James Denny had been a bit wild, and there was a look in his eyes this morning – the suspicion of a glint – which recalled old memories.

A moment or two later Hugh Drummond came in. Slightly under six feet in height, he was broad in proportion. His best friend would not have called him good-looking, but he was the fortunate possessor of that cheerful type of ugliness which inspires immediate confidence in its owner. His nose had never quite recovered from the final year in the Public Schools Heavyweights; his mouth was not small. In fact, to be strictly accurate, only his eyes redeemed his face from being what is known in the vernacular as the Frozen Limit.

Deep-set and steady, with eyelashes that many a woman had envied, they showed the man for what he was – a sportsman and a gentleman. And the combination of the two is an unbeatable production.

He paused as he got to the table, and glanced at the rows of letters. His servant, pretending to busy himself at the other end of the room, was watching him surreptitiously, and noted the grin which slowly spread over Drummond's face as he picked up two or three and examined the envelopes.

'Who would have thought it, James?' he remarked at length. 'Great Scot! I shall have to get a partner.'

With disapproval showing in every line of her face, Mrs Denny entered the room, carrying the kidneys, and Drummond glanced at her with a smile.

'Good morning, Mrs Denny,' he said. 'Wherefore this worried look on your face? Has that reprobate James been misbehaving himself?'

The worthy woman snorted. 'He has not, sir – not yet, leastwise. And if so be that he does' – her eyes travelled up and down the back of the hapless Denny, who was quite unnecessarily pulling books off shelves and putting them back again – 'if so be that he does,' she continued grimly, 'him and me will have words – as I've told him already this morning.' She stalked from the room, after staring pointedly at the letters in Drummond's hand, and the two men looked at one another.

'It's that there reference to crime, sir, that's torn it,' said Denny in a hoarse whisper.

'Thinks I'm going to lead you astray, does she, James?'

Hugh helped himself to bacon. 'My dear fellow, she can think what she likes so long as she continues to grill bacon like this. Your wife is a treasure, James – a pearl among women; and you can tell her so with my love.' He was opening the first envelope, and suddenly he looked up with a twinkle in his eyes. 'Just to set her mind at rest,' he remarked gravely, 'you might tell her that, as far as I can see at present, I shall only undertake murder in exceptional cases.'

He propped the letter up against the toast rack and commenced his breakfast. 'Don't go, James.' With a slight frown he was studying the typewritten sheet.

'I'm certain to want your advice before long. Though not over this one. . . It does not appeal to me – not at all. To assist Messrs. Jones & Jones, whose business is to advance money on note of hand alone, to obtain fresh clients, is a form of amusement which leaves me cold. The waste paper basket, please, James. Tear the effusion up and we will pass on to the next.'

He looked at the mauve envelope doubtfully, and examined the postmark. 'Where is Pudlington, James? And one might almost ask – *why* is Pudlington? No town has any right to such an offensive name.' He glanced through the letter and shook his head. 'Tush! Tush! And the wife of the bank manager, too – the bank manager of Pudlington, James! Can you conceive of anything so dreadful? But I'm afraid Mrs Bank Manager is a puss – a distinct puss. It's when they get on the soul-mate stunt that the furniture begins to fly.'

Drummond tore up the letter and dropped the pieces into the basket beside him. Then he turned to his servant and handed him the remainder of the envelopes.

'Go through them, James, while I assault the kidneys, and pick two or three out for me. I see that you will have to become my secretary. No man could tackle that little bunch alone.'

'Do you want me to open them, sir?' asked Denny doubtfully.

'You've hit it, James – hit it in one. Classify them for me in groups. Criminal; sporting; amatory – that means of or pertaining to love; stupid and merely boring; and as a last resort, miscellaneous.' He stirred his coffee thoughtfully. 'I feel that as a first venture in our new career – ours, I said, James – love appeals to me irresistibly. Find me a damsel in distress; a beautiful girl, helpless in the clutches of knaves. Let me feel that I can fly to her succour, clad in my new grey suiting.'

He finished the last piece of bacon and pushed away his plate. 'Amongst all that mass of paper there must surely be one from a lovely maiden, James, at whose disposal I can place my rusty sword. Incidentally, what has become of the damned thing?'

'It's in the lumber room, sir – tied up with the old hum-brella and the niblick[1] you don't like.'

'Great heavens! Is it?' Drummond helped himself to marmalade. 'And to think that I once pictured myself skew-ering Huns with it. Do you think anybody would be mug enough to buy it, James?'

But that worthy was engrossed in a letter he had just opened, and apparently failed to hear the question. A per-plexed look was spreading over his face, and suddenly he sucked his teeth loudly. It was a sure sign that James was excited, and though Drummond had almost cured him of this distressing habit, he occasionally forgot himself in moments of stress.

His master glanced up quickly, and removed the letter from his hands. 'I'm surprised at you, James,' he remarked severely. 'A secretary should control itself. Don't forget that the perfect secretary is an it: an automatic machine – a thing incapable of feeling. . .'

He read the letter through rapidly, and then, turning back to the beginning, he read it slowly through again.

My dear Box X10 – I don't know whether your advertisement was a joke: I suppose it must have been. But I read it this morn-ing, and it's just possible, X10, just possible, that you mean it. And if you do, you're the man I want. I can offer you excitement and probably crime.

I'm up against it, X10, For a girl I've bitten off rather more than I can chew. I want help – badly. Will you come to the Carlton for tea to-morrow afternoon? I want to have a look at you and see if I think you are genuine. Wear a white flower in your buttonhole.

Drummond laid the letter down, and pulled out his ciga-rette-case. 'To-morrow, James,' he murmured. 'That is to-day – this very afternoon. Verily I believe that we have

[1] A niblick is a golfing term for an iron with a heavy, lofted head, used especially for playing out of bunkers.

impinged upon the goods.' He rose and stood looking out of the window thoughtfully. 'Go out, my trusty fellow, and buy me a daisy or a cauliflower or something white.'

'You think it's genuine, sir?' said James thoughtfully

His master blew out a cloud of smoke. 'I *know* it is,' he answered dreamily. 'Look at that writing; the decision in it – the character. She'll be medium height, and dark, with the sweetest little nose and mouth. Her colouring, James, will be—'

But James had discreetly left the room.

II

At four o'clock exactly Hugh Drummond stepped out of his two-seater at the Haymarket entrance to the Carlton. A white gardenia was in his buttonhole; his grey suit looked the last word in exclusive tailoring. For a few moments after entering the hotel he stood at the top of the stairs outside the dining-room, while his eyes travelled round the tables in the lounge below.

A brother-officer, evidently taking two country cousins round London, nodded resignedly; a woman at whose house he had danced several times smiled at him. But save for a courteous bow he took no notice; slowly and thoroughly he continued his search. It was early, of course, yet, and she might not have arrived, but he was taking no chances.

Suddenly his eyes ceased wandering, and remained fixed on a table at the far end of the lounge. Half hidden behind a plant a girl was seated alone, and for a moment she looked straight at him. Then, with the faintest suspicion of a smile, she turned away, and commenced drumming on the table with her fingers.

The table next to her was unoccupied, and Drummond made his way towards it and sat down. It was characteristic of the man that he did not hesitate; having once made up his mind to go through with a thing, he was in the habit of going and looking neither to the right hand nor to the left.

Which, incidentally, was how he got his D.S.O.; but that, as Kipling would say, is another story.

He felt not the slightest doubt in his mind that this was the girl who had written to him, and, having given an order to the waiter, he started to study her face as unobtrusively as possible. He could only see the profile, but that was quite sufficient to make him bless the moment when more as a jest than anything else he had sent his advertisement to the paper.

Her eyes, he could see, were very blue; and great masses of golden brown hair coiled over her ears, from under a small black hat. He glanced at her feet – being an old stager; she was perfectly shod. He glanced at her hands, and noted, with approval, the absence of any ring. Then he looked once more at her face, and found her eyes were fixed on him.

This time she did not look away. She seemed to think that it was her turn to conduct the examination, and Drummond turned to his tea while the scrutiny continued. He poured himself out a cup, and then fumbled in his waistcoat pocket. After a moment he found what he wanted, and taking out a card he propped it against the teapot so that the girl could see what was on it. In large block capitals he had written 'Box XIO.' Then he added milk and sugar and waited.

She spoke almost at once. 'You'll do, XIO,' she said, and he turned to her with a smile.

'It's very nice of you to say so,' he murmured. 'If I may, I will return the compliment. So will you.'

She frowned slightly. 'This isn't foolishness, you know. What I said in my letter is literally true.'

'Which makes the compliment even more returnable,' he answered. 'If I am to embark on a life of crime, I would sooner collaborate with you than – shall we say? – that earnest eater over there with the tomato in her hat.'

He waved vaguely at the lady in question and then held out his cigarette-case to the girl. 'Turkish on this side – Virginian on that,' he remarked. 'And as I appear satisfactory, will you tell me who I'm to murder?'

With the unlighted cigarette held in her fingers she stared at him gravely. 'I want you to tell me,' she said at length, and there was no trace of jesting in her voice, 'tell me, on your word of honour, whether that advertisement was *bona fide* or a joke.'

He answered her in the same vein. 'It started more or less as a joke. It may now be regarded as absolutely genuine.'

She nodded as if satisfied. 'Are you prepared to risk your life?'

Drummond's eyebrows went up and then he smiled.

'Granted that the inducement is sufficient,' he returned slowly, 'I think that I may say that I am.'

She nodded again. 'You won't be asked to do it in order to obtain a halfpenny bun,' she remarked. 'If you've a match, I would rather like a light.'

Drummond apologized. 'Our talk on trivialities engrossed me for the moment,' he murmured. He held the lighted match for her, and as he did so he saw that she was staring over his shoulder at someone behind his back.

'Don't look round,' she ordered, 'and tell me your name quickly.'

'Drummond – Captain Drummond, late of the Loamshires.' He leaned back in his chair, and lit a cigarette himself.

'And are you going to Henley this year?' Her voice was a shade louder than before.

'I don't know,' he answered casually. 'I may run down for a day possibly, but—'

'My dear Phyllis,' said a voice behind his back, 'this is a pleasant surprise. I had no idea that you were in London.'

A tall, clean-shaven man stopped beside the table, throwing a keen glance at Drummond.

'The world is full of such surprises, isn't it?' answered the girl lightly. 'I don't suppose you know Captain Drummond, do you? Mr Lakington – art connoisseur and – er – collector.'

The two men bowed slightly, and Mr Lakington smiled. 'I do not remember ever having heard my harmless pastimes more concisely described,' he remarked suavely. 'Are you interested in such matters?'

'Not very, I'm afraid,' answered Drummond. 'Just recently I have been rather too busy to pay much attention to art.'

The other man smiled again, and it struck Hugh that rarely, if ever, had he seen such a cold, merciless face.

'Of course, you've been in France,' Lakington murmured. 'Unfortunately a bad heart kept me on this side of the water. One regrets it in many ways – regrets it immensely. Sometimes I cannot help thinking how wonderful it must have been to be able to kill without fear of consequences. There is art in killing, Captain Drummond – profound art. And as you know, Phyllis,' he turned to the girl, 'I have always been greatly attracted by anything requiring the artistic touch'. He looked at his watch and sighed. 'Alas! I must tear myself away. Are you returning home this evening?'

The girl, who had been glancing round the restaurant, shrugged her shoulders. 'Probably,' she answered. 'I haven't quite decided. I might stop with Aunt Kate.'

'Fortunate Aunt Kate.' With a bow Lakington turned away, and through the glass Drummond watched him get his hat and stick from the cloakroom. Then he looked at the girl, and noticed that she had gone a little white.

'What's the matter, old thing?' he asked quickly. 'Are you feeling faint?'

She shook her head, and gradually the colour came back to her face. 'I'm quite all right,' she answered. 'It gave me rather a shock, that man finding us here.'

'On the face of it, it seems a harmless occupation,' said Hugh.

'On the face of it, perhaps,' she said. 'But that man doesn't deal with face values.' With a short laugh she turned to Hugh. 'You've stumbled right into the middle of it, my friend, rather sooner than I anticipated. That is one of the men you will probably have to kill. . .'

Her companion lit another cigarette. 'There is nothing like straightforward candour,' he grinned. 'Except that I disliked his face and his manner, I must admit that I saw nothing about him to necessitate my going to so much trouble. What is his particular worry?'

'First and foremost the brute wants to marry me,' replied the girl.

'I loathe being obvious,' said Hugh, 'but I am not surprised.'

'But it isn't that that matters,' she went on. 'I wouldn't marry him even to save my life.' She looked at Drummond quietly. 'Henry Lakington is the second most dangerous man in England.'

'Only the second,' murmured Hugh. 'Then hadn't I better start my new career with the first?'

She looked at him in silence. 'I suppose you think that I'm hysterical,' she remarked after a while. 'You're probably even wondering whether I'm all there.'

Drummond nicked the ash from his cigarette, then he turned to her dispassionately. 'You must admit,' he remarked, 'that up to now our conversation has hardly proceeded along conventional lines. I am a complete stranger to you; another man who is a complete stranger to me speaks to you while we're at tea. You inform me that I shall probably have to kill him in the near future. The statement is, I think you will agree, a trifle disconcerting.'

The girl threw back her head and laughed merrily.

'You poor young man,' she cried; 'put that way it does sound alarming.' Then she grew serious again. 'There's plenty of time for you to back out now if you like. Just call the waiter, and ask for my bill. We'll say good-bye, and the incident will finish.'

She was looking at him gravely as she spoke, and it seemed to her companion that there was an appeal in the big blue eyes. And they were very big: and the face they were set in was very charming – especially at the angle it was tilted at, in the half-light of the room. Altogether, Drummond reflected, a most adorable girl. And adorable girls had always been a hobby of his. Probably Lakington possessed a letter of hers or something, and she wanted him to get it back. Of course he would, even if he had to thrash the swine to within an inch of his life.

'Well!' The girl's voice cut into his train of thought and he hurriedly pulled himself together.

'The last thing I want is for the incident to finish,' he said fervently. 'Why – it's only just begun.'

'Then you'll help me?'

'That's what I'm here for.' With a smile Drummond lit another cigarette. 'Tell me all about it.'

'The trouble,' she began after a moment, 'is that there is not very much to tell. At present it is largely guesswork, and guesswork without much of a clue. However, to start with, I had better tell you what sort of men you are up against. Firstly, Henry Lakington – the man who spoke to me. He was, I believe, one of the most brilliant scientists who have ever been up at Oxford. There was nothing, in his own line, which would not have been open to him, had he run straight. But he didn't. He deliberately chose to turn his brain to crime. Not vulgar, common sorts of crime – but the big things, calling for a master criminal. He has always had enough money to allow him to take his time over any coup – to perfect his details. And that's what he loves. He regards a crime as an ordinary man regards a complicated business deal – a thing to be studied and looked at from all angles, a thing to be treated as a mathematical problem. He is quite unscrupulous; he is only concerned in pitting himself against the world and winning.'

'An engaging fellah,' said Hugh. 'What particular form of crime does he favour?'

'Anything that calls for brain, iron nerve, and refinement of detail,' she answered. 'Principally, up to date, burglary on a big scale, and murder.'

'My dear soul!' said Hugh incredulously. 'How can you be sure? And why don't you tell the police?'

She smiled wearily. 'Because I've got no proof, and even if I had. . .' She gave a little shudder, and left her sentence unfinished. 'But one day, my father and I were in his house, and, by accident, I got into a room I'd never been in before. It was a strange room, with two large safes let into the wall and steel bars over the skylight in the ceiling. There wasn't a window, and the floor seemed to be made of concrete. And the door was covered with curtains, and was heavy to move – almost as if it was steel or iron. On the desk in the middle of the room lay some miniatures, and, without thinking, I picked them up and looked at them. I happen to know something about miniatures, and, to my horror, I recognized them.' She paused for a moment as a waiter went by their table.

'Do you remember the theft of the celebrated Vatican miniatures belonging to the Duke of Melbourne?'

Drummond nodded; he was beginning to feel interested.

'They were the ones I was holding in my hand,' she said quietly. 'I knew them at once from the description in the papers. And just as I was wondering what on earth to do, the man himself walked into the room.'

'Awkward – deuced awkward.' Drummond pressed out his cigarette and leaned forward expectantly. 'What did he do?'

'Absolutely nothing,' said the girl. 'That's what made it so awful.'

'"Admiring my treasures?" he remarked. "Pretty things, aren't they?"' I couldn't speak a word: I just put them back on the table.

'"Wonderful copies," he went on, "of the Duke of Melbourne's lost miniatures. I think they would deceive most people."

'"They deceived me,"' I managed to get out.

'"Did they?" he said. "The man who painted them will be flattered."

'All the time he was staring at me, a cold, merciless stare that seemed to freeze my brain. Then he went over to one of the safes and unlocked it. "Come here, Miss Benton," he said. "There are a lot more – copies."'

'I only looked inside for a moment, but I have never seen or thought of such a sight. Beautifully arranged on black velvet shelves were ropes of pearls, a gorgeous diamond tiara, and a whole heap of loose, uncut stones. And in one corner I caught a glimpse of the most wonderful gold chaliced cup – just like the one for which Samuel Levy, the Jew moneylender, was still offering a reward. Then he shut the door and locked it, and again stared at me in silence.

'"All copies," he said quietly, "wonderful copies. And should you ever be tempted to think otherwise – ask your father, Miss Benton. Be warned by me; don't do anything foolish. Ask your father first."'

'And did you?' asked Drummond.

She shuddered. 'That very evening,' she answered.

'And Daddy flew into a frightful passion, and told me never to dare to meddle in things that didn't concern me again. Then gradually, as time went on, I realized that Lakington had some hold over Daddy – that he'd got my father in his power. Daddy – of all people – who wouldn't hurt a fly: the best and dearest man who ever breathed.' Her hands were clenched, and her breast rose and fell stormily.

Drummond waited for her to compose herself before he spoke again. 'You mentioned murder, too,' he remarked.

She nodded. 'I've got no proof,' she said, 'less even than over the burglaries. But there was a man called George Dringer, and one evening, when Lakington was dining with us, I heard him discussing this man with Daddy.

'"He's got to go," said Lakington. "He's dangerous!"'

'And then my father got up and closed the door; but I heard them arguing for half an hour. Three weeks later a coroner's jury found that George Dringer had committed suicide while temporarily insane. The same evening Daddy, for the first time in his life, went to bed the worse for drink.'

The girl fell silent, and Drummond stared at the orchestra with troubled eyes. Things seemed to be rather deeper than he had anticipated.

'Then there was another case.' She was speaking again. 'Do you remember that man who was found dead in a railway-carriage at Oxhey station? He was an Italian – Giuseppe by name; and the jury brought in a verdict of death from natural causes. A month before, he had an interview with Lakington which took place at our house: because the Italian, being a stranger, came to the wrong place, and Lakington happened to be with us at the time. The interview finished with a fearful quarrel.' She turned to Drummond with a smile. 'Not much evidence, is there? Only I *know* Lakington murdered him. I *know* it. You may think I'm fanciful – imagining things; you may think I'm exaggerating. I don't mind if you do – because you won't for long.'

Drummond did not answer immediately. Against his saner judgment he was beginning to be profoundly impressed, and, at the moment, he did not quite know what to say. That the girl herself firmly believed in what she was telling him, he was certain; the point was how much of it was – as she expressed it – fanciful imagination.

'What about this other man?' he asked at length.

'I can tell you very little about him,' she answered.

'He came to The Elms – that is the name of Lakington's house – three months ago. He is about medium height and rather thick-set; clean-shaven, with thick brown hair flecked slightly with white. His forehead is broad, and his eyes are a sort of cold grey-blue. But it's his hands that terrify me. They're large and white and utterly ruthless.' She turned to him appealingly. 'Oh! don't think I'm talking wildly,' she implored. 'He frightens me to death – that man: far, far worse than Lakington. He would stop at nothing to gain his ends, and even Lakington himself knows that Mr Peterson is master.'

'Peterson!' murmured Drummond. 'It seems quite a sound old English name.'

The girl laughed scornfully. 'Oh! The name is sound enough, if it was his real one. As it is, it's about as real as his daughter.'

'There is a lady in the case, then?'

'By the name of Irma,' said the girl briefly. 'She lies on the sofa in the garden and yawns. She's no more English than that waiter.'

A faint smile flickered over her companion's face; he had formed a fairly vivid mental picture of Irma. Then he grew serious again.

'And what is it that makes you think there's mischief ahead?' he asked abruptly.

The girl shrugged her shoulders. 'What the novelists call feminine intuition, I suppose,' she answered. 'That – and my father.' She said the last words very low. 'He hardly ever sleeps at night now; I hear him pacing up and down his room – hour after hour, hour after hour. Oh! It makes me mad. . . Don't you understand? I've just got to find out what the trouble is. I've got to get him away from those devils, before he breaks down completely.'

Drummond nodded, and looked away. The tears were bright in her eyes, and, like every Englishman, he detested a scene. While she had been speaking he had made up his mind what course to take, and now, having outsat everybody else, he decided that it was time for the interview to cease. Already an early diner was having a cocktail, while Lakington might return at any moment. And if there was anything in what she had told him, it struck him that it would be as well for that gentleman not to find them still together.

'I think,' he said, 'we'd better go. My address is 60A, Half Moon Street; my telephone 1234 Mayfair. If anything happens, if ever you want me – at any hour of the day or night – ring me up or write. If I'm not in, leave a message with my servant Denny. He is absolutely reliable. The only other thing is your own address.'

29

'The Larches, near Godalming,' answered the girl, as they moved towards the door. 'Oh! if you only knew the glorious relief of feeling one's got someone to turn to. . .' She looked at him with shining eyes, and Drummond felt his pulse quicken suddenly. Imagination or not, so far as her fears were concerned, the girl was one of the loveliest things he had ever seen.

'May I drop you anywhere?' he asked, as they stood on the pavement, but she shook her head.

'No, thank you. I'll go in that taxi.' She gave the man an address, and stepped in, while Hugh stood bareheaded by the door.

'Don't forget,' he said earnestly. 'Any time of the day or night. And while I think of it – we're old friends. Can that be done? In case I come and stay, you see.'

She thought for a moment and then nodded her head. 'All right,' she answered. 'We've met a lot in London during the war.'

With a grinding of gear wheels the taxi drove off, leaving Hugh with a vivid picture imprinted on his mind of blue eyes, and white teeth, and a skin like the bloom of a sun-kissed peach.

For a moment or two he stood staring after it, and then he walked across to his own car. With his mind still full of the interview he drove slowly along Piccadilly, while every now and then he smiled grimly to himself. Was the whole thing an elaborate hoax? Was the girl even now chuckling to herself at his gullibility? If so, the game had only just begun, and he had no objection to a few more rounds with such an opponent. A mere tea at the Carlton could hardly be the full extent of the jest. . . And somehow deep down in his mind, he wondered whether it was a joke – whether, by some freak of fate, he had stumbled on one of those strange mysteries which up to date he had regarded as existing only in the realms of shilling shockers.

He turned into his rooms, and stood in front of the mantelpiece taking off his gloves. It was as he was about to lay them down on the table that an envelope caught his eye, addressed to him in an unknown handwriting. Mechanically he picked it up and opened it. Inside was a single half-sheet of notepaper, on which a few lines had been written in a small, neat hand.

> *There are more things in Heaven and Earth, young man, than a capability for eating steak and onions, and a desire for adventure. I imagine that you possess both: and they are useful assets in the second locality mentioned by the poet. In Heaven, however, one never knows – especially with regard to the onions. Be careful.*

Drummond stood motionless for a moment, with narrowed eyes. Then he leaned forward and pressed the bell.

'Who brought this note, James?' he said quietly, as his servant came into the room.

'A small boy, sir. Said I was to be sure and see you got it most particular.' He unlocked a cupboard near the window and produced a tantalus.[2] 'Whisky, sir, or cocktail?'

'Whisky, I think, James.' Hugh carefully folded the sheet of paper and placed it in his pocket. And his face as he took the drink from his man would have left no doubt in an onlooker's mind as to why, in the past, he had earned the name of 'Bulldog' Drummond.

[2]A tantalus is a stand in which spirit decanters may belocked up though still on view.

Chapter 2

In Which He Journeys to Godalming and the Game Begins

I

'I ALMOST think, James, that I could toy with another kidney.' Drummond looked across the table at his servant, who was carefully arranging two or three dozen letters in groups. 'Do you think it will cause a complete breakdown in the culinary arrangements? I've got a journey in front of me to-day, and I require a large breakfast.'

James Denny supplied the deficiency from a dish that was standing on an electric heater.

'Are you going for long, sir?' he ventured.

'I don't know, James. It all depends on circumstances. Which, when you come to think of it, is undoubtedly one of the most fatuous phrases in the English language. Is there anything in the world that *doesn't* depend on circumstances?'

'Will you be motoring, sir, or going by train?' asked James prosaically. Dialectical arguments did not appeal to him.

'By car,' answered Drummond. 'Pyjamas and a tooth-brush.'

'You won't take evening clothes, sir?'

'No. I want my visit to appear unpremeditated, James, and if one goes about completely encased in boiled shirts, while pretending to be merely out for the afternoon, people have doubts as to one's intellect.'

James digested this great thought in silence.

'Will you be going far, sir?' he asked at length, pouring out a second cup of coffee.

'To Godalming. A charming spot, I believe, though I've never been there. Charming inhabitants, too, James. The lady I met yesterday at the Carlton lives at Godalming.'

'Indeed, sir,' murmured James non-committally.

'You damned old humbug,' laughed Drummond, 'you know you're itching to know all about it. I had a very long and interesting talk with her, and one of two things emerges quite clearly from our conversation. Either, James, I am a congenital idiot, and don't know enough to come in out of the rain; or we've hit the goods. That is what I propose to find out by my little excursion. Either our legs, my friend, are being pulled till they will never resume their normal shape; or that advertisement has succeeded beyond our wildest dreams.'

'There are a lot more answers in this morning, sir.' Denny made a movement towards the letters he had been sorting. 'One from a lovely widow with two children.'

'Lovely,' cried Drummond. 'How forward of her!' He glanced at the letter and smiled. 'Care, James, and accuracy are essential in a secretary. The misguided woman calls herself lonely, not lovely. She will remain so, as far as I am concerned, until the other matter is settled.'

'Will it take long, sir, do you think?'

'To get it settled?' Drummond lit a cigarette and leaned back in his chair. 'Listen, James, and I will outline the case. The maiden lives at a house called The Larches, near Godalming, with her papa. Not far away is another house called The Elms, owned by a gentleman of the name of Henry Lakington – a nasty man, James, with a nasty face – who was also at the Carlton yesterday afternoon for a short time. And now we come to the point. Miss Benton – that is the lady's name – accuses Mr Lakington of being the complete IT in the criminal line. She went even so far as to say that he was the second most dangerous man in England.'

'Indeed, sir. More coffee, sir?'

'Will nothing move you, James?' remarked his master plaintively. 'This man murders people and does things like that, you know.'

'Personally, sir, I prefer a picture-palace. But I suppose there ain't no accounting for 'obbies. May I clear away, sir?'

'No, James, not at present. Keep quite still while I go on, or I shall get it wrong. Three months ago there arrived at The Elms *the* most dangerous man in England – the IT of ITS. This gentleman goes by the name of Peterson, and he owns a daughter. From what Miss Benton said, I have doubts about that daughter, James.' He rose and strolled over to the window. 'Grave doubts. However, to return to the point, it appears that some unpleasing conspiracy is being hatched by IT, the IT of ITS, and the doubtful daughter, into which Papa Benton has been unwillingly drawn. As far as I can make out, the suggestion is that I should unravel the tangled skein of crime and extricate papa.'

In a spasm of uncontrollable excitement James sucked his teeth. 'Lumme, it wouldn't 'alf go on the movies, would it?' he remarked. 'Better than them Red Indians and things.'

'I fear, James, that you are not in the habit of spending your spare time at the British Museum, as I hoped,' said Drummond. 'And your brain doesn't work very quickly. The point is not whether this hideous affair is better than Red Indians and things – but whether it's genuine. Am I to battle with murderers, or shall I find a house-party roaring with laughter on the lawn?'

'As long as you laughs like 'ell yourself, sir, I don't see as 'ow it makes much odds,' answered James philosophically.

'The first sensible remark you've made this morning,' said his master hopefully. 'I will go prepared to laugh.'

He picked up a pipe from the mantelpiece, and proceeded to fill it, while James Denny still waited in silence.

'A lady may ring up to-day,' Drummond continued. 'Miss Benton, to be exact. Don't say where I've gone if she does; but take down any message, and wire it to me at Godalming Post Office. If by any chance you don't hear from me for three days, get in touch with Scotland Yard, and tell 'em where I've gone. That covers everything if it's genuine. If, on the other hand, it's a hoax, and the house-party is a good one, I shall probably want you to come down with my evening clothes and some more kit.'

'Very good, sir. I will clean your small Colt revolver at once.'

Hugh Drummond paused in the act of lighting his pipe, and a grin spread slowly over his face.

'Excellent,' he said. 'And see if you can find that water-squirt pistol I used to have – a Son of a Gun they called it. That ought to raise a laugh, when I arrest the murderer with it.'

II

The 30 h.p. two-seater made short work of the run to Godalming. Under the dickey[1] seat behind lay a small bag, containing the bare necessaries for the night; and as Drummond thought of the two guns rolled up carefully in his pyjamas – the harmless toy and the wicked little automatic – he grinned gently to himself. The girl had not rung him up during the morning, and, after a comfortable lunch at his club, he had started about three o'clock. The hedges, fresh with the glories of spring, flashed past; the smell of the country came sweet and fragrant on the air. There was a gentle warmth, a balminess in the day that made it good to be alive, and once or twice he sang under his breath through sheer lightheartedness of spirit. Surrounded by the peaceful beauty of the fields, with an occasional village half hidden by great trees from under which the tiny houses peeped out, it seemed impossible that crime could exist – laughable. Of

[1]A dickey seat was a folding seat at the back of a car.

course the thing was a hoax, an elaborate leg-pull, but, being not guilty of any mental subterfuge, Hugh Drummond admitted to himself quite truly that he didn't care a damn if it was. Phyllis Benton was at liberty to continue the jest, wherever and whenever she liked. Phyllis Benton was a very nice girl, and very nice girls are permitted a lot of latitude.

A persistent honking behind aroused him from his reverie, and he pulled into the side of the road. Under normal circumstances he would have let his own car out, and as she could touch ninety with ease, he very rarely found himself passed. But this afternoon he felt disinclined to race; he wanted to go quietly and think. Blue eyes and that glorious colouring were a dangerous combination – distinctly dangerous. Most engrossing to a healthy bachelor's thoughts.

An open cream-coloured Rolls-Royce drew level with five people on board, and he looked up as it passed. There were three people in the back – two men and a woman, and for a moment his eyes met those of the man nearest him. Then they drew ahead and Drummond pulled up to avoid the thick cloud of dust.

With a slight frown he stared at the retreating car; he saw the man lean over and speak to the other man; he saw the other man look round. Then a bend in the road hid them from sight, and, still frowning, Drummond pulled out his case and lit a cigarette. For the man whose eye he had caught as the Rolls went by was Henry Lakington. There was no mistaking that hard-lipped, cruel face. Presumably, thought Hugh, the other two occupants were Mr Peterson and the doubtful daughter, Irma; presumably they were returning to The Elms. And incidentally there seemed no pronounced reason why they shouldn't. But, somehow, the sudden appearance of Lakington had upset him; he felt irritable and annoyed. What little he had seen of the man he had not liked; he did not want to be reminded of him, especially just as he was thinking of Phyllis.

He watched the white dust-cloud rise over the hill in front as the car topped it; he watched it settle and drift away in the faint breeze. Then he let in his clutch and followed quite slowly in the big car's wake.

There had been two men in front – the driver and another, and he wondered idly if the latter was Mr Benton. Probably not, he reflected, since Phyllis had said nothing about her father being in London. He accelerated up the hill and swung over the top; the next moment he braked hard and pulled up just in time. The Rolls, with the chauffeur peering into the bonnet, had stopped in such a position that it was impossible for him to get by.

The girl was still seated in the back of the car, also the passenger in front, but the two other men were standing in the road apparently watching the chauffeur, and after a while the one whom Drummond had recognized as Lakington came towards him.

'I'm so sorry,' he began – and then paused in surprise. 'Why, surely it's Captain Drummond?'

Drummond nodded pleasantly. 'The occupant of a car is hardly likely to change in a mile, is he?' he remarked. 'I'm afraid I forgot to wave as you went past, but I got your smile all right.' He leant on his steering-wheel and lit a second cigarette. 'Are you likely to be long?' he asked; 'because if so, I'll stop my engine.'

The other man was now approaching casually, and Drummond regarded him curiously. 'A friend of our little Phyllis, Peterson,' said Lakington, as he came up. 'I found them having tea together yesterday at the Carlton.'

'Any friend of Miss Benton's is, I hope, ours,' said Peterson with a smile. 'You've known her a long time, I expect?'

'Quite a long time,' returned Hugh. 'We have jazzed together on many occasions.'

'Which makes it all the more unfortunate that we should have delayed you,' said Peterson. 'I can't help thinking, Lakington, that that new chauffeur is a bit of a fool.'

'I hope he avoided the crash all right,' murmured Drummond politely.

Both men looked at him. 'The crash!' said Lakington. 'There was no question of a crash. We just stopped.'

'Really,' remarked Drummond, 'I think, sir, that you must be right in your diagnosis of your chauffeur's mentality.' He turned courteously to Peterson. 'When something goes wrong, for a fellah to stop his car by braking so hard that he locks both back wheels is no *bon,* as we used to say in France. I thought, judging by the tracks in the dust, that you must have been in imminent danger of ramming a traction engine. Or perhaps,' he added judicially, 'a sudden order to stop would have produced the same effect.' If he saw the lightning glance that passed between the two men he gave no sign. 'May I offer you a cigarette? Turkish that side – Virginian the other. I wonder if I could help your man,' he continued, when they had helped themselves. 'I'm a bit of an expert with a Rolls.'

'How very kind of you,' said Peterson. 'I'll go and see.' He went over to the man and spoke a few words.

'Isn't it extraordinary,' remarked Hugh, 'how the eye of the boss galvanizes the average man into activity! As long, probably, as Mr Peterson had remained here talking, that chauffeur would have gone on tinkering with the engine. And now – look, in a second – all serene. And yet I dare say Mr Peterson knows nothing about it really. Just the watching eye, Mr Lakington. Wonderful thing – the human optic.'

He rambled on with a genial smile, watching with apparent interest the car in front. 'Who's the quaint bird sitting beside the chauffeur? He appeals to me immensely. Wish to Heaven I'd had a few more like him in France to turn into snipers.'

'May I ask why you think he would have been a success at the job?' Lakington's voice expressed merely perfunctory interest, but his cold, steely eyes were fixed on Drummond.

'He's so motionless,' answered Hugh. 'The bally fellow hasn't moved a muscle since I've been here. I believe he'd sit on a hornet's nest, and leave the inmates guessing. Great gift, Mr Lakington. Shows a strength of will but rarely met with – a mind which rises above mere vulgar curiosity.'

'It is undoubtedly a great gift to have such a mind, Captain Drummond,' said Lakington. 'And if it isn't born in a man, he should most certainly try to cultivate it.' He pitched his cigarette away, and buttoned up his coat. 'Shall we be seeing you this evening?'

Drummond shrugged his shoulders. 'I'm the vaguest man that ever lived,' he said lightly. 'I might be listening to nightingales in the country; or I might be consuming steak and onions preparatory to going to a night club. So long. . . You must let me take you to Hector's one night. Hope you don't break down again so suddenly.'

He watched the Rolls-Royce start, but seemed in no hurry to follow suit. And his many friends, who were wont to regard Hugh Drummond as a mass of brawn not too plentifully supplied with brains, would have been puzzled had they seen the look of keen concentration on his face as he stared along the white, dusty road. He could not say why, but suddenly and very certainly the conviction had come to him that this was no hoax and no leg-pull – but grim and sober reality. In his imagination he heard the sudden sharp order to stop the instant they were over the hill, so that Peterson might have a chance of inspecting him; in a flash of intuition he knew that these two men were no ordinary people, and that he was suspect. And as he slipped smoothly after the big car, now well out of sight, two thoughts were dominant in his mind. The first was that there was some mystery about the motionless, unnatural man who had sat beside the driver; the second was a distinct feeling of relief that his automatic was fully loaded.

III

At half-past five he stopped in front of Godalming Post Office. To his surprise the girl handed him a wire, and Hugh tore the yellow envelope open quickly. It was from Denny, and it was brief and to the point:

Phone message received. AAA. Must see you Carlton tea day after to-morrow. Going Godalming now. AAA. Message ends.

With a slight smile he noticed the military phraseology – Denny at one time in his career had been a signaller – and then he frowned. 'Must see you.' She should – at once.

He turned to the girl and inquired the way to The Larches. It was about two miles, he gathered, on the Guildford road, and impossible to miss – a biggish house standing well back in its own grounds.

'Is it anywhere near a house called The Elms?' he asked.

'Next door, sir,' said the girl. 'The gardens adjoin.'

He thanked her, and having torn up the telegram into small pieces, he got into his car. There was nothing for it, he had decided, but to drive boldly up to the house, and say that he had come to call on Miss Benton. He had never been a man who beat about the bush, and simple methods appealed to him – a trait in his character which many a boxer, addicted to tortuous cunning in the ring, had good cause to remember. What more natural, he reflected, than to drive over and see such an old friend?

He had no difficulty in finding the house, and a few minutes later he was ringing the front-door bell. It was answered by a maidservant, who looked at him in mild surprise. Young men in motor-cars were not common visitors at The Larches.

'Is Miss Benton in?' Hugh asked with a smile which at once won the girl's heart.

'She has only just come back from London, sir,' she answered doubtfully. 'I don't know whether. . .'

'Would you tell her that Captain Drummond has called?' said Hugh as the maid hesitated. 'That I happened to find myself near here, and came on chance of seeing her?

Once again the smile was called into play, and the girl hesitated no longer. 'Will you come inside, sir?' she said. 'I will go and tell Miss Phyllis.'

She ushered him into the drawing-room and closed the door. It was a charming room, just such as he would have expected with Phyllis. Big windows, opening down to the ground, led out on to a lawn, which was already a blaze of colour. A few great oak trees threw a pleasant shade at the end of the garden, and, partially showing through them, he could see another house which he rightly assumed was The Elms. In fact, even as he heard the door open and shut behind him, he saw Peterson come out of a small summer-house and commence strolling up and down, smoking a cigar. Then he turned round and faced the girl.

Charming as she had looked in London, she was doubly so now, in a simple linen frock which showed off her figure to perfection. But if he thought he was going to have any leisure to enjoy the picture undisturbed, he was soon disillusioned.

'Why have you come here, Captain Drummond?' she said, a little breathlessly. 'I said the Carlton – the day after to-morrow.'

'Unfortunately,' said Hugh, 'I'd left London before that message came. My servant wired it on to the post office here. Not that it would have made any difference. I should have come, anyway.'

An involuntary smile hovered round her lips for a moment; then she grew serious again. 'It's very dangerous for you to come here,' she remarked quietly.

'If those men suspect anything, God knows what will happen.'

It was on the tip of his tongue to tell her that it was too late to worry about that; then he changed his mind. 'And what is there suspicious,' he asked, 'in an old friend who happens to be in the neighbourhood dropping in to call? Do you mind if I smoke?'

The girl beat her hands together. 'My dear man,' she cried, 'you don't understand. You're judging those devils by your own standard. They suspect everything – and everybody.'

'What a distressing habit,' he murmured. 'Is it chronic, or merely due to liver? I must send 'em a bottle of good salts. Wonderful thing – good salts. Never without some in France.'

The girl looked at him resignedly. 'You're hopeless,' she remarked – 'absolutely hopeless.'

'Absolutely,' agreed Hugh, blowing out a cloud of smoke. 'Wherefore your telephone message? What's the worry?'

She bit her lip and drummed with her fingers on the arm of her chair. 'If I tell you,' she said at length, 'will you promise me, on your word of honour, that you won't go blundering into The Elms, or do anything foolish like that?'

'At the present moment I'm very comfortable where I am, thanks,' remarked Hugh.

'I know,' she said, 'but I'm so dreadfully afraid that you're the type of person who. . .who. . .' She paused, at a loss for a word.

'Who bellows like a bull, and charges head down,' interrupted Hugh with a grin. She laughed with him, and just for a moment their eyes met, and she read in his something quite foreign to the point at issue. In fact, it is to be feared that the question of Lakington and his companions was not engrossing Drummond's mind, as it doubtless should have been, to the exclusion of all else.

'They're so utterly unscrupulous,' she continued hurriedly, 'so fiendishly clever, that even you would be like a child in their hands.'

Hugh endeavoured to dissemble his pleasure at that little word 'even,' and only succeeded in frowning horribly.

'I will be discretion itself,' he assured her firmly.

'I promise you.'

'I suppose I shall have to trust you,' she said.

'Have you seen the evening papers today?'

'I looked at the ones that come out in the morning labelled 6 p.m. before I had lunch,' he answered.

'Is there anything of interest?'

She handed him a copy of the *Planet.* 'Read that little paragraph in the second column.' She pointed to it, as he took the paper and Hugh read it aloud.

'Mr Hiram C. Potts – the celebrated American millionaire – is progressing favourably. He has gone into the country for a few days, but is sufficiently recovered to conduct business as usual.' He laid down the paper and looked at the girl sitting opposite. 'One is pleased,' he remarked in a puzzled tone, 'for the sake of Mr Potts. To be ill and have a name like that is more than most men could stand. . . But I don't quite see. . .'

'That man was stopping at the Carlton, where he met Lakington,' said the girl. 'He is a multimillionaire, over here in connection with some big steel trust; and when multi-millionaires get friendly with Lakington, their health frequently does suffer.'

'But this paper says he's getting better,' objected Drummond. '"Sufficiently recovered to conduct business as usual." What's wrong with that?'

'If he is sufficiently recovered to conduct business as usual, why did he send his confidential secretary away yesterday morning on an urgent mission to Belfast?'

'Search me,' said Hugh. 'Incidentally, how do you know he did?'

'I asked at the Carlton this morning,' she answered.

'I said I'd come after a job as typist for Mr Potts. They told me at the inquiry office that he was ill in bed and unable to see anybody. So I asked for his secretary, and they told me what I've just told you – that he had left for Belfast that morning and would be away several days. It may be that there's nothing in it; on the other hand, it may be that there's a lot. And it's only by following up every possible clue,' she continued fiercely, 'that I can hope to beat those fiends and get Daddy out of their clutches.'

Drummond nodded gravely, and did not speak. For into his mind had flashed suddenly the remembrance of that sinister, motionless figure seated by the chauffeur. The wildest guesswork certainly – no vestige of proof – and yet, having once come, the thought stuck. And as he turned it over in his mind, almost prepared to laugh at himself for his credulity – millionaires are not removed against their will, in broad daylight, from one of the biggest hotels in London, to sit in immovable silence in an open car – the door opened and an elderly man came in.

Hugh rose, and the girl introduced the two men. 'An old friend, Daddy,' she said. 'You must have heard me speak of Captain Drummond.'

'I don't recall the name at the moment, my dear,' he answered courteously – a fact which was hardly surprising – 'but I fear I'm getting a little forgetful. I am pleased to meet you, Captain Drummond. You'll stop and have some dinner, of course.'

Hugh bowed. 'I should like to, Mr Benton. Thank you very much. I'm afraid the hour of my call was a little informal, but being round in these parts, I felt I must come and look Miss Benton up.'

His host smiled absent-mindedly, and walking to the window, stared through the gathering dusk at the house opposite, half hidden in the trees. And Hugh, who was watching him from under lowered lids, saw him suddenly clench both hands in a gesture of despair.

It cannot be said that dinner was a meal of sparkling gaiety. Mr Benton was palpably ill at ease, and beyond a few desultory remarks spoke hardly at all: while the girl, who sat opposite Hugh, though she made one or two valiant attempts to break the long silences, spent most of the meal in covertly watching her father. If anything more had been required to convince Drummond of the genuineness of his interview with her at the Carlton the preceding day, the atmosphere at this strained and silent party supplied it.

As if unconscious of anything peculiar, he rambled on in his usual inconsequent method, heedless of whether he was answered or not; but all the time his mind was busily working. He had already decided that a Rolls-Royce was not the only car on the market which could break down mysteriously, and with the town so far away, his host could hardly fail to ask him to stop the night. And then – he had not yet quite settled how – he proposed to have a closer look at The Elms.

At length the meal was over, and the maid, placing the decanter in front of Mr Benton, withdrew from the room.

'You'll have a glass of port, Captain Drummond,' remarked his host, removing the stopper and pushing the bottle towards him. 'An old pre-war wine which I can vouch for.'

Hugh smiled, and even as he lifted the heavy old cut glass, he stiffened suddenly in his chair. A cry – half shout, half scream, and stifled at once – had come echoing through the open windows. With a crash the stopper fell from Mr Benton's nerveless fingers, breaking the finger-bowl in front of him, while every vestige of colour left his face.

'It's something these days to be able to say that,' remarked Hugh, pouring himself out a glass. 'Wine, Miss Benton?' He looked at the girl, who was staring fearfully out of the window, and forced her to meet his eye. 'It will do you good.'

His tone was compelling, and after a moment's hesitation she pushed the glass over to him. 'Will you pour it out?' she said, and he saw that she was trembling all over.

'Did you – did you hear – anything?' With a vain endeavour to speak calmly, his host looked at Hugh.

'That night-bird?' he answered easily. 'Eerie noises they make, don't they? Sometimes in France, when everything was still, and only the ghostly green flares went hissing up, one used to hear 'em. Startled nervous sentries out of their lives.' He talked on, and gradually the colour came back to the other man's face. But Hugh noticed that he drained his port at a gulp, and immediately refilled his glass. . .

Outside everything was still; no repetition of that short, strangled cry again disturbed the silence. With the training bred of many hours in No Man's Land, Drummond was listening, even while he was speaking, for the faintest suspicious sound – but he heard nothing. The soft whispering night-noises came gently through the window; but the man who had screamed once did not even whimper again. He remembered hearing a similar cry near the brickstacks at Guinchy, and two nights later he had found the giver of it, at the edge of a mine-crater, with glazed eyes that still held in them the horror of the final second. And more persistently than ever, his thoughts centred on the fifth occupant of the Rolls-Royce. . .

It was with almost a look of relief that Mr Benton listened to his tale of woe about his car.

'Of course you must stop here for the night,' he cried. 'Phyllis, my dear, will you tell them to get a room ready?'

With an inscrutable look at Hugh, in which thankfulness and apprehension seemed mingled, the girl left the room. There was an unnatural glitter in her father's eyes – a flush on his cheeks hardly to be accounted for by the warmth of the evening; and it struck Drummond that, during the time he had been pretending to look at his car, Mr Benton had been fortifying himself. It was obvious, even to the soldier's unprofessional eye, that the man's nerves had gone to pieces; and that unless something was done soon, his daughter's worst forebodings were likely to be fulfilled. He talked disjointedly and fast; his hands were not steady, and he seemed to be always waiting for something to happen.

Hugh had not been in the room ten minutes before his host produced the whisky, and during the time that he took to drink a mild nightcap, Mr Benton succeeded in lowering three extremely strong glasses of spirit. And what made it the more sad was that the man was obviously not a heavy drinker by preference.

At eleven o'clock Hugh rose and said good night.

'You'll ring if you want anything, won't you?' said his host. 'We don't have very many visitors here, but I hope you'll find everything you require. Breakfast at nine.'

Drummond closed the door behind him, and stood for a moment in silence, looking round the hall. It was deserted, but he wanted to get the geography of the house firmly imprinted on his mind. Then a noise from the room he had just left made him frown sharply – his host was continuing the process of fortification – and he stepped across towards the drawing-room. Inside, as he hoped, he found the girl.

She rose the instant he came in, and stood by the mantelpiece with her hands locked.

'What was it?' she half whispered – 'that awful noise at dinner?'

He looked at her gravely for a while, and then he shook his head. 'Shall we leave it as a night-bird for the present?' he said quietly. Then he leaned towards her, and took her hands in his own. 'Go to bed, little girl,' he ordered; 'this is my show. And, may I say, I think you're just wonderful. Thank God you saw my advertisement!'

Gently he released her hands, and walking to the door, held it open for her. 'If by any chance you should hear things in the night – turn over and go to sleep again.'

'But what are you going to do?' she cried.

Hugh grinned. 'I haven't the remotest idea,' he answered. 'Doubtless the Lord will provide.'

The instant the girl had left the room Hugh switched off the lights and stepped across to the curtains which covered the long windows. He pulled them aside, letting them come together behind him; then, cautiously, he unbolted one side of the big centre window. The night was dark, and the moon was not due to rise for two or three hours, but he was too old a soldier to neglect any precautions. He wanted to see more of the The Elms and its inhabitants; he did not want them to see more of him.

Silently he dodged across the lawn towards the big trees at the end, and leaning up against one of them, he proceeded to make a more detailed survey of his objective. It was the same type of house as the one he had just left, and the grounds seemed about the same size. A wire fence separated the two places, and in the darkness Hugh could just make out a small wicket-gate, closing a path which connected both houses. He tried it, and found to his satisfaction that it opened silently.

Passing through, he took cover behind some bushes from which he could command a better view of Mr Lakington's abode. Save for one room on the ground floor the house was in darkness, and Hugh determined to have a look at that room. There was a chink in the curtains, through which the light was streaming out, which struck him as having possibilities.

Keeping under cover, he edged towards it, and at length, he got into a position from which he could see inside. And what he saw made him decide to chance it, and go even closer.

Seated at the table was a man he did not recognize; while on either side of him sat Lakington and Peterson. Lying on a sofa smoking a cigarette and reading a novel was a tall, dark girl, who seemed completely uninterested in the proceedings of the other three. Hugh placed her at once as the doubtful daughter Irma, and resumed his watch on the group at the table.

A paper was in front of the man, and Peterson, who was smoking a large cigar, was apparently suggesting that he should make use of the pen which Lakington was obligingly holding in readiness. In all respects a harmless tableau, save for one small thing – the expression on the man's face. Hugh had seen it before often – only then it had been called shell-shock. The man was dazed, semi-unconscious. Every now and then he stared round the room, as if bewildered; then he would shake his head and pass his hand wearily over his forehead. For a quarter of an hour the scene continued; then Lakington produced an instrument from his pocket. Hugh saw the man shrink back in terror, and reach for the pen. He saw the girl lie back on the sofa as if disappointed and pick up her novel again; and he saw Lakington's face set in a cold sneer. But what impressed him most in that momentary flash of action was Peterson. There was something inhuman in his complete passivity. By not the fraction of a second did he alter the rate at which he was smoking – the slow, leisurely rate of the connoisseur; by not the twitch of an eyelid did his expression change. Even as he watched the man signing his name, no trace of emotion showed on his face – whereas on Lakington's there shone a fiendish satisfaction.

The document was still lying on the table, when Hugh produced his revolver. He knew there was foul play about, and the madness of what he had suddenly made up his mind to do never struck him: being that manner of fool, he was made that way. But he breathed a pious prayer that he would shoot straight – and then he held his breath. The crack of the shot and the bursting of the only electric-light bulb in the room were almost simultaneous; and the next second, with a roar of 'Come on, boys,' he burst through the window. At an immense advantage over the others, who could see nothing for the moment, he blundered round the room. He timed the blow at Lakington to a nicety; he hit him straight on the point of the jaw and he felt the man go down like a log. Then he grabbed at the paper on the table, which tore in his hand, and picking the dazed signer up bodily, he rushed through the window on to the lawn. There was not an instant to be lost; only the impossibility of seeing when suddenly plunged into darkness had enabled him to pull the thing off so far. And before that advantage disappeared he had to be back at The Larches with his burden, no light weight for even a man of his strength to carry.

But there seemed to be no pursuit, no hue and cry. As he reached the little gate he paused and looked back, and he fancied he saw outside the window a gleam of white, such as a shirt-front. He lingered for an instant, peering into the darkness and recovering his breath, when with a vicious phut something buried itself in the tree beside him. Drummond lingered no more; long years of experience left no doubt in his mind as to what that something was.

'Compressed-air rifle – or electric,' he muttered to himself, stumbling on, and half dragging, half carrying his dazed companion.

He was not very clear in his own mind what to do next, but the matter was settled for him unexpectedly. Barely had he got into the drawing-room, when the door opened and the girl rushed in.

'Get him away at once,' she cried. 'In your car. . . Don't waste a second. I've started her up.'

'Good girl,' he cried enthusiastically. 'But what about you?'

She stamped her foot impatiently. 'I'm all right – absolutely all right. Get him away – that's all that matters.'

Drummond grinned. 'The humorous thing is that I haven't an idea who the bird is – except that—'

He paused, with his eyes fixed on the man's left thumb. The top joint was crushed into a red, shapeless pulp, and suddenly the meaning of the instrument Lakington had produced from his pocket became clear. Also the reason of that dreadful cry at dinner. . .

'By God!' whispered Drummond, half to himself, while his jaws set like a steel vice. 'A thumbscrew. The devils. . .the bloody swine. . .'

'Oh! Quick, quick,' the girl urged in an agony. 'They may be here at any moment.' She dragged him to the door, and together they forced the man into the car.

'Lakington won't,' said Hugh with a grin. 'And if you see him to-morrow – don't ask after his jaw. . . Good night, Phyllis.

With a quick movement he raised her hand to his lips; then he slipped in the clutch and the car disappeared down the drive. . .

He felt a sense of elation and of triumph at having won the first round, and as the car whirled back to London through the cool night air his heart was singing with the joy of action. And it was perhaps as well for his peace of mind that he did not witness the scene in the room at The Elms.

Lakington still lay motionless on the floor; Peterson's cigar still glowed steadily in the darkness. It was hard to believe that he had ever moved from the table; only the bullet imbedded in a tree proved that somebody must have got busy. Of course, it might have been the girl, who was just lighting another cigarette from the stump of the old one.

At length Peterson spoke. 'A young man of dash and temperament,' he said genially. 'It will be a pity to lose him.'

'Why not keep him and lose the girl?' yawned Irma. 'I think he might amuse me—'

'We have always our dear Henry to consider,' answered Peterson. 'Apparently the girl appeals to him. I'm afraid, Irma, he'll have to go. . .and at once. . .'

The speaker was tapping his left knee softly with his hand; save for that slight movement he sat as if nothing had happened. And yet ten minutes before a carefully planned coup had failed at the instant of success. Even his most fearless accomplices had been known to confess that Peterson's inhuman calmness sent cold shivers down their backs.

Chapter 3

In Which Things Happen in Half Moon Street

I

HUGH DRUMMOND folded up the piece of paper he was studying and rose to his feet as the doctor came into the room. He then pushed a silver box of cigarettes across the table and waited.

'Your friend,' said the doctor, 'is in a very peculiar condition, Captain Drummond – very peculiar.' He sat down and, putting the tips of his fingers together, gazed at Drummond in his most professional manner. He paused for a moment, as if expecting an awed agreement with this profound utterance, but the soldier was calmly lighting a cigarette. 'Can you,' resumed the doctor, 'enlighten me at all as to what he has been doing during the last few days?'

Drummond shook his head. 'Haven't an earthly, doctor.'

'There is, for instance, that very unpleasant wound in his thumb,' pursued the other. 'The top joint is crushed to a pulp.'

'I noticed that last night,' answered Hugh non-committally. 'Looks as if it had been mixed up between a hammer and an anvil, don't it?'

'But you have no idea how it occurred?'

'I'm full of ideas,' said the soldier. 'In fact, if it's any help to you in your diagnosis, that wound was caused by the application of an unpleasant mediaeval instrument known as a thumbscrew.'

The worthy doctor looked at him in amazement. 'A thumbscrew! You must be joking, Captain Drummond.'

'Very far from it,' answered Hugh briefly. 'If you want to know, it was touch and go whether the other thumb didn't share the same fate.' He blew out a cloud of smoke, and smiled inwardly as he noticed the look of scandalized horror on his companion's face. 'It isn't his thumb that concerns me,' he continued; 'it's his general condition. What's the matter with him?'

The doctor pursed his lips and looked wise, while Drummond wondered that no one had ever passed a law allowing men of his type to be murdered on sight.

'His heart seems sound,' he answered after a weighty pause, 'and I found nothing wrong with him constitutionally. In fact, I may say, Captain Drummond, he is in every respect a most healthy man. Except – er – except for this peculiar condition.'

Drummond exploded. 'Damnation take it, and what on earth do you suppose I asked you to come round for? It's of no interest to me to hear that his liver is working properly.' Then he controlled himself. 'I beg your pardon, doctor: I had rather a trying evening last night. Can you give me any idea as to what has caused this peculiar condition?'

His companion accepted the apology with an acid bow. 'Some form of drug,' he answered.

Drummond heaved a sigh of relief. 'Now we're getting on,' he cried. 'Have you any idea what drug?'

'It is, at the moment, hard to say,' returned the other. 'It seems to have produced a dazed condition mentally, without having affected him physically. In a day or two, perhaps, I might be able to – er – arrive at some conclusion. . .'

'Which, at present, you have not. Right; now we know where we are.' A pained expression flitted over the doctor's face: this young man was very direct. 'To continue,' Hugh went on, 'as you don't know what the drug is, presumably you don't know either how long it will take for the effect to wear off.'

'That – er – is, within limits, correct,' concluded the doctor.

'Right; once again we know where we are. What about diet?'

'Oh! Light. . . Not too much meat. . . No alcohol. . .' He rose to his feet as Hugh opened the door; really the war seemed to have produced a distressing effect on people's manners. Diet was the one question on which he always let himself go. . .

'Not much meat – no alcohol. Right. Good morning, doctor. Down the stairs and straight on. Good morning.' The door closed behind him, and he descended to his waiting car with cold disapproval on his face. The whole affair struck him as most suspicious – thumbscrews, strange drugs. . . Possibly it was his duty to communicate with the police. . .

'Excuse me, sir.' The doctor paused and eyed a well-dressed man who had spoken to him uncompromisingly.

'What can I do for you, sir?' he said.

'Am I right in assuming that you are a doctor?'

'You are perfectly correct, sir, in your assumption.'

The man smiled: obviously a gentleman, thought the practitioner, with his hand on the door of his car.

'It's about a great pal of mine, Captain Drummond, who lives in here,' went on the other. 'I hope you won't think it unprofessional, but I thought I'd ask you privately how you find him.'

The doctor looked surprised. 'I wasn't aware that he was ill,' he answered.

'But I heard he'd had a bad accident,' said the man, amazed.

The doctor smiled. 'Reassure yourself, my dear sir,' he murmured in his best professional manner. 'Captain Drummond, so far as I am aware, has never been better. I – er – cannot say the same of his friend.' He stepped into his car. 'Why not go up and see for yourself?'

The car rolled smoothly into Piccadilly, but the man showed no signs of availing himself of the doctor's suggestion. He turned and walked rapidly away, and a few moments later – in an exclusive West End club – a trunk call was put through to Godalming – a call which caused the recipient to nod his head in satisfaction and order the Rolls-Royce.

Meanwhile, unconscious of this sudden solicitude for his health, Hugh Drummond was once more occupied with the piece of paper he had been studying on the doctor's entrance. Every now and then he ran his fingers through his crisp brown hair and shook his head in perplexity. Beyond establishing the fact that the man in the peculiar condition was Hiram C. Potts, the American multi-millionaire, he could make nothing out of it.

'If only I'd managed to get the whole of it,' he muttered to himself for the twentieth time. 'That damn fellah Peterson was too quick.' The scrap he had torn off was typewritten, save for the American's scrawled signature, and Hugh knew the words by heart.

> plete paralysis
> ade of Britain
> months I do
> the holder of
> of five million
> do desire and
> earl necklace and the
> are at present
> chess of Lamp-
> k no questions
> btained.
> AM C. POTTS.

At length he replaced the scrap in his pocket-book and rang the bell.

'James,' he remarked as his servant came in, 'will you whisper "very little meat and no alcohol" in your wife's ear, so far as the bird next door is concerned? Fancy paying a doctor to come round and tell one that?'

'Did he say anything more, sir?'

'Oh! A lot. But that was the only thing of the slightest practical use, and I knew that already.' He stared thoughtfully out of the window. 'You'd better know,' he continued at length, 'that as far as I can see we're up against a remarkably tough proposition.'

'Indeed, sir,' murmured his servant. 'Then perhaps I had better stop any further insertion of that advertisement. It works out at six shillings a time.'

Drummond burst out laughing. 'What would I do without you, oh! my James,' he cried. 'But you may as well stop it. Our hands will be quite full for some time to come, and I hate disappointing hopeful applicants for my services.'

'The gentleman is asking for you, sir.' Mrs Denny's voice from the door made them look round, and Hugh rose.

'Is he talking sensibly, Mrs Denny?' he asked eagerly, but she shook her head.

'Just the same, sir,' she announced. 'Looking round the room all dazed like. And he keeps on saying "Danger."'

Hugh walked quickly along the passage to the room where the millionaire lay in bed.

'How are you feeling?' said Drummond cheerfully.

The man stared at him uncomprehendingly, and shook his head.

'Do you remember last night?' Hugh continued, speaking very slowly and distinctly. Then a sudden idea struck him and he pulled the scrap of paper out of his case. 'Do you remember signing that?' he asked, holding it out to him.

For a while the man looked at it; then with a sudden cry of fear he shrank away. 'No, no,' he muttered, 'not again.'

Hugh hurriedly replaced the paper. 'Bad break on my part, old bean; you evidently remember rather too well. It's quite all right,' he continued reassuringly; 'no one will hurt you.' Then after a pause: 'Is your name Hiram C. Potts?'

The man nodded his head doubtfully and muttered 'Hiram Potts' once or twice, as if the words sounded familiar.

'Do you remember driving in a motor-car last night?' persisted Hugh.

But what little flash of remembrance had pierced the drug-clouded brain seemed to have passed; the man only stared dazedly at the speaker. Drummond tried him with a few more questions, but it was no use, and after a while he got up and moved towards the door.

'Don't you worry, old son,' he said with a smile. 'We'll have you jumping about like a two-year-old in a couple of days.'

Then he paused: the man was evidently trying to say something. 'What is it you want?' Hugh leant over the bed.

'Danger, danger.' Faintly the words came, and then, with a sigh, he lay back exhausted.

With a grim smile Drummond watched the motionless figure.

'I'm afraid,' he said half aloud, 'that you're rather like your medical attendant. Your only contribution to the sphere of pure knowledge is something I know already.'

He went out and quietly closed the door. And as he re-entered his sitting-room he found his servant standing motionless behind one of the curtains watching the street below.

'There's a man, sir,' he remarked without turning round, 'watching the house.'

For a moment Hugh stood still, frowning. Then he gave a short laugh. 'The devil there is!' he remarked. 'The game has begun in earnest, my worthy warrior, with the first nine points to us. For possession, even of a semi-dazed lunatic, is nine points of the law, is it not, James?'

His servant retreated cautiously from the curtain and came back into the room. 'Of the law – yes, sir,' he repeated enigmatically. 'It is time, sir, for your morning glass of beer.'

II

At twelve o'clock precisely the bell rang, announcing a visitor, and Drummond looked up from the columns of the *Sportsman* as his servant came into the room.

'Yes, James,' he remarked. 'I think we are at home. I want you to remain within call, and under no circumstances let our sick visitor out of your sight for more than a minute. In fact, I think you'd better sit in his room.'

He resumed his study of the paper, and James, with a curt 'Very good, sir,' left the room. Almost at once he returned, and flinging open the door announced Mr Peterson.

Drummond looked up quickly and rose with a smile.

'Good morning,' he cried. 'This is a very pleasant surprise, Mr Peterson.' He waved his visitor to a chair. 'Hope you've had no more trouble with your car.'

Mr Peterson drew off his gloves, smiling amiably.

'None at all, thank you, Captain Drummond. The chauffeur appears to have mastered the defect.'

'It was your eye on him that did it. Wonderful thing – the human optic, as I said to your friend, Mr – Mr Laking. I hope that he's quite well and taking nourishment.'

'Soft food only,' said the other genially. 'Mr Lakington had a most unpleasant accident last night – most unpleasant.'

Hugh's face expressed his sympathy. 'How very unfortunate!' he murmured. 'I trust nothing serious.'

'I fear his lower jaw was fractured in two places.'

Peterson helped himself to a cigarette from the box beside him. 'The man who hit him must have been a boxer.'

'Mixed up in a brawl, was he?' said Drummond, shaking his head. 'I should never have thought, from what little I've seen of Mr Lakington, that he went in for painting the town red. I'd have put him down as a most abstemious man – but one never can tell, can one? I once knew a fellah who used to get fighting drunk on three whiskies, and to look at him you'd have put him down as a Methodist parson. Wonderful the amount of cheap fun that chap got out of life.'

Peterson nicked the ash from his cigarette into the grate.

'Shall we come to the point, Captain Drummond?' he remarked affably.

Hugh looked bewildered. 'The point, Mr Peterson? Er – by all manner of means.'

Peterson smiled even more affably. 'I felt certain that you were a young man of discernment,' he remarked, 'and I wouldn't like to keep you from your paper a minute longer than necessary.'

'Not a bit,' cried Hugh. 'My time is yours – though I'd very much like to know your real opinion of The Juggernaut for the Chester Cup. It seems to me that he cannot afford to give Sumatra seven pounds on their form up to date.'

'Are you interested in gambling?' asked Peterson politely.

'A mild flutter, Mr Peterson, every now and then,' returned Drummond. 'Strictly limited stakes.'

'If you confine yourself to that you will come to no harm,' said Peterson. 'It is when the stakes become unlimited that the danger of the crash becomes unlimited too.'

'That is what my mother always told me,' remarked Hugh. 'She even went farther, dear good woman that she was. 'Never bet except on a certainty, my boy,' was her constant advice, 'and then put your shirt on!' I can hear her saying it now, Mr Peterson, with the golden rays of the setting sun lighting up her sweet face.'

Suddenly Peterson leant forward in his chair. 'Young man,' he remarked, 'we've got to understand one another. Last night you butted in on my plans, and I do not like people who do that. By an act which, I must admit, appealed to me greatly, you removed something I require – something, moreover, which I intend to have. Breaking the electric bulb with a revolver-shot shows resource and initiative. The blow which smashed Henry Lakington's jaw in two places shows strength. All qualities which I admire, Captain Drummond – admire greatly. I should dislike having to deprive the world of those qualities.'

Drummond gazed at the speaker open-mouthed. 'My dear sir,' he protested feebly, 'you overwhelm me. Are you really accusing me of being a sort of wild west show?' He waggled a finger at Peterson.

'You know you've been to the movies too much, like my fellah, James. He's got revolvers and things on the brain.'

Peterson's face was absolutely impassive; save for a slightly tired smile it was expressionless. 'Finally, Captain Drummond, you tore in half a piece of paper which I require – and removed a very dear old friend of my family, who is now in this house. I want them both back, please, and if you like I'll take them now.'

Drummond shrugged his shoulders resignedly.

'There is something about you, Mr Peterson,' he murmured, 'which I like. You strike me as being the type of man to whom a young girl would turn and pour out her maidenly secrets. So masterful, so compelling, so unruffled. I feel sure – when you have finally disabused your mind of this absurd hallucination – that we shall become real friends.'

Peterson still sat motionless save for a ceaseless tapping with his hand on his knee.

'Tell me,' continued Hugh, 'why did you allow this scoundrel to treat you in such an off-hand manner? It doesn't seem to me to be the sort of thing that ought to happen at all, and I suggest your going to the police at once.'

'Unfortunately a bullet intended for him just missed,' answered Peterson casually. 'A pity – because there would have been no trace of him by now.'

'Might be awkward for you,' murmured Hugh. 'Such methods, Mr Peterson, are illegal, you know. It's a dangerous thing to take the law into your own hands. May I offer you a drink?'

Peterson declined courteously. 'Thank you – not at this hour.' Then he rose. 'I take it, then, that you will not return me my property here and now.'

'Still the same delusion, I see!' remarked Hugh with a smile.

'Still the same delusion,' repeated Peterson. 'I shall be ready to receive both the paper and the man up till six o'clock to-night at 32A, Berners Street; and it is possible, I might even say probable, should they turn up by then, that I shall not find it necessary to kill you.'

Hugh grinned. 'Your kindly forbearance amazes me,' he cried. 'Won't you really change your mind and have a drink?

'Should they not arrive by then, I shall be put to the inconvenience of taking them, and in that case – much as I regret it – you may have to be killed. You're such an aggressive young man, Captain Drummond – and, I fear, not very tactful.' He spoke regretfully, drawing on his gloves; then as he got to the door he paused. 'I'm afraid that my words will not have much effect,' he remarked, 'but the episode last night *did* appeal to me. I would like to spare you – I would really. It's a sign of weakness, my young friend, which I view with amazement – but nevertheless, it is there. So be warned in time. Return my property to Berners Street, and leave England for a few months.' His eyes seemed to burn into the soldier's brain. 'You are meddling in affairs,' he went on gently, 'of the danger of which you have no conception. A fly in the gear-box of a motor-car would be a sounder proposition for a life insurance than you will be – if you continue on your present course.'

There was something so incredibly menacing in the soft, quiet voice, that Drummond looked at the speaker fascinated. He had a sudden feeling that he must be dreaming – that in a moment or two he would wake up and find that they had really been talking about the weather the whole time. Then the cynical gleam of triumph in Peterson's eyes acted on him like a cold douche; quite clearly that gentleman had misinterpreted his silence.

'Your candour is as refreshing,' he answered genially, 'as your similes are apt. I shudder to think of that poor little fly, Mr Peterson, especially with your chauffeur grinding his gears to pieces.' He held open the door for his visitor, and followed him into the passage. At the other end stood Denny, ostentatiously dusting a book-shelf, and Peterson glanced at him casually. It was characteristic of the man that no trace of annoyance showed on his face. He might have been any ordinary visitor taking his leave.

And then suddenly from the room outside which Denny was dusting there came a low moaning and an incoherent babble. A quick frown passed over Drummond's face, and Peterson regarded him thoughtfully.

'An invalid in the house?' he remarked. 'How inconvenient for you!' He laid his hand for a moment on the soldier's arm. 'I sadly fear you're going to make a fool of yourself. And it will be such a pity.' He turned towards the stairs. 'Don't bother, please; I can find my own way out.'

III

Hugh turned back into his own room, and lighting a particularly noisy pipe, sat down in his own special chair, where James Denny found him five minutes later, with his hands deep in his pockets, and his legs crossed, staring out of the window. He asked him about lunch twice without result, and having finally been requested to go to hell, he removed himself aggrievedly to the kitchen. Drummond was under no delusions as to the risks he was running. Underrating his opponent had never been a fault of his, either in the ring or in France, and he had no intention of beginning now. The man who could abduct an American millionaire, and drug him till he was little better than a baby, and then use a thumbscrew to enforce his wishes, was not likely to prove overscrupulous in the future. In fact, the phut of that bullet still rang unpleasantly in his ears.

After a while he began half unconsciously to talk aloud to himself. It was an old trick of his when he wanted to make up his mind on a situation, and he found that it helped him to concentrate his thoughts.

'Two alternatives, old buck,' he remarked, stabbing the air with his pipe. 'One – give the Potts bird up at Berners Street; two – do not. Number one – out of court at once. Preposterous – absurd. Therefore – number two holds the field.' He recrossed his legs, and ejected a large wineglassful of nicotine juice from the stem of his pipe on to the carpet. Then he sank back exhausted, and rang the bell.

'James,' he said, as the door opened, 'take a piece of paper and a pencil – if there's one with a point – and sit down at the table. I'm going to think, and I'd hate to miss out anything.'

His servant complied, and for a while silence reigned.

'First,' remarked Drummond, 'put down – "They know where Potts is."'

'Is, sir, or are?' murmured Denny, sucking his pencil.

'Is, you fool. It's a man, not a collection. And don't interrupt, for Heaven's sake. Two – "They will try to get Potts."'

'Yes, sir,' answered Denny, writing busily.

'Three – "They will not get Potts." That is as far as I've got at the moment, James – but every word of it stands. Not bad for a quarter of an hour, my trusty fellah – what?'

'That's the stuff to give the troops, sir,' agreed his audience, sucking his teeth.

Hugh looked at him in displeasure. 'That noise is not, James,' he remarked severely. 'Now you've got to do something else. Rise and with your well-known stealth approach the window, and see if the watcher still watcheth without.'

The servant took a prolonged survey, and finally announced that he failed to see him.

'Then that proves conclusively that he's there,' said Hugh. 'Write it down, James: four – "Owing to the watcher without, Potts cannot leave the house without being seen."'

'That's two withouts, sir,' ventured James tentatively; but Hugh, with a sudden light dawning in his eyes, was staring at the fire-place.

'I've got it, James,' he cried. 'I've got it. . . Five – "Potts must leave the house without being seen." I want him, James, I want him all to myself. I want to make much of him and listen to his childish prattle. He shall go to my cottage on the river, and you shall look after him.'

'Yes, sir,' returned James dutifully.

'And in order to get him there, we must get rid of the watcher without. How can we get rid of the bird – how can we, James, I ask you? Why, by giving him nothing further to watch for. Once let him think that Potts is no longer within, unless he's an imbecile he will no longer remain without.'

'I see, sir,' said James.

'No, you don't – you don't see anything. Now trot along over, James, and give my compliments to Mr Darrell. Ask him to come in and see me for a moment. Say I'm thinking and daren't move.'

James rose obediently, and Drummond heard him cross over the passage to the other suite of rooms that lay on the same floor. Then he heard the murmur of voices, and shortly afterwards his servant returned.

'He is in his bath, sir, but he'll come over as soon as he's finished.' He delivered the message and stood waiting. 'Anything more, sir?'

'Yes, James. I feel certain that there's a lot. But just to carry on with, I'll have another glass of beer.' As the door closed, Drummond rose and started to pace up and down the room. The plan he had in his mind was simple, but he was a man who believed in simplicity.

'Peterson will not come himself – nor will our one and only Henry. Potts has not been long in the country, which is all to the good. And if it fails – we shan't be any worse off than we are now. Luck – that's all; and the more you tempt her, the kinder she is.' He was still talking gently to himself when Peter Darrell strolled into the room.

'Can this thing be true, old boy,' remarked the new-comer. 'I hear you're in the throes of a brainstorm.'

'I am, Peter – and not even that repulsive dressing-gown of yours can stop it. I want you to help me.'

'All that I have, dear old flick, is yours for the asking. What can I do?'

'Well, first of all, I want you to come along and see the household pet.' He piloted Darrell along the passage to the American's room, and opened the door. The millionaire looked at them dazedly from the pillows, and Darrell stared back in startled surprise.

'My God! What's the matter with him?' he cried.

'I would give a good deal to know,' said Hugh grimly. Then he smiled reassuringly at the motionless man, and led the way back to the sitting-room.

'Sit down, Peter,' he said. 'Get outside that beer and listen to me carefully.'

For ten minutes he spoke, while his companion listened in silence. Gone completely was the rather vacuous-faced youth clad in a gorgeous dressing-gown; in his place there sat a keen-faced man nodding from time to time as a fresh point was made clear. Even so had both listened in the years that were past to their battalion commander's orders before an attack.

At length Hugh finished. 'Will you do it, old man?' he asked.

'Of course,' returned the other. 'But wouldn't it be better, Hugh,' he said pleadingly, 'to whip up two or three of the boys and have a real scrap? I don't seem to have anything to do.'

Drummond shook his head decidedly. 'No, Peter, my boy – not this show. We're up against a big thing; and if you like to come in with me, I think you'll have all you want in the scrapping line before you've finished. But this time, low cunning is the order.'

Darrell rose. 'Right you are, dearie. Your instructions shall be carried out to the letter. Come and feed your face with me. Got a couple of birds from the Gaiety lunching at the Cri.'

'Not today,' said Hugh. 'I've got quite a bit to get through this afternoon.'

As soon as Darrell had gone, Drummond again rang the bell for his servant.

'This afternoon, James, you and Mrs Denny will leave here and go to Paddington. Go out by the front door, and should you find yourself being followed – as you probably will be – consume a jujube and keep your heads. Having arrived at the booking-office, take a ticket to Cheltenham, say good-bye to Mrs Denny in an impassioned tone, and exhort her not to miss the next train to that delectable inland resort. You might even speak slightingly about her sick aunt at Westbourne Grove, who alone prevents your admirable wife from accompanying you. Then, James, you will board the train for Cheltenham and go there. You will remain there for two days, during which period you must remember that you're a married man – even if you do go to the movies. You will then return here, and await further orders. Do you get me?'

'Yes, sir.' James stood to attention with a smart heel-click.

'Your wife – she has a sister or something, hasn't she, knocking about somewhere?'

'She 'as a palsied cousin in Camberwell, sir,' remarked James with justifiable pride.

'Magnificent,' murmured Hugh. 'She will dally until even-tide with her palsied cousin – if she can bear it – and then she must go by Underground to Ealing, where she will take a ticket to Goring. I don't think there will be any chance of her being followed – you'll have drawn them off. When she gets to Goring, I want the cottage got ready at once, for two vis-itors.' He paused and lit a cigarette. 'Above all, James – mum's the word. As I told you a little while ago, the game has begun. Now just repeat what I've told you.'

He listened while his servant ran through his instructions, and nodded approvingly. 'To think there are still people who think military service a waste of time!' he murmured. 'Four years ago you couldn't have got one word of it right.'

He dismissed Denny, and sat down at his desk. First he took the half-torn sheet out of his pocket, and putting it in an envelope, sealed it carefully. Then he placed it in another envelope, with a covering letter to his bank, requesting them to keep the enclosure intact.

Then he took a sheet of notepaper, and with much deliberation proceeded to pen a document which afforded him considerable amusement, judging by the grin which appeared from time to time on his face. This effusion he also enclosed in a sealed envelope, which he again addressed to his bank. Finally, he stamped the first, but not the second – and placed them both in his pocket.

For the next two hours he apparently found nothing better to do than eat a perfectly grilled chop prepared by Mrs Denny, and superintend his visitor unwillingly consuming a sago pudding. Then, with the departure of the Dennys for Paddington, which coincided most aptly with the return of Peter Darrell, a period of activity commenced in Half Moon Street. But being interior activity, interfering in no way with the placid warmth of the street outside, the gentleman without, whom a keen observer might have thought strangely interested in the beauties of that well-known thoroughfare – seeing that he had been there for three hours – remained serenely unconscious of it. His pal had followed the Dennys to Paddington. Drummond had not come out – and the watcher who watched without was beginning to get bored.

About 4.30 he sat up and took notice again as someone left the house; but it was only the superbly dressed young man whom he had discovered already was merely a clothes-peg calling himself Darrell.

The sun was getting low and the shadows were lengthening when a taxi drove up to the door. Immediately the watcher drew closer, only to stop with a faint smile as he saw two men get out of it. One was the immaculate Darrell; the other was a stranger, and both were quite obviously what in the vernacular is known as 'oiled.'

'You prisheless ole bean,' he heard Darrell say affectionately, 'thish blinking cabsh my show.'

The other man hiccoughed assent, and leant wearily against the palings.

'Right,' he remarked, 'ole friend of me youth. It shall be ash you wish.'

With a tolerant eye he watched them tack up the stairs, singing lustily in chorus. Then the door above closed, and the melody continued to float out through the open window.

Ten minutes later he was relieved. It was quite an unostentatious relief: another man merely strolled past him. And since there was nothing to report, he merely strolled away. He could hardly be expected to know that up in Peter Darrell's sitting-room two perfectly sober young men were contemplating with professional eyes an extremely drunk gentleman singing in a chair, and that one of those two sober young men was Peter Darrell.

Then further interior activity took place in Half Moon Street, and as the darkness fell, silence gradually settled on the house.

Ten o'clock struck, then eleven – and the silence remained unbroken. It was not till eleven-thirty that a sudden small sound made Hugh Drummond sit up in his chair, with every nerve alert. It came from the direction of the kitchen – and it was the sound he had been waiting for.

Swiftly he opened his door and passed along the passage to where the motionless man lay still in bed. Then he switched on a small reading-lamp, and with a plate of semolina in his hand he turned to the recumbent figure.

'Hiram C. Potts,' he said in a low, coaxing tone, 'sit up and take your semolina. Force yourself, laddie, force yourself. I know it's nauseating, but the doctor said no alcohol and very little meat.'

In the silence that followed, a board creaked outside, and again he tempted the sick man with food.

'Semolina, Hiram – semolina. Makes bouncing babies. I'd just love to see you bounce, my Potts.'

His voice died away, and he rose slowly to his feet. In the open door four men were standing, each with a peculiar-shaped revolver in his hand.

'What the devil,' cried Drummond furiously, 'is the meaning of this?'

'Cut it out,' cried the leader contemptuously. 'These guns are silent. If you utter – you die. Do you get me?'

The veins stood out on Drummond's forehead, and he controlled himself with an immense effort.

'Are you aware that this man is a guest of mine, and sick?' he said, his voice shaking with rage.

'You don't say,' remarked the leader, and one of the others laughed. 'Rip the bed-clothes off, boys, and gag the young cock-sparrow.'

Before he could resist, a gag was thrust in Drummond's mouth, and his hands were tied behind his back. Then, helpless and impotent, he watched three of them lift up the man from the bed, and putting a gag in his mouth also, carry him out of the room.

'Move,' said the fourth to Hugh. 'You join the picnic.'

With fury gathering in his eyes he preceded his captor along the passage and downstairs. A large car drove up as they reached the street, and in less time than it takes to tell, the two helpless men were pushed in, followed by the leader; the door was shut and the car drove off.

'Don't forget,' he said to Drummond suavely, 'this gun *is* silent. You had better be the same.'

At one o'clock the car swung up to The Elms. For the last ten minutes Hugh had been watching the invalid in the corner, who was making frantic efforts to loosen his gag. His eyes were rolling horribly, and he swayed from side to side in his seat, but the bandages round his hands held firm and at last he gave it up.

Even when he was lifted out and carried indoors he did not struggle; he seemed to have sunk into a sort of apathy.

Drummond followed with dignified calmness, and was led into a room off the hall.

In a moment or two Peterson entered, followed by his daughter. 'Ah! my young friend,' cried Peterson affably. 'I hardly thought you'd give me such an easy run as this.' He put his hand into Drummond's pockets, and pulled out his revolver and a bundle of letters. 'To your bank,' he murmured. 'Oh! surely, surely not that as well. Not even stamped. Ungag him, Irma – and untie his hands. My very dear young friend – you pain me.'

'I wish to know, Mr Peterson,' said Hugh quietly, 'by what right this dastardly outrage has been committed. A friend of mine, sick in bed – removed; abducted in the middle of the night: to say nothing of me.'

With a gentle laugh Irma offered him a cigarette. '*Mon Dieu!*' she remarked, 'but you are most gloriously ugly, my Hugh!' Drummond looked at her coldly, while Peterson, with a faint smile, opened the envelope in his hand. And, even as he pulled out the contents, he paused suddenly and the smile faded from his face. From the landing upstairs came a heavy crash, followed by a flood of the most appalling language.

'What the—hell do you think you're doing, you flat-faced son of a Maltese goat? And where the—am I, anyway?'

'I must apologise for my friend's language,' murmured Hugh gently, 'but you must admit he has some justification. Besides, he was, I regret to state, quite wonderfully drunk earlier this evening, and just as he was sleeping it off these desperadoes abducted him.'

The next moment the door burst open, and an infuriated object rushed in. His face was wild, and his hand was bandaged, showing a great red stain on the thumb.

'What's this—jest?' he howled furiously.

'And this damned bandage all covered with red ink?'

'You must ask our friend here, Mullings,' said Hugh. 'He's got a peculiar sense of humour. Anyway, he's got the bill in his hand.'

In silence they watched Peterson open the paper and read the contents, while the girl leant over his shoulder.

To Mr Peterson, The Elms, Godalming.

	£	s.	d.
To hire of one demobilized soldier	5	0	0
To making him drunk (in this item present strength and cost of drink and said soldier's capacity must be allowed for)	5	0	0
To bottle of red ink	0	0	1
To shock to system	10	0	0
TOTAL	£20	0	1

It was Irma who laughed.

'Oh! but, my Hugh,' she gurgled, *'que vous etes adorable!'*

But he did not look at her. His eyes were on Peterson, who with a perfectly impassive face was staring at him fixedly.

Chapter 4

In Which He Spends a Quiet Night at The Elms

I

'IT is a little difficult to know what to do with you, young man,' said Peterson gently, after a long silence. 'I knew you had no tact.'

Drummond leaned back in his chair and regarded his host with a faint smile.

'I must come to you for lessons, Mr Peterson. Though I frankly admit,' he added genially, 'that I have never been brought up to regard the forcible abduction of a harmless individual and a friend who is sleeping off the effects of what low people call a jag as being exactly typical of that admirable quality.'

Peterson's glance rested on the dishevelled man still standing by the door, and after a moment's thought he leaned forward and pressed a bell.

'Take that man away,' he said abruptly to the servant who came into the room, 'and put him to bed. I will consider what to do with him in the morning.'

'Consider be damned,' howled Mullings, starting forward angrily. 'You'll consider a thick ear, Mr Blooming Knowall. What I wants to know—'

The words died away in his mouth, and he gazed at Peterson like a bird looks at a snake. There was something so ruthlessly malignant in the stare of the grey-blue eyes, that the ex-soldier who had viewed going over the top with comparative equanimity, as being part of his job, quailed and looked apprehensively at Drummond.

'Do what the kind gentleman tells you, Mullings,' said Hugh, 'and go to bed.' He smiled at the man reassuringly. 'And if you're very, very good, perhaps, as a great treat, he'll come and kiss you goodnight.'

'Now *that*,' he remarked as the door closed behind them, 'is what I call tact.'

He lit a cigarette, and thoughtfully blew out a cloud of smoke.

'Stop this fooling,' snarled Peterson. 'Where have you hidden Potts?'

'Tush, tush,' murmured Hugh. 'You surprise me. I had formed such a charming mental picture of you, Mr Peterson, as the strong, silent man who never lost his temper, and here you are disappointing me at the beginning of our acquaintance.'

For a moment he thought that Peterson was going to strike him, and his own fist clenched under the table.

'I wouldn't, my friend,' he said quietly, 'indeed I wouldn't. Because if you hit me, I shall most certainly hit you. And it will not improve your beauty.'

Slowly Peterson sank back in his chair, and the veins which had been standing out on his forehead became normal again. He even smiled; only the ceaseless tapping of his hand on his left knee betrayed his momentary loss of composure. Drummond's fist unclenched, and he stole a look at the girl. She was in her favourite attitude on the sofa, and had not even looked up.

'I suppose that it is quite useless for me to argue with you,' said Peterson after a while.

'I was a member of my school debating society,' remarked Hugh reminiscently. 'But I was never much good. I'm too obvious for argument, I'm afraid.'

'You probably realize from what has happened to-night,' continued Peterson, 'that I am in earnest.'

'I should be sorry to think so,' answered Hugh. 'If that is the best you can do, I'd cut it right out and start a tomato farm.'

The girl gave a little gurgle of laughter and lit another cigarette.

'Will you come and do the dangerous part of the work for us, Monsieur Hugh?' she asked.

'If you promise to restrain the little fellows, I'll water them with pleasure,' returned Hugh lightly.

Peterson rose and walked over to the window, where he stood motionless, staring out into the darkness. For all his assumed flippancy, Hugh realized that the situation was what in military phraseology might be termed 'critical'. There were in the house probably half a dozen men who, like their master, were absolutely unscrupulous. If it suited Peterson's book to kill him, he would not hesitate to do so for a single second. And Hugh realized, when he put it that way in his own mind, that it was no exaggeration, no *façon de parler,* but a plain, unvarnished statement of fact. Peterson would no more think twice of killing a man if he wished to, than the normal human being would of crushing a wasp.

For a moment the thought crossed his mind that he would take no chances by remaining in the house; that he would rush Peterson from behind and escape into the darkness of the garden. But it was only momentary – gone almost before it had come, for Hugh Drummond was not that manner of man – gone even before he noticed that Peterson was standing in such a position that he could see every detail of the room behind him reflected in the glass through which he stared.

A fixed determination to know what lay in that sinister brain replaced his temporary indecision. Events up to date had moved so quickly that he had hardly had time to get his bearings; even now the last twenty-four hours seemed almost a dream. And as he looked at the broad back and massive head of the man at the window, and from him to the girl idly smoking on the sofa, he smiled a little grimly. He had just remembered the thumbscrew of the preceding evening. Assuredly the demobilized officer who found peace dull was getting his money's worth; and Drummond had a shrewd suspicion that the entertainment was only just beginning.

A sudden sound outside in the garden made him look up quickly. He saw the white gleam of a shirt front, and the next moment a man pushed open the window and came unsteadily into the room. It was Mr Benton, and quite obviously he had been seeking consolation in the bottle.

'Have you got him?' he demanded thickly, steadying himself with a hand on Peterson's arm.

'I have not,' said Peterson shortly, eyeing the swaying figure in front of him contemptuously.

'Where is he?'

'Perhaps if you ask your daughter's friend Captain Drummond, he might tell you. For Heaven's sake, sit down, man, before you fall down.' He pushed Benton roughly into a chair, and resumed his impassive stare into the darkness.

The girl took not the slightest notice of the new arrival, who gazed stupidly at Drummond across the table.

'We seem to be moving in an atmosphere of cross-purposes, Mr Benton,' said the soldier affably. 'Our host will not get rid of the idea that I am a species of bandit. I hope your daughter is quite well.'

'Er – quite, thank you,' muttered the other.

'Tell her, will you, that I propose to call on her before returning to London to-morrow. That is, if she won't object to my coming early.'

With his hands in his pockets, Peterson was regarding Drummond from the window.

'You propose leaving us to-morrow, do you?' he said quietly.

Drummond stood up.

'I ordered my car for ten o'clock,' he answered. 'I hope that will not upset the household arrangements,' he continued,

75

turning to the girl, who was laughing softly and polishing her nails.

'*Vraiment!* but you grow on one, my Hugh,' she smiled. 'Are we really losing you so soon?'

'I am quite sure that I shall be more useful to Mr Peterson at large, than I am cooped up here,' said Hugh. 'I might even lead him to this hidden treasure which he thinks I've got.'

'You will do that all right,' remarked Peterson.

'But at the moment I was wondering whether a little persuasion now – might not give me all the information I require more quickly and with less trouble.'

A fleeting vision of a mangled, pulplike thumb flashed across Hugh's mind; once again he heard that hideous cry, half animal, half human, which had echoed through the darkness the preceding night, and for an instant his breath came a little faster. Then he smiled, and shook his head.

'I think you are rather too good a judge of human nature to try anything so foolish,' he said thoughtfully. 'You see, unless you kill me, which I don't think would suit your book, you might find explanations a little difficult to-morrow.'

For a while there was silence in the room, broken at length by a short laugh from Peterson.

'For a young man truly your perspicacity is great,' he remarked. 'Irma, is the blue room ready? If so, tell Luigi to show Captain Drummond to it.'

'I will show him myself,' she answered, rising.

'And then I shall go to bed. *Mon Dieu!* my Hugh, but I find your country *très ennuyeux.*' She stood in front of him for a moment, and then led the way to the door, glancing at him over her shoulder.

Hugh saw a quick look of annoyance pass over Peterson's face as he turned to follow the girl, and it struck him that that gentleman was not best pleased at the turn of events. It vanished almost as soon as it came, and Peterson waved a friendly hand at him, as if the doings of the night had been the most ordinary thing in the world. Then the door closed, and he followed his guide up the stairs.

The house was beautifully furnished. Hugh was no judge of art, but even his inexperienced eye could see that the prints on the walls were rare and valuable. The carpets were thick, and his feet sank into them noiselessly; the furniture was solid and in exquisite taste. And it was as he reached the top of the stairs that a single deep-noted clock rang a wonderful chime and then struck the hour. The time was just three o'clock.

The girl opened the door of a room and switched on the light. Then she faced him smiling, and Hugh looked at her steadily. He had no wish whatever for any conversation, but as she was standing in the centre of the doorway it was impossible for him to get past her without being rude.

'Tell me, you ugly man,' she murmured, 'why you are such a fool.'

Hugh smiled, and, as has been said before, Hugh's smile transformed his face.

'I must remember that opening,' he said. 'So many people, I feel convinced, would like to say it on first acquaintance, but confine themselves to merely thinking it. It establishes a basis of intimacy at once, doesn't it?'

She swayed a little towards him, and then, before he realized her intention, she put a hand on his shoulder.

'Don't you understand,' she whispered fiercely, 'that they'll kill you?' She peered past him half fearfully, and then turned to him again. 'Go, you idiot, go – while there's time. Oh! If I could only make you understand; if you'd only believe me! Get out of it – go abroad; do anything – but don't fool round here.'

In her agitation she was shaking him to and fro.

'It seems a cheerful household,' remarked Hugh with a smile. 'May I ask why you're all so concerned about me? Your estimable father gave me the same advice yesterday morning.'

'Don't ask why,' she answered feverishly, 'because I can't tell you. Only you must believe that what I say is the truth – you must. It's just possible that if you go now and tell them where you've hidden the American you'll be all right. But if you don't—'

Her hand dropped to her side suddenly. 'Breakfast will be at nine, my Hugh: until then, *au revoir.*'

He turned as she left the room, a little puzzled by her change of tone. Standing at the top of the stairs was Peterson, watching them both in silence. . .

II

In the days when Drummond had been a platoon commander, he had done many dangerous things. The ordinary joys of the infantry subaltern's life – such as going over the top, and carrying out raids – had not proved sufficient for his appetite. He had specialized in peculiar stunts of his own: stunts over which he was singularly reticent; stunts over which his men formed their own conclusions, and worshipped him accordingly.

But Drummond was no fool, and he had realized the vital importance of fitting himself for these stunts to the best of his ability. Enormous physical strength is a great asset, but it carries with it certain natural disadvantages. In the first place, its possessor is frequently clumsy: Hugh had practised in France till he could move over ground without a single blade of grass rustling. Van Dyck – a Dutch trapper – had first shown him the trick, by which a man goes forward on his elbows like a snake, and is here one moment and gone the next, with no one the wiser.

Again, its possessor is frequently slow: Hugh had practised in France till he could kill a man with his bare hands in a second. Olaki – a Japanese – had first taught him two or three of the secrets of his trade, and in the intervals of resting behind the lines he had perfected them until it was even money whether the Jap or he would win in a practice bout.

And there were nights in No Man's Land when his men would hear strange sounds, and knowing that Drummond was abroad on his wanderings, would peer eagerly over the parapet into the desolate torn-up waste in front. But they never saw anything, even when the green ghostly flares went hissing up into the darkness and the shadows danced fantastically. All was silent and still; the sudden shrill whimper was not repeated.

Perhaps a patrol coming back would report a German, lying huddled in a shell-hole, with no trace of a wound, but only a broken neck; perhaps the patrol never found anything. But whatever the report, Hugh Drummond only grinned and saw to his men's breakfasts. Which is why there are in England today quite a number of civilians who acknowledge only two rulers – the King and Hugh Drummond. And they would willingly die for either.

The result on Drummond was not surprising: as nearly as a man may be he was without fear. And when the idea came to him as he sat on the edge of his bed thoughtfully pulling off his boots, no question of the possible risk entered into his mind. To explore the house seemed the most natural thing in the world, and with characteristic brevity he summed up the situation as it struck him.

'They suspect me anyhow: in fact, they know I took Potts. Therefore, even if they catch me passage-creeping, I'm no worse off than I am now. And I might find something of interest. Therefore, carry on, brave heart.'

The matter was settled; the complete bench of bishops headed by their attendant satellites would not have stopped him, nor the fact that the German front-line trench was a far safer place for a stranger than The Elms at night. But he didn't know that fact, and it would have cut no more ice than the episcopal dignitaries, if he had. . .

It was dark in the passage outside as he opened the door of his room and crept towards the top of the stairs. The collar of his brown lounge coat was turned up, and his stockinged feet made no sound on the heavy pile carpet. Like a huge shadow he vanished into the blackness, feeling his way forward with the uncanny instinct that comes from much practice. Every now and then he paused and listened intently, but the measured ticking of the clock below and the occasional creak of a board alone broke the stillness.

For a moment his outline showed up against the faint grey light which was coming through a window half-way down the stairs; then he was gone again, swallowed up in the gloom of the hall. To the left lay the room in which he had spent the evening, and Drummond turned to the right. As he had gone up to bed he had noticed a door screened by a heavy curtain which he thought might be the room Phyllis Benton had spoken of – the room where Henry Lakington kept his ill-gotten treasures. He felt his way along the wall, and at length his hand touched the curtain – only to drop it again at once. From close beside him had come a sharp, angry hiss. . .

He stepped back a pace and stood rigid, staring at the spot from which the sound had seemed to come – but he could see nothing. Then he leaned forward and once more moved the curtain. Instantly it came again, sharper and angrier than before.

Hugh passed a hand over his forehead and found it damp. Germans he knew, and things on two legs, but what was this that hissed so viciously in the darkness? At length he determined to risk it, and drew from his pocket a tiny electric torch. Holding it well away from his body, he switched on the light. In the centre of the beam, swaying gracefully to and fro, was a snake. For a moment he watched it fascinated as it spat at the light angrily; he saw the flat hood where the vicious head was set on the upright body; then he switched off the torch and retreated rather faster than he had come.

'A convivial household,' he muttered to himself through lips that were a little dry. 'A hooded cobra is an unpleasing pet.'

He stood leaning against the banisters regaining his self-control. There was no further sound from the cobra; seemingly it only got annoyed when its own particular domain was approached. In fact, Hugh had just determined to reconnoitre the curtained doorway again to see if it was possible to circumvent the snake, when a low chuckle came distinctly to his ears from the landing above.

He flushed angrily in the darkness. There was no doubt whatever as to the human origin of that laugh, and Hugh suddenly realized that he was making the most profound fool of himself. And such a realization, though possibly salutary to all of us at times, is most unpleasant.

For Hugh Drummond, who, with all his lack of conceit, had a very good idea of Hugh Drummond's capabilities, to be at an absolute disadvantage – to be laughed at by some dirty swine whom he could strangle in half a minute – was impossible! His fists clenched, and he swore softly under his breath. Then as silently as he had come down, he commenced to climb the stairs again. He had a hazy idea that he would like to hit something – hard.

There were nine stairs in the first half of the flight, and it was as he stood on the fifth that he again heard the low chuckle. At the same instant something whizzed past his head so low that it almost touched his hair, and there was a clang on the wall beside him. He ducked instinctively, and regardless of noise raced up the remaining stairs, on all-fours. His jaw was set like a vice, his eyes were blazing; in fact, Hugh Drummond was seeing red.

He paused when he reached the top, crouching in the darkness. Close to him he could feel someone else, and holding his breath, he listened. Then he heard the man move – only the very faintest sound – but it was enough. Without a second's thought he sprang, and his hands closed on human flesh. He laughed gently; then he fought in silence.

His opponent was strong above the average, but after a minute he was like a child in Hugh's grasp. He choked once or twice and muttered something; then Hugh slipped his right hand gently on to the man's throat. His fingers moved slowly round, his thumb adjusted itself lovingly, and the man felt his head being forced back irresistibly. He gave one strangled cry, and then the pressure relaxed. . .

'One half-inch more, my gentle humorist,' Hugh whispered in his ear, 'and your neck would have been broken. As it is, it will be very stiff for some days. Another time – don't laugh. It's dangerous.'

Then, like a ghost, he vanished along the passage in the direction of his own room.

'I wonder who the bird was,' he murmured thoughtfully to himself. 'Somehow I don't think he'll laugh quite so much in future – damn him.'

III

At eight o'clock the next morning a burly-looking ruffian brought in some hot water and a cup of tea. Hugh watched him through half-closed eyes, and eliminated him from the competition. His bullet head moved freely on a pair of massive shoulders; his neck showed no traces of nocturnal trouble. As he pulled up the blinds the light fell full on his battered, rugged face, and suddenly Hugh sat up in bed and stared at him.

'Good Lord!' he cried, 'aren't you Jem Smith?'

The man swung round like a flash and glared at the bed.

'Wot the 'ell 'as that got to do wiv you?' he snarled, and then his face changed. 'Why, strike me pink, if it ain't young Drummond.'

Hugh grinned.

'Right in one, Jem. What in the name of fortune are you doing in this outfit?'

But the man was not to be drawn.

'Never you mind, sir,' he said grimly. 'I reckon that's my own business.'

'Given up the game, Jem?' asked Hugh.

'It give me up, when that cross-eyed son of a gun Young Baxter fought that fake down at 'oxton. Gawd! If I could get the swine – just once again – s'welp me, I'd–' Words failed the ex-bruiser; he could only mutter. And Hugh, who remembered the real reason why the game had given Jem up, and a period of detention at His Majesty's expense had taken its place, preserved a discreet silence.

The pug paused as he got to the door, and looked at Drummond doubtfully. Then he seemed to make up his mind, and advanced to the side of the bed.

'It ain't none o' my business,' he muttered hoarsely, 'but seeing as 'ow you're one of the boys, if I was you I wouldn't get looking too close at things in this 'ere 'ouse. It ain't 'ealthy: only don't say as I said so.'

Hugh smiled.

'Thank you, Jem. By the way, has anyone got a stiff neck in the house this morning?'

'Stiff neck!' echoed the man. 'Strike me pink if that ain't funny – you're asking, I mean. The bloke's sitting up in 'is bed swearing awful. Can't move 'is 'ead at all.'

'And who, might I ask, is the bloke?' said Drummond, stirring his tea.

'Why, Peterson, o' course. Oo else? Breakfast at nine.'

The door closed behind him, and Hugh lit a cigarette thoughtfully. Most assuredly he was starting in style: Lakington's jaw one night, Peterson's neck the second, seemed a sufficiently energetic opening to the game for the veriest glutton. Then that cheerful optimisn which was the envy of his friends asserted itself.

'Supposin' I'd killed 'em,' he murmured, aghast. 'Just supposin'. Why, the bally show would have been over, and I'd have had to advertise again.'

Only Peterson was in the dining-room when Hugh came down. He had examined the stairs on his way, but he could see nothing unusual which would account for the thing which had whizzed past his head and clanged sullenly against the wall. Nor was there any sign of the cobra by the curtained door; merely Peterson standing in a sunny room behind a bubbling coffee-machine.

'Good morning,' remarked Hugh affably. 'How are we all to-day? By Jove! That coffee smells good.'

'Help yourself,' said Peterson. 'My daughter is never down as early as this.'

'Rarely conscious before eleven – what?' murmured Hugh. 'Deuced wise of her. May I press you to a kidney?' He returned politely towards his host, and paused in dismay. 'Good heavens! Mr Peterson, is your neck hurting you?'

'It is,' answered Peterson grimly.

'A nuisance, having a stiff neck. Makes everyone laugh, and one gets no sympathy. Bad thing – laughter. . . At times, anyway.' He sat down and commenced to eat his breakfast.

'Curiosity is a great deal worse, Captain Drummond. It was touch and go whether I killed you last night.'

The two men were staring at one another steadily.

'I think I might say the same,' returned Drummond.

'Yes and no,' said Peterson. 'From the moment you left the bottom of the stairs, I had your life in the palm of my hand. Had I chosen to take it, my young friend, I should not have had this stiff neck.'

Hugh returned to his breakfast unconcernedly.

'Granted, laddie, granted. But had I not been of such a kindly and forbearing nature, you wouldn't have had it, either.' He looked at Peterson critically. 'I'm inclined to think it's a great pity I didn't break your neck, while I was about it.' Hugh sighed, and drank some coffee. 'I see that I shall have to do it some day, and probably Lakington's as well. . . By the way, how is our Henry? I trust his jaw is not unduly inconveniencing him.'

Peterson, with his coffee cup in his hand, was staring down the drive.

'Your car is a little early, Captain Drummond,' he said at length. 'However, perhaps it can wait two or three minutes, while we get matters perfectly clear. I should dislike you not knowing where you stand.' He turned round and faced the soldier. 'You have deliberately, against my advice, elected to fight me and the interests I represent. So be it. From now on, the gloves are off. You embarked on this course from a spirit of adventure, at the instigation of the girl next door. She, poor little fool, is concerned over that drunken waster – her father. She asked you to help her – you agreed; and, amazing though it may seem, up to now you have scored a certain measure of success. I admit it, and I admire you for it. I apologize now for having played the fool with you last night: you're the type of man whom one should kill outright – or leave alone.'

He set down his coffee cup, and carefully snipped the end off a cigar.

'You are also the type of man who will continue on the path he has started. You are completely in the dark; you have no idea whatever what you are up against.' He smiled grimly, and turned abruptly on Hugh. 'You fool – you stupid young fool. Do you *really* imagine that you can beat me?'

The soldier rose and stood in front of him.

'I have a few remarks of my own to make,' he answered, 'and then we might consider the interview closed. I ask nothing better than that the gloves should be off – though with your filthy methods of fighting, anything you touch will get very dirty. As you say, I am completely in the dark as to your plans; but I have a pretty shrewd idea what I'm up against. Men who can employ a thumbscrew on a poor defenceless brute seem to me to be several degrees worse than an aboriginal cannibal, and therefore if I put you down as one of the lowest types of degraded criminal I shall not be very wide of the mark. There's no good you snarling at me, you swine; it does everybody good to hear some home truths – and don't forget it was you who pulled off the gloves.'

Drummond lit a cigarette; then his merciless eyes fixed themselves again on Peterson.

'There is only one thing more,' he continued. 'You have kindly warned me of my danger: let me give you a word of advice in my turn. I'm going to fight you; if I can, I'm going to beat you. Anything that may happen to me is part of the game. But if anything happens to Miss Benton during the course of operations, then, as surely as there is a God above, Peterson, I'll get at you somehow and murder you with my own hands.'

For a few moments there was silence, and then with a short laugh Drummond turned away.

'Quite melodramatic,' he remarked lightly. 'And very bad for the digestion so early in the morning. My regards to your charming daughter, also to him of the broken jaw. Shall we meet again soon?' He paused at the door and looked back.

Peterson was still standing by the table, his face expressionless.

'Very soon indeed, young man,' he said quietly. 'Very soon indeed. . .'

Hugh stepped out into the warm sunshine, and spoke to his chauffeur.

'Take her out into the main road, Jenkins,' he said, 'and wait for me outside the entrance to the next house. I shan't be long.'

Then he strolled through the garden towards the little wicket-gate that led to The Larches. Phyllis! The thought of her was singing in his heart to the exclusion of everything else. Just a few minutes with her; just the touch of her hand, the faint smell of the scent she used – and then back to the game.

He had almost reached the gate, when, with a sudden crashing in the undergrowth, Jem Smith blundered out into the path. His naturally ruddy face was white, and he stared round fearfully.

'Gawd! sir,' he cried, 'mind out. 'Ave yer seen it?'

'Seen what, Jem?' asked Drummond.

'That there brute. 'E's escaped; and if 'e meets a stranger—' He left the sentence unfinished, and stood listening. From somewhere behind the house came a deep-throated, snarling roar; then the clang of a padlock shooting home in metal, followed by a series of heavy thuds as if some big animal was hurling itself against the bars of a cage.

'They've got it,' murmured Jem, mopping his brow.

'You seem to have a nice little crowd of pets about the house,' remarked Drummond, putting a hand on the man's arm as he was about to move off. 'What was that docile creature we've just heard calling to its young?'

The ex-pugilist looked at him sullenly.

'Never you mind, sir; it ain't no business of yours. An' if I was you, I wouldn't make it your business to find out.'

A moment later he had disappeared into the bushes, and Drummond was left alone. Assuredly a cheerful household, he reflected; just the spot for a rest-cure. Then he saw a figure on the lawn of the next house which banished everything else from his mind; and opening the gate, he walked eagerly towards Phyllis Benton.

IV

'I heard you were down here,' she said gravely, holding out her hand to him. 'I've been sick with anxiety ever since father told me he'd seen you.'

Hugh imprisoned the little hand in his own huge ones, and smiled at the girl.

'I call that just sweet of you,' he answered. 'Just sweet. . . Having people worry about me is not much in my line, but I think I rather like it.'

'You're the most impossible person,' she remarked, releasing her hand. 'What sort of a night did you have?'

'Somewhat parti-coloured,' returned Hugh lightly. 'Like the hoary old curate's egg – calm in parts.'

'But why did you go at all?' she cried, beating her hands together. 'Don't you realize that if anything happens to you, I shall never forgive myself?'

The soldier smiled reassuringly.

'Don't worry, little girl,' he said. 'Years ago I was told by an old gipsy that I should die in my bed of old age and excessive consumption of invalid port. . . As a matter of fact, the cause of my visit was rather humorous. They abducted me in the middle of the night, with an ex-soldier of my old battalion, who was, I regret to state, sleeping off the effects of much indifferent liquor in my rooms.'

'What are you talking about?' she demanded.

'They thought he was your American millionaire cove, and the wretched Mullings was too drunk to deny it. In fact, I don't think they ever asked his opinion at all.' Hugh grinned reminiscently. 'A pathetic spectacle.'

'Oh! But splendid,' cried the girl a little breathlessly. 'And where was the American?'

'Next door – safe with a very dear old friend of mine, Peter Darrell. You must meet Peter some day – you'll like him.' He looked at her thoughtfully.

'No,' he added, 'on second thoughts, I'm not at all sure that I shall let you meet Peter. You might like him too much; and he's a dirty dog.'

'Don't be ridiculous,' she cried with a faint blush. 'Tell me, where is the American now?'

'Many miles out of London,' answered Hugh.

'I think we'll leave it at that. The less you know, Miss Benton, at the moment – the better.'

'Have you found out anything?' she demanded eagerly.

Hugh shook his head.

'Not a thing. Except that your neighbours are as pretty a bunch of scoundrels as I ever want to meet.'

'But you'll let me know if you do.' She laid a hand beseechingly on his arm. 'You know what's at stake for me, don't you? Father, and – oh! but you know.'

'I know,' he answered gravely. 'I know, old thing. I promise I'll let you know anything I find out. And in the meantime I want you to keep an eye fixed on what goes on next door, and let me know anything of importance by letter to the Junior Sports Club.' He lit a cigarette thoughtfully. 'I have an idea that they feel so absolutely confident in their own power, that they are going to make the fatal mistake of underrating their opponents. We shall see.' He turned to her with a twinkle in his eye. 'Anyway, our Mr Lakington will see that you don't come to any harm.'

'The brute!' she cried, very low. 'How I hate him!' Then – with a sudden change of tone, she looked up at Drummond. 'I don't know whether it's worth mentioning,' she said slowly, 'but yesterday afternoon four men came at different times to The Elms. They were the sort of type one sees tub-thumping in Hyde Park, all except one, who looked like a respectable working-man.'

Hugh shook his head.

'Don't seem to help much, does it? Still, one never knows. Let me know anything like that in future at the club.'

'Good morning, Miss Benton.' Peterson's voice behind them made Drummond swing round with a smothered curse. 'Our inestimable friend Captain Drummond brought such a nice young fellow to see me last night, and then left him lying about the house this morning.'

Hugh bit his lip with annoyance; until that moment he had clean forgotten that Mullings was still in The Elms.

'I have sent him along to your car,' continued Peterson suavely, 'which I trust was the correct procedure. Or did you want to give him to me as a pet?'

'From a rapid survey, Mr Peterson, I should think you have quite enough already,' said Hugh. 'I trust you paid him the money you owe him.'

'I will allot it to him in my will,' remarked Peterson. ' If you do the same in yours, doubtless he will get it from one of us sooner or later. In the meantime, Miss Benton, is your father up?'

The girl frowned.

'No – not yet.'

'Then I will go and see him in bed. For the present, au revoir.' He walked towards the house, and they watched him go in silence. It was as he opened the drawing-room window that Hugh called after him:

'Do you like the horse Elliman's or the ordinary brand?' he asked. 'I'll send you a bottle for that stiff neck of yours.'

Very deliberately Peterson turned round.

'Don't trouble, thank you, Captain Drummond. I have my own remedies, which are far more efficacious.'

Chapter 5

In Which There is Trouble at Goring

I

'DID you have a good night, Mullings?' remarked Hugh as he got into his car.

The man grinned sheepishly.

'I dunno what the game was, sir, but I ain't for many more of them. They're about the ugliest crowd of blackguards in that there 'ouse that I ever wants to see again.'

'How many did you see altogether?' asked Drummond.

'I saw six actual like, sir; but I 'eard others talking.'

The car slowed up before the post office and Hugh got out. There were one or two things he proposed to do in London before going to Goring, and it struck him that a wire to Peter Darrell might allay that gentleman's uneasiness if he was late in getting down. So new was he to the tortuous ways of crime, that the foolishness of the proceeding never entered his head: up to date in his life, if he had wished to send a wire he had sent one. And so it may be deemed a sheer fluke on his part, that a man dawdling by the counter aroused his suspicions. He was a perfectly ordinary man, chatting casually with the girl on the other side; but it chanced that, just as Hugh was holding the post office pencil up, and gazing at its so-called point with an air of resigned anguish, the perfectly ordinary man ceased chatting and looked at him. Hugh caught his eye for a fleeting second; then the conversation continued. And as he turned to pull out the pad of forms, it struck him that the man had looked away just a trifle too quickly. . .

A grin spread slowly over his face, and after a moment's hesitation he proceeded to compose a short wire. He wrote it in block letters for additional clearness; he also pressed his hardest as befitted a blunt pencil. Then with the form in his hand he advanced to the counter.

'How long will it take to deliver in London?' he asked the girl. . .

The girl was not helpful. It depended, he gathered, on a variety of circumstances, of which not the least was the perfectly ordinary man who talked so charmingly. She did not say so, in so many words, but Hugh respected her none the less for her maidenly reticence.

'I don't think I'll bother, then,' he said, thrusting the wire into his pocket. 'Good morning. . .'

He walked to the door, and shortly afterwards his car rolled down the street. He would have liked to remain and see the finish of his little jest, but, as is so often the case, imagination is better than reality. Certain it is that he chuckled consumedly the whole way up to London, whereas the actual finish was tame.

With what the girl considered peculiar abruptness, the perfectly ordinary man concluded his conversation with her, and decided that he, too, would send a wire. And then, after a long and thoughtful pause at the writing-bench, she distinctly heard an unmistakable 'Damn.' Then he walked out, and she saw him no more.

Moreover, it is to be regretted that the perfectly ordinary man told a lie a little later in the day, when giving his report to someone whose neck apparently inconvenienced him greatly. But then a lie is frequently more tactful than the truth, and to have announced that the sole result of his morning's labours had been to decipher a wire addressed to The Elms, which contained the cryptic remark, 'Stung again, stiff neck, stung again,' would not have been tactful. So he lied, as has been stated, thereby showing his wisdom. . .

But though Drummond chuckled to himself as the car rushed through the fresh morning air, once or twice a gleam that was not altogether amusement shone in his eyes. For four years he had played one game where no mistakes were allowed; the little incident of the post office had helped to bring to his mind the certainty that he had now embarked on another where the conditions were much the same. That he had scored up to date was luck rather than good management, and he was far too shrewd not to realize it. Now he was marked, and luck with a marked man cannot be tempted too far.

Alone and practically unguarded he had challenged a gang of international criminals: a gang not only utterly unscrupulous but controlled by a mastermind. Of its power as yet he had no clear idea; of its size and immediate object he had even less. Perhaps it was as well. Had he realized even dimly the immensity of the issues he was up against, had he had but an inkling of the magnitude of the plot conceived in the sinister brain of his host of the previous evening, then, cheery optimist though he was, even Hugh Drummond might have wavered. But he had no such inkling, and so the gleam in his eyes was but transitory, the chuckle that succeeded it more whole-hearted than before. Was it not sport in a land flowing with strikes and profiteers; sport such as his soul loved?

'I am afraid, Mullings,' he said as the car stopped in front of his club, 'that the kindly gentleman with whom we spent last night has repudiated his obligations. He refuses to meet the bill I gave him for your services. Just wait here a moment.'

He went inside, returning in a few moments with a folded cheque.

'Round the corner, Mullings, and an obliging fellah in a black coat will shove you out the necessary Bradburys.'

The man glanced at the cheque.

'Fifty quid, sir!' he gasped. 'Why – it's too much, sir. . . I. . .'

'The labourer, Mullings, is worthy of his hire. You have been of the very greatest assistance to me; and, incidentally, it is more than likely that I may want you again. Now, where can I get hold of you?'

'13, Green Lane, 'oxton, sir, 'll always find me. And any time, sir, as you wants me, I'd like to come just for the sport of the thing.'

Hugh grinned.

'Good lad. And it may be sooner than you think.'

With a cheery laugh he turned back into his club, and for a moment or two the ex-soldier stood looking after him. Then with great deliberation he turned to the chauffeur, and spat reflectively.

'If there was more like 'im, and less like *'im'* – he indicated a stout vulgarian rolling past in a large car and dreadful clothes – 'things wouldn't 'appen such as is 'appening to-day. Ho! no. . .'

With which weighty dictum Mr Mullings, late private of the Royal Loamshires, turned his steps in the direction of the 'obliging fellah in a black coat.'

II

Inside the Junior Sports Club, Hugh Drummond was burying his nose in a large tankard of the ale for which that cheery pot-house was still famous. And in the intervals of this most delightful pastime he was trying to make up his mind on a peculiarly knotty point. Should he or should he not communicate with the police on the matter? He felt that as a respectable citizen of the country it was undoubtedly his duty to tell somebody something. The point was who to tell and what to tell him. On the subject of Scotland Yard his ideas were nebulous; he had a vague impression that one filled in a form and waited – tedious operations, both.

'Besides, dear old flick,' he murmured abstractedly to the portrait of the founder of the club, who had drunk the cellar dry and then died, 'am I a respectable citizen? Can it be said with any certainty, that if I filled in a form saying all that had happened in the last two days, I shouldn't be put in quod[1] myself?'

He sighed profoundly and gazed out into the sunny square. A waiter was arranging the first editions of the evening papers on a table, and Hugh beckoned to him to bring one. His mind was still occupied with his problem, and almost mechanically he glanced over the columns. Cricket, racing, the latest divorce case and the latest strike – all the usual headings were there. And he was just putting down the paper, to again concentrate on his problem, when a paragraph caught his eye.

'STRANGE MURDER IN BELFAST.

'The man whose body was discovered in such peculiar circumstances near the docks has been identified as Mr James Granger, the confidential secretary to Mr Hiram Potts, the American multi-millionaire, at present in this country. The unfortunate victim of this dastardly outrage – his head, as we reported in out last night's issue, was nearly severed from his body – had apparently been sent over on business by Mr Potts, and had arrived the preceding day. What he was doing in the locality in which he was found is a mystery.

'We understand that Mr Potts, who has recently been indisposed, has returned to the Carlton, and is greatly upset at the sudden tragedy.

'The police are confident that they will shortly obtain a clue, though the rough element in the locality where the murder was committed presents great difficulties. It seems clear that the motive was robbery, as all the murdered man's pockets were rifled. But the most peculiar thing about the case is the extraordinary care taken by the murderer to prevent the identification of the body. Every article of clothing, even down to the murdered man's socks, had had the name torn out, and it was only through the criminal overlooking the

[1]Quod is slang for prison.

tailor's tab inside the inner breast-pocket of Mr Granger's coat that the police were enabled to identify the body.'

Drummond laid down the paper on his knees, and stared a little dazedly at the club's immoral founder.

'Holy smoke! Laddie,' he murmured, 'that man Peterson ought to be on the committee here. Verily, I believe, he could galvanize the staff into some semblance of activity.'

'Did you order anything, sir?' A waiter paused beside him.

'No,' murmured Drummond, 'but I will rectify the omission. Another large tankard of ale.'

The waiter departed, and Hugh picked up the paper again.

'*We understand*,' he murmured gently to himself, '*that Mr Potts, who has recently been indisposed, has returned to the Carlton*. . . Now that's very interesting. . .' He lit a cigarette and lay back in his chair. 'I was under the impression that Mr Potts was safely tucked up in bed, consuming semolina pudding, at Goring. It requires elucidation.'

'I beg your pardon, sir,' remarked the waiter, placing the beer on the table beside him.

'You needn't,' returned Hugh. 'Up to date you have justified my fondest expectations. And as a further proof of my good will, I would like you to get me a trunk call – 2 X Goring.'

A few minutes later he was in the telephone box.

'Peter, I have seldom been so glad to hear your voice. Is all well? Good. Don't mention any names. Our guest is there, is he? Gone on strike against more milk puddings, you say. Coax him, Peter. Make a noise like a sturgeon, and he'll think it's caviare. Have you seen the papers? There are interesting doings in Belfast, which concern us rather intimately. I'll be down later, and we'll have a powwow.'

He hung up the receiver and stepped out of the box.

'If, Algy,' he remarked to a man who was looking at the tape machine outside, ' the paper says a blighter's somewhere and you know he's somewhere else – what do you do?'

'Up to date in such cases I have always shot the editor,' murmured Algy Longworth. 'Come and feed.'

'You're so helpful, Algy. A perfect rock of strength. Do you want a job?'

'What sort of a job?' demanded the other suspiciously.

'Oh! not work, dear old boy. Damn it, man – you know me better than that, surely!'

'People are so funny nowadays,' returned Longworth gloomily. 'The most unlikely souls seem to be doing things and trying to look as if they were necessary. What is this job?'

Together the two men strolled into the luncheon-room, and long after the cheese had been finished, Algy Longworth was still listening in silence to his companion.

'My dear old bean,' he murmured ecstatically as Hugh finished, 'my *very* dear old bean. I think it's the most priceless thing I ever heard. Enrol me as a member of the band. And, incidentally, Toby Sinclair is running round in circles asking for trouble. Let's rope him in.'

'Go and find him this afternoon, Algy,' said Hugh rising. 'And tell him to keep his mouth shut. I'd come with you, but it occurs to me that the wretched Potts, bathed in tears at the Carlton, is in need of sympathy. I would have him weep on my shoulder awhile. So long, old dear. You'll hear from me in a day or two.'

It was as he reached the pavement that Algy dashed out after him, with genuine alarm written all over his face.

'Hugh,' he spluttered, 'there's only one stipulation. An armistice must be declared during Ascot week.'

With a thoughtful smile on his face Drummond sauntered along Pall Mall. He had told Longworth more or less on the spur of the moment, knowing that gentleman's capabilities to a nicety. Under a cloak of assumed flippancy he concealed an iron nerve which had never yet failed him; and, in spite of the fact that he wore an entirely unnecessary eyeglass, he could see farther into a brick wall than most of the people who called him a fool.

It was his suggestion of telling Toby Sinclair that caused the smile. For it had started a train of thought in Drummond's mind which seemed to him to be good. If Sinclair – why not two or three more equally trusty sportsmen? Why not a gang of the boys?

Toby possessed a V.C., and a good one – for there are grades of the V.C., and those grades are appreciated to a nicety by the recipient's brother officers if not by the general public. The show would fit Toby like a glove. . . Then there was Ted Jerningham, who combined the rôles of an amateur actor of more than average merit with an ability to hit any-thing at any range with every conceivable type of firearm. And Jerry Seymour in the Flying Corps. . . Not a bad thing to have a flying man – up one's sleeve. . . And possibly someone versed in the ways of tanks might come in handy. . .

The smile broadened to a grin; surely life was very good. And then the grin faded, and something suspiciously like a frown took its place. For he had arrived at the Carlton, and reality had come back to him. He seemed to see the almost headless body of a man lying in a Belfast slum. . .

'Mr Potts will see no one, sir,' remarked the man to whom he addressed his question. 'You are about the twentieth gentleman who has been here already today.'

Hugh had expected this, and smiled genially.

'Precisely, my stout fellow,' he remarked, 'but I'll lay a small amount of money that they were newspaper men. Now, I'm not. And I think that if you will have this note delivered to Mr Potts, he will see me.'

He sat down at a table, and drew a sheet of paper towards him. Two facts were certain: first, that the man upstairs was not the real Potts; second, that he was one of Peterson's gang. The difficulty was to know exactly how to word the note. There might be some mystic pass-word, the omission of which would prove him an impostor at once. At length he took a pen and wrote rapidly; he would have to chance it.

Urgent. A message from headquarters.

He sealed the envelope and handed it with the necessary five shillings for postage to the man. Then he sat down to wait. It was going to be a ticklish interview if he was to learn anything, but the thrill of the game had fairly got him by now, and he watched eagerly for the messenger's return. After what seemed an interminable delay he saw him crossing the lounge.

'Mr Potts will see you, sir. Will you come this way?'

'Is he alone?' said Hugh, as they were whirled up in the lift.

'Yes, sir. I think he was expecting you.'

'Indeed,' murmured Hugh. 'How nice it is to have one's expectations realized.'

He followed his guide along a corridor, and paused outside a door while he went into a room. He heard a murmur of voices, and then the man reappeared.

'This way, sir,' he said, and Hugh stepped inside, to stop with an involuntary gasp of surprise. The man seated in the chair *was* Potts, to all intents and purposes. The likeness was extraordinary, and had he not known that the real article was at Goring he would have been completely deceived himself.

The man waited till the door was closed: then he rose and stepped forward suspiciously.

'I don't know you,' he said. 'Who are you?'

'Since when has everyone employed by headquarters known one another?' Drummond returned guardedly. 'And, incidentally, your likeness to our lamented friend is wonderful. It very nearly deceived even me.'

The man, not ill-pleased, gave a short laugh.

'It'll pass, I think. But it's risky. These cursed reporters have been badgering the whole morning. . . And if his wife or somebody comes over, what then?'

Drummond nodded in agreement.

'Quite so. But what can you do?'

'It wasn't like Rosca to bungle in Belfast. He's never left a clue before, and he had plenty of time to do the job properly.'

'A name inside a breast-pocket might easily be over-looked,' remarked Hugh, seizing the obvious clue.

'Are you making excuses for him?' snarled the other. 'He's failed, and failure is death. Such is our rule. Would you have it altered?'

'Most certainly not. The issues are far too great for any weakness. . .'

'You're right, my friend – you're right. Long live the Brotherhood.' He stared out of the window with smoulder-ing eyes, and Hugh preserved a discreet silence. Then sud-denly the other broke out again. . . 'Have they killed that insolent puppy of a soldier yet?'

'Er – not yet,' murmured Hugh mildly.

'They must find the American at once.' The man thumped the table emphatically. 'It was important before – at least his money was. Now with this blunder – it's vital.'

'Precisely,' said Hugh. 'Precisely.'

'I've already interviewed one man from Scotland Yard, but every hour increases the danger. However, you have a mes-sage for me. What is it?'

Hugh rose and casually picked up his hat. He had got more out of the interview than he had hoped for, and there was noth-ing to be gained by prolonging it. But it struck him that Mr Potts's impersonator was a man of unpleasant disposition, and that tactically a flanking movement to the door was indicated. And, being of an open nature himself, it is possible that the real state of affairs showed for a moment on his face. Be that as it may, something suddenly aroused the other's suspicions, and with a snarl of fury he sprang past Hugh to the door.

'Who are you?' He spat the words out venomously, at the same time whipping an ugly-looking knife out of his pocket.

Hugh replaced his hat and stick on the table and grinned gently.

'I am the insolent puppy of a soldier, dear old bird,' he remarked, watching the other warily. 'And if I was you I'd put the tooth-pick away. . . You might hurt yourself—'

As he spoke he was edging, little by little, towards the other man, who crouched snarling by the door. His eyes, grim and determined, never left the other's face; his hands, apparently hanging listless by his sides, were tingling with the joy of what he knew was coming.

'And the penalty of failure is death, isn't it, dear one?' He spoke almost dreamily; but not for an instant did his attention relax. The words of Olaki, his Japanese instructor, were ringing through his brain: 'Distract his attention if you can; but, as you value your life, don't let him distract yours.'

And so, almost imperceptibly, he crept towards the other man, talking gently.

'Such is your rule. And I think you have failed, haven't you, you unpleasant specimen of humanity? How will they kill you, I wonder?'

It was at that moment that the man made his mistake. It is a mistake that has nipped the life of many a promising pussy in the bud, at the hands, or rather the teeth, of a dog that knows. He looked away; only for a moment – but he looked away. Just as a cat's nerves give after a while and it looks round for an avenue of escape, so did the crouching man take his eyes from Hugh. And quick as any dog, Hugh sprang.

With his left hand he seized the man's right wrist, with his right he seized his throat. Then he forced him upright against the door and held him there. Little by little the grip of his right hand tightened, till the other's eyes were starting from his head, and he plucked at Hugh's face with an impotent left arm, an arm not long enough by three inches to do any damage. And all the while the soldier smiled gently, and stared into the other's eyes. Even when inch by inch he shifted his grip on the man's knife hand he never took his eyes from his opponent's face; even when with a sudden gasp of agony the man dropped his knife from fingers which, of a sudden, had become numb, the steady, merciless glance still bored into his brain.

'You're not very clever at it, are you?' said Hugh softly. 'It would be so easy to kill you now, and, except for the inconvenience I should undoubtedly suffer, it mightn't be a bad idea. But they know me downstairs, and it would make it so awkward when I wanted to dine here again. . . So, taking everything into account, I think—'

There was a sudden lightning movement, a heave and a quick jerk. The impersonator of Potts was dimly conscious of flying through the air, and of hitting the floor some yards from the door. He then became acutely conscious that the floor was hard, and that being winded is a most painful experience. Doubled up and groaning, he watched Hugh pick up his hat and stick, and make for the door. He made a frantic effort to rise, but the pain was too great, and he rolled over cursing, while the soldier, his hand on the door-knob, laughed gently.

'I'll keep the tooth-pick,' he remarked, 'as a memento.'

The next moment he was striding along the corridor towards the lift. As a fight it had been a poor one, but his brain was busy with the information he had heard. True, it had been scrappy in the extreme, and, in part, had only confirmed what he had suspected all along. The wretched Granger had been foully done to death, for no other reason than that he was the millionaire's secretary. Hugh's jaw tightened; it revolted his sense of sport. It wasn't as if the poor blighter had done anything; merely because he existed and might ask inconvenient questions he had been removed. And as the lift shot downwards, and the remembrance of the grim struggle he had had in the darkness of The Elms the night before came back to his mind, he wondered once again if he had done wisely in not breaking Peterson's neck while he had had the chance.

He was still debating the question in his mind as he crossed the tea-lounge. And almost unconsciously he glanced towards the table where three days before he had had tea with Phyllis Benton, and had been more than half inclined to believe that the whole thing was an elaborate leg-pull. . .

'Why, Captain Drummond, you look pensive.' A well-known voice from a table at his side made him look down, and he bowed a little grimly. Irma Peterson was regarding him with a mocking smile.

He glanced at her companion, a young man whose face seemed vaguely familiar to him, and then his eyes rested once more on the girl. Even his masculine intelligence could appreciate the perfection – in a slightly foreign style – of her clothes; and, as to her beauty, he had never been under any delusions. Nor, apparently, was her escort, whose expression was not one of unalloyed pleasure at the interruption to his *tête-à-tête*.

'The Carlton seems rather a favourite resort of yours,' she continued, watching him through half-closed eyes. 'I think you're very wise to make the most of it while you can.'

'While I can?' said Hugh. 'That sounds rather depressing.'

'I've done my best,' continued the girl, 'but matters have passed out of my hands, I'm afraid.'

Again Hugh glanced at her companion, but he had risen and was talking to some people who had just come in.

'Is he one of the firm?' he remarked. 'His face seems familiar.'

'Oh, no!' said the girl. 'He is – just a friend. What have you been doing this afternoon?'

'That, at any rate, is straight and to the point,' laughed Hugh. 'If you want to know, I've just had a most depressing interview.'

'You're a very busy person, aren't you, my ugly one?' she murmured.

'The poor fellow, when I left him, was quite prostrated with grief, and – er – pain,' he went on mildly.

'Would it be indiscreet to ask who the poor fellow is?' she asked.

'A friend of your father's, I think,' said Hugh, with a profound sigh. 'So sad. I hope Mr Peterson's neck is less stiff by now?'

The girl began to laugh softly.

'Not very much, I'm afraid. And it's made him a little irritable. Won't you wait and see him?'

'Is he here now?' said Hugh quickly.

'Yes,' answered the girl. 'With his friend whom you've just left. You're quick, *mon ami* – quite quick.' She leaned forward suddenly. 'Now, why don't you join us instead of so foolishly trying to fight us? Believe me, Monsieur Hugh, it is the only thing that can possibly save you. You know too much.'

'Is the invitation to amalgamate official, or from your own charming brain?' murmured Hugh.

'Made on the spur of the moment,' she said lightly. 'But it may be regarded as official.'

'I'm afraid it must be declined on the spur of the moment,' he answered in the same tone. 'And equally to be regarded as official. Well, au revoir. Please tell Mr Peterson how sorry I am to have missed him.'

'I will most certainly,' answered the girl. 'But then, *mon ami,* you will be seeing him again soon, without doubt. . .'

She waved a charming hand in farewell, and turned to her companion, who was beginning to manifest symptoms of impatience. But Drummond, though he went into the hall outside, did not immediately leave the hotel. Instead, he buttonholed an exquisite being arrayed in gorgeous apparel, and led him to a point of vantage.

'You see that girl,' he remarked, 'having tea with a man at the third table from the big palm? Now, can you tell me who the man is? I seem to know his face, but I can't put a name to it.'

'That, sir,' murmured the exquisite being, with the faintest perceptible scorn of such ignorance, 'is the Marquis of Laidley. His lordship is frequently here.'

'Laidley!' cried Hugh, is sudden excitement. 'Laidley! The Duke of Lampshire's son! You priceless old stuffed tomato – the plot thickens.'

Completely regardless of the scandalised horror on the exquisite being's face, he smote him heavily in the stomach and stepped into Pall Mall. For clear before his memory had come three lines on the scrap of paper he had torn from the table at The Elms that first night, when he had grabbed the dazed millionaire from under Peterson's nose.

> earl necklace and the
> are at present
> chess of Lamp-

The Duchess of Lampshire's pearls were world-famous; the Marquis of Laidley was apparently enjoying his tea. And between the two there seemed to be a connection rather too obvious to be missed.

III

'I'm glad you two fellows came down,' said Hugh thoughtfully, as he entered the sitting-room of his bungalow at Goring. Dinner was over, and stretched in three chairs were Peter Darrell, Algy Longworth, and Toby Sinclair. The air was thick with smoke, and two dogs lay curled up on the mat, asleep. 'Did you know that a man came here this afternoon, Peter?'

Darrell yawned and stretched himself.

'I did not. Who was it?'

'Mrs Denny has just told me.' Hugh reached out a hand for his pipe, and proceeded to stuff it with tobacco. 'He came about the water.'

'Seems a very righteous proceeding, dear old thing,' said Algy lazily.

'And he told her that I had told him to come. Unfortunately, I'd done nothing of the sort.'

His three listeners sat up and stared at him.

'What do you mean, Hugh?' asked Toby Sinclair at length.

'It's pretty obvious, old boy,' said Hugh grimly. 'He no more came about the water than he came about my aunt.

I should say that about five hours ago Peterson found out that our one and only Hiram C. Potts was upstairs.'

'Good Lord!' spluttered Darrell, by now very wide awake. 'How the devil has he done it?'

'There are no flies on the gentleman,' remarked Hugh. 'I didn't expect he'd do it quite so quick, I must admit. But it wasn't very difficult for him to find out that I had a bungalow here, and so he drew the covert.'

'And he's found the bally fox,' said Algy. 'What do we do, sergeant-major?'

'We take it in turns – two at a time – to sit up with Potts.' Hugh glanced at the other three. 'Damn it – you blighters – wake up!'

Darrell struggled to his feet and walked up and down the room.

'I don't know what it is,' he said, rubbing his eyes, 'I feel most infernally sleepy.'

'Well, listen to me – confound you. . . Toby!' Hugh hurled a tobacco-pouch at the offender's head.

'Sorry, old man.' With a start Sinclair sat up in his chair and blinked at Hugh.

'They're almost certain to try and get him to-night,' went on Hugh. 'Having given the show away by leaving a clue on the wretched secretary, they must get the real man as soon as possible. It's far too dangerous to leave the – leave the—' His head dropped forward on his chest: a short, half-strangled snore came from his lips. It had the effect of waking him for the moment, and he staggered to his feet.

The other three, sprawling in their chairs, were openly and unashamedly asleep; even the dogs lay in fantastic attitudes, breathing heavily, inert like logs.

'Wake up!' shouted Hugh wildly. 'For God's sake – wake up! We've been drugged!'

An iron weight seemed to be pressing down on his eyelids: the desire for sleep grew stronger and stronger. For a few moments more he fought against it, hopelessly, despairingly;

while his legs seemed not to belong to him, and there was a roaring noise in his ears. And then, just before unconsciousness overcame him, there came to his bemused brain the sound of a whistle thrice repeated from outside the window. With a last stupendous effort he fought his way towards it, and for a moment he stared into the darkness. There were dim figures moving through the shrubs, and suddenly one seemed to detach itself. It came nearer, and the light fell on the man's face. His nose and mouth were covered with a sort of pad, but the cold, sneering eyes were unmistakable.

'Lakington!' gasped Hugh, and then the roaring noise increased in his head; his legs struck work altogether. He collapsed on the floor and lay sprawling, while Lakington, his face pressed against the glass outside, watched in silence.

'Draw the curtains.' Lakington was speaking, his voice muffled behind the pad, and one of the men did as he said. There were four in all, each with a similar pad over his mouth and nose. 'Where did you put the generator, Brownlow?'

'In the coal-scuttle.' A man whom Mrs Denny would have no difficulty in recognizing, even with the mask on his face, carefully lifted a small black box out of the scuttle from behind some coal, and shook it gently, holding it to his ear. 'It's finished,' he remarked, and Lakington nodded.

'An ingenious invention is gas,' he said, addressing another of the men. 'We owe your nation quite a debt of gratitude for the idea.'

A guttural grunt left no doubt as to what that nation was, and Lakington dropped the box into his pocket.

'Go and get him,' he ordered briefly, and the others left the room.

Contemptuously Lakington kicked one of the dogs; it rolled over and lay motionless in its new position. Then he went in turn to each of the three men sprawling in the chairs. With no attempt at gentleness he turned their faces up to the light, and studied them deliberately; then he let their heads roll back again with a thud. Finally, he went to the window and stared down at Drummond. In his eyes was a look of cold fury, and he kicked the unconscious man savagely in the ribs.

'You young swine,' he muttered. 'Do you think I'll forget that blow on the jaw?'

He took another box out of his pocket and looked at it lovingly.

'Shall I?' With a short laugh he replaced it. 'It's too good a death for you, Captain Drummond, D.S.O., M.C. Just to snuff out in your sleep. No, my friend, I think I can devise something better than that; something really artistic.'

Two other men came in as he turned away, and Lakington looked at them.

'Well,' he asked, 'have you got the old woman?'

'Bound and gagged in the kitchen,' answered one of them laconically. 'Are you going to do this crowd in?'

The speaker looked at the unconscious men with hatred in his eyes.

'They encumber the earth – this breed of puppy.'

'They will not encumber it for long,' said Lakington softly. 'But the one in the window there is not going to die quite so easily. I have a small unsettled score with him. . .'

'All right; he's in the car.' A voice came from outside the window, and with a last look at Hugh Drummond, Lakington turned away.

'Then we'll go,' he remarked. 'Au revoir, my blundering young bull. Before I've finished with you, you'll scream for mercy. And you won't get it. . .'

Through the still night air there came the thrumming of the engine of a powerful car. Gradually it died away and there was silence. Only the murmur of the river over the weir broke the silence, save for an owl which hooted mournfully in a tree near by. And then, with a sudden crack, Peter Darrell's head rolled over and hit the arm of his chair.

Chapter 6

In Which a Very Old Game Takes Place on the Hog's Back

I

A THICK grey mist lay over the Thames. It covered the water and the low fields to the west like a thick white carpet; it drifted sluggishly under the old bridge which spans the river between Goring and Streatley. It was the hour before dawn, and sleepy passengers, rubbing the windows of their carriages as the Plymouth boat express rushed on towards London, shivered and drew their rugs closer around them. It looked cold. . .cold and dead.

Slowly, almost imperceptibly, the vapour rose, and spread outwards up the wooded hills by Basildon. It drifted through the shrubs and rose-bushes of a little garden, which stretched from a bungalow down to the water's edge, until at length wisps of it brushed gently round the bungalow itself. It was a daily performance in the summer, and generally the windows of the lower rooms remained shut till long after the mist had gone and the sun was glinting through the trees on to the river below. But on this morning there was a change in the usual programme. Suddenly the window of one of the downstair rooms was flung open, and a man with a white haggard face leant out drawing great gulps of fresh air into his lungs. Softly the white wraiths eddied past him into the room behind – a room in which a queer, faintly sweet smell still hung – a room in which three other men lay sprawling uncouthly in chairs, and two dogs lay motionless on the hearthrug.

After a moment or two the man withdrew, only to appear again with one of the others in his arms. And then, having dropped his burden through the window on to the lawn outside, he repeated his performance with the remaining two. Finally he pitched the two dogs after them, and then, with his hand to his forehead, he staggered down to the water's edge.

'Holy smoke!' he muttered to himself, as he plunged his head into the cold water; 'talk about the morning after! . . . Never have I thought of such a head.'

After a while, with the water still dripping from his face, he returned to the bungalow and found the other three in varying stages of partial insensibility.

'Wake up, my heroes,' he remarked, 'and go and put your fat heads in the river.'

Peter Darrell scrambled unsteadily to his feet. 'Great Scott! Hugh,' he muttered thickly, 'what's happened?"

'We've been had for mugs,' said Drummond grimly.

Algy Longworth blinked at him foolishly from his position in the middle of a flower-bed.

'Dear old soul,' he murmured at length, 'you'll have to change your wine merchants. Merciful Heavens! is the top of my head still on?'

'Don't be a fool, Algy,' grunted Hugh. 'You weren't drunk last night. Pull yourself together, man; we were all of us drugged or doped somehow. And now,' he added bitterly, 'we've all got heads, and we have not got Potts.'

'I don't remember anything,' said Toby Sinclair, 'except falling asleep. Have they taken him?'

'Of course they have,' said Hugh. 'Just before I went off I saw 'em all in the garden, and that swine Lakington was with them. However, while you go and put your nuts in the river, I'll go up and make certain.'

With a grim smile he watched the three men lurch down to the water; then he turned and went upstairs to the room which had been occupied by the American millionaire. It was empty, as he had known it would be, and with a smothered curse he made his way downstairs again. And it was as he stood in the little hall saying things gently under his breath that he heard a muffled moaning noise coming from the kitchen. For a moment he was nonplussed; then, with an oath at his stupidity, he dashed through the door. Bound tightly to the table, with a gag in her mouth, the wretched Mrs Denny was sitting on the floor, blinking at him wrathfully. . .

'What on earth will Denny say to me when he hears about this!' said Hugh, feverishly cutting the cords. He helped her to her feet, and then forced her gently into a chair. 'Mrs Denny, have those swine hurt you?'

Five minutes served to convince him that the damage, if any, was mental rather than bodily, and that her vocal powers were not in the least impaired. Like a dam bursting, the flood of the worthy woman's wrath surged over him; she breathed a hideous vengeance on every one impartially. Then she drove Hugh from the kitchen, and slammed the door in his face.

'Breakfast in half an hour,' she cried from inside – 'not that one of you deserves it.'

'We are forgiven,' remarked Drummond, as he joined the other three on the lawn. 'Do any of you feel like breakfast? Fat sausages and crinkly bacon.'

'Shut up,' groaned Algy, ' or we'll throw you into the river. What I want is a brandy-and-soda – half a dozen of 'em.'

'I wish I knew what they did to us,' said Darrell. 'Because, if I remember straight, I drank bottled beer at dinner, and I'm damned if I see how they could have doped that.'

'I'm only interested in one thing, Peter,' remarked Drummond grimly, 'and that isn't what they did to us. It's what we're going to do to them.'

'Count me out,' said Algy. 'For the next year I shall be fully occupied resting my head against a cold stone. Hugh, I positively detest your friends. . .'

It was a few hours later that a motor-car drew up outside that celebrated chemist in Piccadilly whose pick-me-ups are known from Singapore to Alaska. From it there descended four young men, who ranged themselves in a row before the counter and spoke no word. Speech was unnecessary. Four foaming drinks were consumed, four acid-drops were eaten, and then, still in silence, the four young men got back into the car and drove away. It was a solemn rite, and on arrival at the Junior Sports Club the four performers sank into four large chairs, and pondered gently on the vileness of the morning after. Especially when there hadn't been a night before. An unprofitable meditation evidently, for suddenly, as if actuated by a single thought, the four young men rose from their four large chairs and again entered the motor-car.

The celebrated chemist whose pick-me-ups are known from Singapore to Alaska gazed at them severely.

'A very considerable bend, gentlemen,' he remarked.

'Quite wrong,' answered the whitest and most haggard of the row. 'We are all confirmed Pussyfoots, and have been consuming non-alcoholic beer.'

Once more to the scrunch of acid-drops the four young men entered the car outside; once more, after a brief and silent drive, four large chairs in the smoking-room of the Junior Sports Club received an occupant. And it was so, even until luncheon time. . .

'Are we better?' said Hugh, getting to his feet, and regarding the other three with a discerning eye.

'No,' murmured Toby, 'but I am beginning to hope that I may live. Four Martinis and then we will gnaw a cutlet.'

II

'Has it struck you fellows,' remarked Hugh, at the conclusion of lunch, ' that seated around this table are four officers who fought with some distinction and much discomfort in the recent historic struggle?'

'How beautifully you put it, old flick!' said Darrell.

'Has it further struck you fellows,' continued Hugh, 'that last night we were done down, trampled on, had for mugs by a crowd of dirty blackguards composed largely of the dregs of the universe?'

'A veritable Solomon,' said Algy, gazing at him admiringly through his eyeglass. 'I told you this morning I detested your friends.'

'Has it still further struck you,' went on Hugh, a trifle grimly, 'that we aren't standing for it? At any rate, I'm not. It's my palaver this, you fellows, and if you like. . . Well, there's no call on you to remain in the game. I mean – er—'

'Yes, we're waiting to hear what the devil you do mean,' said Toby uncompromisingly.

'Well – er,' stammered Hugh, 'there's a big element of risk – er – don't you know, and there's no earthly reason why you fellows should get roped in and all that. I mean – er – I'm sort of pledged to see the thing through, don't you know, and—' He relapsed into silence, and stared at the tablecloth, uncomfortably aware of three pairs of eyes fixed on him.

'Well – er – ' mimicked Algy, 'there's a big element of risk – er – don't you know, and I mean – er – we're sort of pledged to bung you through the window, old bean, if you talk such consolidated drivel.'

Hugh grinned sheepishly.

'Well, I had to put it to you fellows. Not that I ever thought for a moment you wouldn't see the thing through – but last evening is enough to show you that we're up against a tough crowd. A damned tough crowd,' he added thoughtfully. 'That being so,' he went on briskly, after a moment or two, 'I propose that we should tackle the blighters tonight.'

'To-night!' echoed Darrell. 'Where?'

'At The Elms, of course. That's where the wretched Potts is for a certainty.'

'And how do you propose that we should set about it?' demanded Sinclair.

Drummond drained his port and grinned gently.

'By stealth, dear old beans – by stealth. You – and I thought we might rake in Ted Jerningham, and perhaps Jerry Seymour, to join the happy throng – will make a demonstration in force, with the idea of drawing off the enemy, thereby leaving the coast clear for me to explore the house for the unfortunate Potts.'

'Sounds very nice in theory,' said Darrell dubiously, 'but. . .'

'And what do you mean by a demonstration?' said Longworth. 'You don't propose we should sing carols outside the drawing-room window, do you?'

'My dear people,' Hugh murmured protestingly, 'surely you know me well enough by now to realize that I can't possibly have another idea for at least ten minutes. That is just the general scheme; doubtless the mere vulgar details will occur to us in time. Besides, it's someone else's turn now.' He looked round the table hopefully.

'We might dress up or something,' remarked Toby Sinclair, after a lengthy silence.

'What in the name of Heaven is the use of that?' said Darrell witheringly. 'It's not private theatricals, nor a beauty competition.'

'Cease wrangling, you two,' said Hugh suddenly, a few moments later. 'I've got a perfect cerebral hurricane raging. An accident. . . A car. . . What is the connecting link. . . Why, drink. Write it down, Algy, or we might forget. Now, can you beat that?'

'We might have some chance,' said Darrell kindly, 'if we had the slightest idea what you were talking about.'

'I should have thought it was perfectly obvious,' returned Hugh coldly. 'You know, Peter, your worry is that you're too quick on the uptake. Your brain is too sharp.'

'How do you spell connecting?' demanded Algy, looking up from his labours. 'And, anyway, the damn pencil won't write.'

'Pay attention, all of you,' said Hugh. 'Tonight, some time about ten of the clock, Algy's motor will proceed along the Godalming-Guildford road. It will contain you three – also Ted and Jerry Seymour, if we can get 'em. On approaching the gate of The Elms, you will render the night hideous with your vocal efforts. Stray passers-by will think that you are all tight. Then will come the dramatic moment, when, with a heavy crash, you ram the gate.'

'How awfully jolly!' spluttered Algy. 'I beg to move that your car be used for the event.'

'Can't be done, old son,' laughed Hugh. 'Mine's faster than yours, and I'll be wanting it myself. Now – to proceed. Horrified at this wanton damage to property, you will leave the car and proceed in mass formation up the drive.'

'Still giving tongue?' queried Darrell.

'Still giving tongue. Either Ted or Jerry or both of 'em will approach the house and inform the owner in heart-broken accents that they have damaged his gatepost. You three will remain in the garden – you might be recognized. Then it will be up to you. You'll have several men all round you. Keep 'em occupied – somehow. They won't hurt you; they'll only be concerned with seeing that you don't go where you're not wanted. You see, as far as the world is concerned, it's just an ordinary country residence. The last thing they want to do is to draw any suspicion on themselves – and, on the face of it, you are merely five convivial wanderers who have looked on the wine when it was red. I think,' he added thoughtfully, 'that ten minutes will be enough for me. . .'

'What will you be doing?' said Toby.

'I shall be looking for Potts. Don't worry about me. I may find him; I may not. But when you have given me ten minutes – you clear off. I'll look after myself. Now is that clear?'

'Perfectly,' said Darrell, after a short silence. 'But I don't know that I like it, Hugh. It seems to me, old son, that you're running an unnecessary lot of risk.'

'Got any alternative?' demanded Drummond.

'If we're all going down,' said Darrell, 'why not stick together and rush the house in a gang?'

'No go, old bean,' said Hugh decisively. 'Too many of 'em to hope to pull it off. No, low cunning is the only thing that's got an earthly of succeeding.'

'There is one other possible suggestion,' remarked Toby slowly. 'What about the police? From what you say, Hugh, there's enough in that house to jug the whole bunch.'

'Toby!' gasped Hugh. ' I thought better of you. You seriously suggest that we should call in the police! And then return to a life of toping and ease! Besides,' he continued, removing his eyes from the abashed author of this hideous suggestion, 'there's a very good reason for keeping the police out of it. You'd land the girl's father in the cart, along with the rest of them. And it makes it so devilish awkward if one's father-in-law is in prison!'

'When are we going to see this fairy?' demanded Algy.

'You, personally, never. You're far too immoral. I might let the others look at her from a distance in a year or two.' With a grin he rose, and then strolled towards the door. 'Now go and rope in Ted and Jerry, and for the love of Heaven don't ram the wrong gate.'

'What are you going to do yourself?' demanded Peter suspiciously.

'I'm going to look at her from close to. Go away, all of you, and don't listen outside the telephone box.'

III

Hugh stopped his car at Guildford station and, lighting a cigarette, strolled restlessly up and down. He looked at his watch a dozen times in two minutes; he threw away his smoke before it was half finished. In short he manifested every symptom usually displayed by the male of the species when awaiting the arrival of the opposite sex. Over the telephone he had arranged that SHE should come by train from Godalming to confer with him on a matter of great importance; SHE had said she would, but what was it? He, having no suitable answer ready, had made a loud buzzing noise indicative of a telephone exchange in pain, and then rung off. And now he was waiting in that peculiar condition of mind which reveals itself outwardly in hands that are rather too warm, and feet that are rather too cold.

'When is this bally train likely to arrive?' He accosted a phlegmatic official, who regarded him coldly, and doubted the likelihood of its being more than a quarter of an hour early.

At length it was signalled, and Hugh got back into his car. Feverishly he scanned the faces of the passengers as they came out into the street, until, with a sudden quick jump of his heart, he saw her, cool and fresh, coming towards him with a faint smile on her lips.

'What is this very important matter you want to talk to me about?' she demanded, as he adjusted the rug round her.

'I'll tell you when we get out on the Hog's Back,' he said, slipping in his clutch. 'It's absolutely vital.'

He stole a glance at her, but she was looking straight in front of her, and her face seemed expressionless.

'You must stand a long way off when you do,' she said demurely. 'At least if it's the same thing as you told me over the phone.'

Hugh grinned sheepishly.

'The exchange went wrong,' he remarked at length. 'Astonishing how rotten the telephones are in Town these days.'

'Quite remarkable,' she returned. 'I thought you weren't feeling very well or something. Of course, if it was the exchange. . .'

'They sort of buzz and blow, don't you know,' he explained helpfully.

'That must be most fearfully jolly for them,' she agreed. And there was silence for the next two miles. . .

Once or twice he looked at her out of the corner of his eye, taking in every detail of the sweet profile so near to him. Except for their first meeting at the Carlton, it was the only time he had ever had her completely to himself, and Hugh was determined to make the most of it. He felt as if he could go on driving for ever, just he and she alone. He had an overwhelming longing to put out his hand and touch a soft tendril of hair which was blowing loose just behind her ear; he had an overwhelming longing to take her in his arms, and. . . It was then that the girl turned and looked at him. The car swerved dangerously. . .

'Let's stop,' she said, with the suspicion of a smile. 'Then you can tell me.'

Hugh drew into the side of the road, and switched off the engine.

'You're not fair,' he remarked, and if the girl saw his hand tremble a little as he opened the door, she gave no sign. Only her breath came a shade faster, but a mere man could hardly be expected to notice such a trifle as that. . .

He came and stood beside her, and his right arm lay along the seat just behind her shoulders.

'You're not fair,' he repeated gravely. 'I haven't swerved like that since I first started to drive.'

'Tell me about this important thing,' she said a little nervously.

He smiled, and no woman yet born could see Hugh Drummond smile without smiling too.

'You darling!' he whispered, under his breath – 'you adorable darling!' His arm closed around her, and almost before she realized it, she felt his lips on hers. For a moment she sat motionless, while the wonder of it surged over her, and the sky seemed more gloriously blue, and the woods a richer green. Then, with a little gasp, she pushed him away.

'You mustn't. . .oh! you mustn't, Hugh,' she whispered.

'And why not, little girl?' he said exultingly. 'Don't you know I love you?'

'But look, there's a man over there, and he'll see.'

Hugh glanced at the stolid labourer in question and smiled.

'Go an absolute mucker over the cabbages, what! Plant carrots by mistake.' His face was still very close to hers. 'Well?'

'Well, what?' she murmured.

'It's your turn,' he whispered. 'I love you, Phyllis – just love you.'

'But it's only two or three days since we met,' she said feebly.

'And phwat the divil has that got to do with it, at all?' he demanded. 'Would I be wanting longer to decide such an obvious fact? Tell me,' he went on, and she felt his arm round her again forcing her to look at him – 'tell me, don't you care. . .a little?'

'What's the use?' She still struggled, but, even to her, it wasn't very convincing. 'We've got other things to do. . . We can't think of. . .'

And then this very determined young man settled matters in his usual straightforward fashion. She felt herself lifted bodily out of the car as if she had been a child: she found herself lying in his arms, with Hugh's eyes looking very tenderly into her own and a whimsical grin round his mouth.

'Cars pass here,' he remarked, 'with great regularity. I know you'd hate to be discovered in this position.'

'Would I?' she whispered. 'I wonder. . .'

She felt his heart pound madly against her; and with a sudden quick movement she put both her arms round his neck and kissed him on the mouth.

'Is that good enough?' she asked, very low: and just for a few moments, time stood still. . . Then, very gently, he put her back in the car.

'I suppose,' he remarked resignedly, 'that we had better descend to trivialities. We've had lots of fun and games since I last saw you a year or two ago.'

'Idiot boy,' she said happily. 'It was yesterday morning.'

'The interruption is considered trivial. Mere facts don't count when it's you and me.' There was a further interlude of uncertain duration, followed rapidly by another because the first was so nice.

'To resume,' continued Hugh. 'I regret to state that they've got Potts.'

The girl sat up quickly and stared at him.

'Got him? Oh, Hugh! how did they manage it?'

'I'm damned if I know,' he answered grimly. 'They found out that he was in my bungalow at Goring during the afternoon by sending round a man to see about the water. Somehow or other he must have doped the drink or the food, because after dinner we all fell asleep. I can just remember seeing Lakington's face outside in the garden, pressed against the window, and then everything went out. I don't remember anything more till I woke this morning with the most appalling head. Of course, Potts had gone.'

'I heard the car drive up in the middle of the night,' said the girl thoughtfully. 'Do you think he's at The Elms now?'

'That is what I propose to find out to-night,' answered Hugh. 'We have staged a little comedy for Peterson's especial benefit, and we are hoping for the best.'

'Oh, boy, do be careful!' She looked at him anxiously. 'I'd never forgive myself if anything happened to you. I'd feel it was all due to me, and I just couldn't bear it.'

'Dear little girl,' he whispered tenderly, 'you're simply adorable when you look like that. But not even for you would I back out of this show now.' His mouth set in a grim line. 'It's gone altogether too far, and they've shown themselves to be so completely beyond the pale that it's got to be fought out. And when it has been,' he caught both her hands in his. . . 'and we've won. . . why, then, girl o' mine, we'll get Peter Darrell to be best man.'

Which was the cue for the commencement of the last and longest interlude, terminated only by the sudden and unwelcome appearance of a motor-bus covered within and without by unromantic sightseers, and paper bags containing bananas.

They drove slowly back to Guildford, and on the way he told her briefly of the murder of the American's secretary in Belfast, and his interview the preceding afternoon with the impostor at the Carlton.

'It's a tough proposition,' he remarked quietly. 'They're absolutely without scruple, and their power seems unlimited. I know they are after the Duchess of Lampshire's pearls: I found the beautiful Irma consuming tea with young Laidley yesterday – you know, the Duke's eldest son. But there's something more in the wind than that, Phyllis – something which, unless I'm a mug of the first water, is an infinitely larger proposition than that.'

The car drew up at the station, and he strolled with her on to the platform. Trivialities were once more banished: vital questions concerning when it had first happened – by both; whether he was quite sure it would last for ever – by her; what she could possibly see in him – by him; and wasn't everything just too wonderful for words – mutual and carried *nem. con.*[1]

Then the train came in, and he put her into a carriage. And two minutes later, with the touch of her lips warm on his, and her anxious little cry, 'Take care, my darling! – take care!' still ringing in his ears, he got into his car and drove off to an hotel to get an early dinner. Love for the time was over; the next round of the other game was due. And it struck Drummond that it was going to be a round where a mistake would not be advisable.

[1]From the Latin *nemine contradicente* meaning 'with no one dissenting'. Unanimously.

IV

At a quarter to ten he backed his car into the shadow of
some trees not far from the gate of The Elms. The sky was
overcast, which suited his purpose, and through the gloom of
the bushes he dodged rapidly towards the house. Save for a
light in the sitting-room and one in a bedroom upstairs, the
front of the house was in darkness, and, treading noiselessly
on the turf, he explored all round it. From a downstairs
room on one side came the hoarse sound of men's voices,
and he placed that as the smoking-room of the gang of
ex-convicts and blackguards who formed Peterson's staff.
There was one bedroom light at the back of the house, and
thrown on the blind he could see the shadow of a man. As
he watched, the man got up and moved away, only to return
in a moment or two and take up his old position.

'It's one of those two bedrooms,' he muttered to himself,
'if he's here at all.'

Then he crouched in the shadow of some shrubs and
waited. Through the trees to his right he could see The
Larches, and once, with a sudden quickening of his heart, he
thought he saw the outline of the girl show up in the light
from the drawing-room. But it was only for a second, and
then it was gone. . .

He peered at his watch: it was just ten o'clock. The trees
were creaking gently in the faint wind; all around him the
strange night noises – noises which play pranks with a man's
nerves – were whispering and muttering. Bushes seemed
suddenly to come to life, and move; eerie shapes crawled
over the ground towards him – figures which existed only in
his imagination. And once again the thrill of the night stalker
gripped him.

He remembered the German who had lain motionless for
an hour in a little gully by Hebuterne, while he from behind
a stunted bush had tried to locate him. And then that one
creak as the Boche had moved his leg. And then. . .the end.
On that night, too, the little hummocks had moved and

taken themselves strange shapes: fifty times he had imagined he saw him; fifty times he knew he was wrong – in time. He was used to it; the night held no terrors for him, only a fierce excitement. And thus it was that as he crouched in the bushes, waiting for the game to start, his pulse was as normal, and his nerves as steady, as if he had been sitting down to supper. The only difference was that in his hand he held something tight-gripped.

At last faintly in the distance he heard the hum of a car. Rapidly it grew louder, and he smiled grimly to himself as the sound of five unmelodious voices singing lustily struck his ear. They passed along the road in front of the house. There was a sudden crash – then silence; but only for a moment.

Peter's voice came first:

'You priceless old ass, you've rammed the blinking gate.'

It was Jerry Seymour who then took up the ball. His voice was intensely solemn – also extremely loud.

'Preposhterous. Perfectly preposhterous. We must go and apologize to the owner. . . I. . . I. . .absholutely. . .musht apologize. . . Quite unpardonable. . . You can't go about country. . . knocking down gates. . . Out of queshtion. . .'

Half consciously Hugh listened, but, now that the moment for action had come, every faculty was concentrated on his own job. He saw half a dozen men go rushing out into the garden through a side door, and then two more ran out and came straight towards him. They crashed past him and went on into the darkness, and for an instant he wondered what they were doing. A little later he was destined to find out. . .

Then came a peal at the front-door bell, and he determined to wait no longer. He darted through the garden door, to find a flight of back stairs in front of him, and in another moment he was on the first floor. He walked rapidly along the landing, trying to find his bearings, and, turning a corner, he found himself at the top of the main staircase – the spot where he had fought Peterson two nights previously.

From below Jerry Seymour's voice came clearly.

'Are you the pro-propri-tor, ole friend? Because there's been. . .acchident. . .'

He waited to hear no more, but walked quickly on to the room which he calculated was the one where he had seen the shadow on the blind. Without a second's hesitation he flung the door open and walked in. There, lying in the bed, was the American, while crouched beside him, with a revolver in his hand, was a man. . .

For a few seconds they watched one another in silence, and then the man straightened up.

'The soldier!' he snarled. 'You young pup!'

Deliberately, almost casually, he raised his revolver, and then the unexpected happened. A jet of liquid ammonia struck him full in the face, and with a short laugh Hugh dropped his water-pistol in his pocket, and turned his attention to the bed. Wrapping the millionaire in a blanket, he picked him up, and, paying no more attention to the man gasping and choking in a corner, he raced for the back stairs.

Below he could still hear Jerry hiccoughing gently, and explaining to the pro. . .pro. . .pritor that he pershonally would repair. . .inshisted on repairing. . .any and every gateposht he posshessed. . . And then he reached the garden. . .

Everything had fallen out exactly as he had hoped, but had hardly dared to expect. He heard Peterson's voice, calm and suave as usual, answering Jerry. From the garden in front came the dreadful sound of a duet by Algy and Peter. Not a soul was in sight; the back of the house was clear. All that he had to do was to walk quietly through the wicket-gate to The Larches with his semi-conscious burden, get to his car and drive off. It all seemed so easy that he laughed. . .

But there were one or two factors that he had forgotten, and the first and most important one was the man upstairs. The window was thrown up suddenly, and the man leaned out waving his arms. He was still gasping with the strength of the ammonia, but Hugh saw him clearly in the light from the room behind. And as he cursed himself for a fool in not having tied him up, from the trees close by there came the sharp clang of metal.

With a quick catch in his breath he began to run. The two men who had rushed past him before he had entered the house, and whom, save for a passing thought, he had disregarded, had become the principal danger. For he had heard that clang before; he remembered Jem Smith's white horror-struck face, and then his sigh of relief as the thing – whatever it was – was shut in its cage. And now it was out, dodging through the trees, let loose by the two men.

Turning his head from side to side, peering into the gloom, he ran on. What an interminable distance it seemed to the gate. . .and even then. . . He heard something crash into a bush on his right, and give a snarl of anger. Like a flash he swerved into the undergrowth on the left.

Then began a dreadful game. He was still some way from the fence, and he was hampered at every step by the man slung over his back. He could hear the thing blundering about searching for him, and suddenly with a cold feeling of fear, he realized that the animal was in front of him – that his way to the gate was barred. The next moment he saw it. . .

Shadowy, indistinct, in the darkness, he saw something glide between two bushes. Then it came out into the open and he knew it had seen him, though as yet he could not make out what it was. Grotesque and horrible it crouched on the ground, and he could hear its heavy breathing, as it waited for him to move.

Cautiously he lowered the millionaire to the ground, and took a step forward. It was enough; with a snarl of fury the crouching form rose and shambled towards him. Two hairy arms shot towards his throat, he smelt the brute's fetid breath, hot and loathsome, and he realized what he was up against. It was a partially grown gorilla.

For a full minute they fought in silence, save for the hoarse grunts of the animal as it tried to tear away the man's hand from its throat, and then encircle him with its powerful arms. And with his brain cold as ice Hugh saw his danger and kept his head. It couldn't go on: no human being could last the pace, whatever his strength. And there was only one chance of finishing it quickly, the possibility that the grip taught him by Olaki would serve with a monkey as it did with a man.

He shifted his left thumb an inch or two on the brute's throat, and the gorilla, thinking he was weakening, redoubled its efforts. But still those powerful hands clutched its throat; try as it would, it failed to make them budge. And then, little by little, the fingers moved, and the grip which had been tight before grew tighter still.

Back went its head; something was snapping in its neck. With a scream of fear and rage it wrapped its legs round Drummond, squeezing and writhing. And then suddenly there was a tearing snap, and the great limbs relaxed and grew limp.

For a moment the man stood watching the still quivering brute lying at his feet; then, with a gasp of utter exhaustion, he dropped on the ground himself. He was done – utterly cooked; even Peterson's voice close behind scarcely roused him.

'Quite one of the most amusing entertainments I've seen for a long time.' The calm, expressionless voice made him look up wearily, and he saw that he was surrounded by men. The inevitable cigar glowed red in the darkness, and after a moment or two he scrambled unsteadily to his feet.

'I'd forgotten your damned menagerie, I must frankly confess,' he remarked. 'What's the party for?' He glanced at the men who had closed in round him.

'A guard of honour, my young friend,' said Peterson suavely, 'to lead you to the house. I wouldn't hesitate. . .it's very foolish. Your friends have gone, and, strong as you are, I don't think you can manage ten.'

Hugh commenced to stroll towards the house.

'Well, don't leave the wretched Potts lying about. I dropped him over there.' For a moment the idea of making a dash for it occurred to him, but he dismissed it at once. The odds were too great to make the risk worth while, and in the centre of the group he and Peterson walked side by side.

'The last man whom poor Sambo had words with,' said Peterson reminiscently, 'was found next day with his throat torn completely out.'

'A lovable little thing,' murmured Hugh. 'I feel quite sorry at having spoilt his record.'

Peterson paused with his hand on the sitting-room door, and looked at him benevolently.

'Don't be despondent, Captain Drummond. We have ample time at our disposal to ensure a similar find to-morrow morning.'

Chapter 7

In Which He Spends an Hour or Two on a Roof

I

DRUMMOND paused for a moment at the door of the sitting-room, then with a slight shrug he stepped past Peterson. During the last few days he had grown to look on this particular room as the private den of the principals of the gang. He associated it in his mind with Peterson himself, suave, impassive, ruthless; with the girl Irma, perfectly gowned, lying on the sofa, smoking innumerable cigarettes, and manicuring her already faultless nails; and in a lesser degree, with Henry Lakington's thin, cruel face, and blue, staring eyes.

But to-night a different scene confronted him. The girl was not there: her accustomed place on the sofa was occupied by an unkempt-looking man with a ragged beard. At the end of the table was a vacant chair, on the right of which sat Lakington regarding him with malevolent fury. Along the table on each side there were half a dozen men, and he glanced at their faces. Some were obviously foreigners; some might have been anything from murderers to Sunday School teachers. There was one with spectacles and the general appearance of an intimidated rabbit, while his neighbour, helped by a large red scar right across his cheek, and two bloodshot eyes, struck Hugh as being the sort of man with whom one would not share a luncheon basket.

'I know he'd snatch both drumsticks and gnaw them simultaneously,' he reflected, staring at him fascinated; 'and then he'd throw the bones in your face.'

Peterson's voice from just behind his shoulder roused him from his distressing reverie.

'Permit me, gentlemen, to introduce to you Captain Drummond, D.S.O., M.C., the originator of the little entertainment we have just had.'

Hugh bowed gravely.

'My only regret is that it failed to function,' he remarked. 'As I told you outside, I'd quite forgotten your menagerie. In fact' – his glance wandered slowly and somewhat pointedly from face to face at the table – 'I had no idea it was such a large one.'

'So this is the insolent young swine, is it?' The bloodshot eyes of the man with the scarred face turned on him morosely. 'What I cannot understand is why he hasn't been killed by now.'

Hugh waggled an accusing finger at him.

'I knew you were a nasty man as soon as I saw you. Now look at Henry up at the end of the table; he doesn't say that sort of thing. And you do hate me, don't you, Henry? How's the jaw?'

'Captain Drummond,' said Lakington, ignoring Hugh and addressing the first speaker, 'was very nearly killed last night. I thought for some time as to whether I would or not, but I finally decided it would be much too easy a death. So it can be remedied to-night.'

If Hugh felt a momentary twinge of fear at the calm, expressionless tone, and the half-satisfied grunt which greeted the words, no trace of it showed on his face. Already the realization had come to him that if he got through the night alive he would be more than passing lucky, but he was too much of a fatalist to let that worry him unduly. So he merely stifled a yawn, and again turned to Lakington.

'So it was you, my little one, whose fairy face I saw pressed against the window. Would it be indiscreet to ask you how you got the dope into us?'

Lakington looked at him with an expression of grim satisfaction on his face.

'You were gassed, if you want to know. An admirable invention of my friend Kauffner's nation.'

A guttural chuckle came from one of the men, and Hugh looked at him grimly.

'The scum certainly would not be complete,' he remarked to Peterson, 'without a filthy Boche in it.'

The German pushed back his chair with an oath, his face purple with passion.

'A filthy Boche,' he muttered thickly, lurching towards Hugh. 'Hold him the arms of, and I will the throat tear out. . .'

The intimidated rabbit rose protestingly at this prospect of violence; the scarred sportsman shot out of his chair eagerly, the lust of battle in his bloodshot eyes. The only person save Hugh who made no movement was Peterson, and he, very distinctly, chuckled. Whatever his failings, Peterson had a sense of humour. . .

It all happened so quickly. At one moment Hugh was apparently intent upon selecting a cigarette, the next instant the case had fallen to the floor; there was a dull, heavy thud, and the Boche crashed back, overturned a chair, and fell like a log to the floor, his head hitting the wall with a vicious crack. The bloodshot being resumed his seat a little limply; the intimidated bunny gave a stifled gasp and breathed heavily; Hugh resumed his search for a cigarette.

'After which breezy interlude,' remarked Peterson, 'let us to business get.'

Hugh paused in the act of striking a match, and for the first time a genuine smile spread over his face.

'There are moments, Peterson,' he murmured, 'when you really appeal to me.'

Peterson took the empty chair next to Lakington.

'Sit down,' he said shortly. 'I can only hope that I shall appeal to you still more before we kill you.' Hugh bowed and sat down.

'Consideration,' he murmured, 'was always your strong point. May I ask how long I have to live?'

Peterson smiled genially.

'At the very earnest request of Mr Lakington you are to be spared until to-morrow morning. At least, that is our present intention. Of course, there might be an accident in the night: in a house like this one can never tell. Or' – he carefully cut the end off a cigar – 'you might go mad, in which case we shouldn't bother to kill you. In fact, it would really suit our book better if you did: the disposal of corpses, even in these days of advanced science, presents certain difficulties – not insuperable – but a nuisance. And so, if you go mad, we shall not be displeased.'

Once again he smiled genially.

'As I said before, in a house like this, you never can tell. . .'

The intimidated rabbit, still breathing heavily, was staring at Hugh, fascinated; and after a moment Hugh turned to him with a courteous bow.

'Laddie,' he remarked, 'you've been eating onions. Do you mind deflecting the blast in the opposite direction?'

His calm imperturbability seemed to madden Lakington, who with a sudden movement rose from his chair and leaned across the table, while the veins stood out like whipcord on his usually expressionless face.

'You wait,' he snarled thickly; 'you wait till I've finished with you. You won't be so damned humorous then. . .'

Hugh regarded the speaker languidly.

'Your supposition is more than probable,' he remarked, in a bored voice. 'I shall be too intent on getting into a Turkish bath to remove the contamination to think of laughing.'

Slowly Lakington sank back in his chair, a hard, merciless smile on his lips; and for a moment or two there was silence in the room. It was broken by the unkempt man on the sofa, who, without warning, exploded unexpectedly.

'A truce to all this fooling,' he burst forth in a deep rumble; 'I confess I do not understand it. Are we assembled here to-night, comrades, to listen to private quarrels and stupid talk?'

A murmur of approval came from the others, and the speaker stood up waving his arms.

'I know not what this young man has done: I care less. In Russia such trifles matter not. He has the appearance of a bourgeois, therefore he must die. Did we not kill thousands – aye, tens of thousands of his kidney, before we obtained the great freedom? Are we not going to do the same in this accursed country?' His voice rose to the shrill, strident note of the typical tub-thumper. 'What is this wretched man,' he continued, waving a hand wildly at Hugh, 'that he should interrupt the great work for one brief second? Kill him now – throw him in a corner, and let us proceed.'

He sat down again, amidst a further murmur of approval, in which Hugh joined heartily.

'Splendid,' he murmured. 'A magnificent peroration. Am I right, sir, in assuming that you are what is vulgarly known as a Bolshevist?'

The man turned his sunken eyes, glowing with the burning fires of fanaticism, on Drummond.

'I am one of those who are fighting for the freedom of the world,' he cried harshly, 'for the right to live of the proletariat. The workers were the bottom dogs in Russia till they killed the rulers. Now – they rule, and the money they earn goes into their own pockets, not those of incompetent snobs.' He flung out his arms wildly. 'It is freedom; it is the dawn of the new age.' He seemed to shrivel up suddenly, as if exhausted with the violence of his passion. Only his eyes still gleamed with the smouldering madness of his soul.

Hugh looked at him with genuine curiosity; it was the first time he had actually met one of these wild visionaries in the flesh. And then the curiosity was succeeded by a very definite amazement; what had Peterson to do with such as he?

He glanced casually at his principal enemy, but his face showed nothing. He was quietly turning over some papers; his cigar glowed as evenly as ever. He seemed to be no whit surprised by the unkempt one's outburst; in fact, it appeared to be quite in order. And once again Hugh stared at the man on the sofa with puzzled eyes.

For the moment his own deadly risk was forgotten; a growing excitement filled his mind. Could it be possible that here, at last, was the real object of the gang; could it be possible that Peterson was organizing a deliberate plot to try and Bolshevize England? If so, where did the Duchess of Lampshire's pearls come in? What of the American, Hiram Potts? Above all, what did Peterson hope to make out of it himself? And it was as he arrived at that point in his deliberations that he looked up to find Peterson regarding him with a faint smile.

'It is a little difficult to understand, isn't it, Captain Drummond?' he said, carefully flicking the ash off his cigar. 'I told you you'd find yourself in deep water.' Then he resumed the contemplation of the papers in front of him, as the Russian burst out again.

'Have you ever seen a woman skinned alive?' he howled wildly, thrusting his face forward at Hugh. 'Have you ever seen men killed with the knotted rope; burned almost to death and then set free, charred and mutilated wrecks? But what does it matter provided only freedom comes, as it has in Russia. To-morrow it will be England: in a week the world. . . Even if we have to wade through rivers of blood up to our throats, nevertheless it will come. And in the end we shall have a new earth.'

Hugh lit a cigarette and leaned back in his chair.

'It seems a most alluring programme,' he murmured. 'And I shall have much pleasure in recommending you as manager of a babies' créche. I feel certain the little ones would take to you instinctively.'

He half closed his eyes, while a general buzz of conversation broke out round the table. Tongues had been loosened, wonderful ideals conjured up by the Russian's inspiring words; and for the moment he was forgotten. Again and again the question hammered at his brain – what in the name of Buddha had Peterson and Lakington to do with this crowd? Two intensely brilliant, practical criminals mixed up with a bunch of ragged-trousered visionaries, who, to all intents and purposes, were insane. . .

Fragments of conversation struck his ears from time to time. The intimidated rabbit, with the light of battle in his watery eye, was declaiming on the glories of Workmen's Councils; a bullet-headed man who looked like a down-at-heels racing tout was shouting an inspiring battle-cry about no starvation wages and work for all.

'Can it be possible,' thought Hugh grimly, 'that such as these have the power to control big destinies?' And then, because he had some experience of what an unbalanced brain, whose owner could talk, was capable of achieving; because he knew something about mob psychology, his half-contemptuous amusement changed to a bitter foreboding.

'You fool,' he cried suddenly to the, Russian; and everyone ceased talking. 'You poor, damned boob! You – and your new earth! In Petrograd to-day bread is two pounds four shillings a pound; tea, fifteen pounds a pound. Do you call that freedom? Do you suggest that we should wade to *that,* through rivers of blood?' He gave a contemptuous laugh. 'I don't know which distresses me most, your maggoty brain or your insanitary appearance.'

Too surprised to speak, the Russian sat staring at him; and it was Peterson who broke the silence with his suave voice.

'Your distress, I am glad to say, is not likely to be one of long duration,' he remarked. 'In fact, the time has come for you to retire for the night, my young friend.'

He stood up smiling; then he walked over to the bell behind Hugh and rang it.

'Dead or mad – I wonder which.' He threw the end of his cigar into the grate as Hugh rose. 'While we deliberate down here on various matters of importance, we shall be thinking of you upstairs – that is to say, if you get there. I see that Lakington is even now beginning to gloat in pleasant anticipation.'

Not a muscle on the soldier's face twitched; not by the hint of a look did he show the keenly watching audience that he realized his danger. He might have been an ordinary guest preparing to go to bed; and in Peterson's face there shone for a moment a certain unwilling admiration. Only Lakington's was merciless, with its fiendish look of anticipation, and Hugh stared at him with level eyes for a while before he turned towards the door.

'Then I will say good night,' he remarked casually. 'Is it the same room that I had last time?'

'No,' said Peterson. 'A different one – specially prepared for you. If you get to the top of the stairs a man will show you where it is.' He opened the door and stood there smiling. And at that moment all the lights went out.

II

The darkness could be felt, as real darkness inside a house always can be felt. Not the faintest glimmer even of greyness showed anywhere, and Hugh remained motionless, wondering what the next move was going to be. Now that the night's ordeal had commenced, all his nerve had returned to him. He felt ice cold; and as his powerful hands clenched and unclenched by his sides, he grinned faintly to himself.

Behind him in the room he could hear an occasional movement in one of the chairs, and once from the hall outside he caught the sound of whispering. He felt that he was surrounded by men, thronging in on him from all sides, and suddenly he gave a short laugh. Instantly silence settled; strain as he would he could not hear a sound. Then very cautiously he commenced to feel his way towards the door.

Outside a car went by honking discordantly, and with a sort of cynical amusement he wondered what its occupants would think if they knew what was happening in the house so near to them. And at that moment someone brushed past him. Like a flash Hugh's hand shot out and gripped him by the arm. The man wriggled and twisted, but he was powerless as a child, and with another short laugh Hugh found his throat with his other hand. And again silence settled on the room. . .

Still holding the unknown man in front of him, he reached the foot of the stairs, and there he paused. He had suddenly remembered the mysterious thing which had whizzed past his head that other night, and then clanged sullenly into the wall beside him. He had gone up five stairs when it had happened, and now with his foot on the first he started to do some rapid thinking.

If, as Peterson had kindly assured him, they proposed to try and send him mad, it was unlikely that they would kill him on the stairs. At the same time it was obviously an implement capable of accurate adjustment and therefore it was more than likely that they would use it to frighten him. And if they did – if they did. . . The unknown man wriggled feebly in his hands, and a sudden unholy look came on to Hugh's face.

'It's the only possible chance,' he said to himself, 'and if it's you or me, laddie, I guess it's got to be you.'

With a quick heave he jerked the man off his feet, and lifted him up till his head was above the level of his own. Then clutching him tight, he commenced to climb. His own head was bent down, somewhere in the region of the man's back, and he took no notice of the feebly kicking legs.

Then at last he reached the fourth step, and gave a final adjustment to his semi-conscious burden. He felt that the hall below was full of men, and suddenly Peterson's voice came to him out of the darkness.

'That is four, Captain Drummond. What about the fifth step?'

'A very good-looking one as far as I remember,' answered Hugh. 'I'm just going to get on to it.'

'That should prove entertaining,' remarked Peterson. 'I'm just going to switch on the current.'

Hugh pressed his head even lower in the man's back, and lifted him up another three inches.

'How awfully jolly!' he murmured. 'I hope the result will please you.'

'I'd stand quite still if I were you,' said Peterson suavely. 'Just listen.'

As Hugh had gambled on, the performance was designed to frighten. Instead of that, something hit the neck of the man he was holding with such force that it wrenched him clean out of his arms. Then came the clang beside him, and with a series of ominous thuds a body rolled down the stairs into the hall below.

'You fool.' He heard Lakington's voice, shrill with anger. 'You've killed him. Switch on the light. . .'

But before the order could be carried out Hugh had disappeared, like a great cat, into the darkness of the passage above. It was neck or nothing; he had at the most a minute to get clear. As luck would have it the first room he darted into was empty, and he flung up the window and peered out.

A faint, watery moon showed him a twenty-foot drop on to the grass, and without hesitation he flung his legs over the sill. Below a furious hubbub was going on; steps were already rushing up the stairs. He heard Peterson's calm voice, and Lakington's hoarse with rage, shouting inarticulate orders. And at that moment something prompted him to look upwards.

It was enough – that one look; he had always been mad, he always would be. It was a dormer window, and to an active man access to the roof was easy. Without an instant's hesitation he abandoned all thoughts of retreat; and when two excited men rushed into the room he was firmly ensconced, with his legs astride of the ridge of the window, not a yard from their heads.

Securely hidden in the shadow he watched the subsequent proceedings with genial toleration. A raucous bellow from the two men announced that they had discovered his line of escape; and in half a minute the garden was full of hurrying figures. One, calm and impassive, his identity betrayed only by the inevitable cigar, stood by the garden door, apparently taking no part in the game; Lakington, blind with fury, was running round in small circles, cursing everyone impartially.

'The car is still there.' A man came up to Peterson, and Hugh heard the words distinctly.

'Then he's probably over at Benton's house. I will go and see.'

Hugh watched the thick-set, massive figure stroll down towards the wicket gate, and he laughed gently to himself. Then he grew serious again, and with a slight frown he pulled out his watch and peered at it. Half-past one. . . Two more hours before dawn. And in those two hours he wanted to explore the house from on top; especially he wanted to have a look at the mysterious central room of which Phyllis had spoken to him – the room where Lakington kept his treasures. But until the excited throng below went indoors, it was unsafe to move. Once out of the shadow, anyone would be able to see him crawling over the roof in the moonlight.

At times the thought of the helpless man for whose death he had in one way been responsible recurred to him, and he shook his head angrily. It had been necessary, he realized: you can carry someone upstairs in a normal house without him having his neck broken – but still. . . And then he wondered who he was.

It had been one of the men who sat round the table – of that he was tolerably certain. But which. . .? Was it the frightened bunny, or the Russian, or the gentleman with the bloodshot eye? The only comfort was that whoever it had been, the world would not be appreciably the poorer for his sudden decease. The only regret was that it hadn't been dear

Henry. . . He had a distaste for Henry which far exceeded his dislike of Peterson.

'He's not over there.' Peterson's voice came to him from below. 'And we've wasted time enough as it is.'

The men had gathered together in a group, just below where Hugh was sitting, evidently awaiting further orders.

'Do you mean to say we've lost the young swine again?' said Lakington angrily.

'Not lost – merely mislaid,' murmured Peterson. 'The more I see of him the more do I admire his initiative.'

Lakington snorted.

'It was that damned fool Ivolsky's own fault,' he snarled; 'why didn't he keep still as he was told to do?'

'Why, indeed?' returned Peterson, his cigar glowing red. 'And I'm afraid we shall never know. He is very dead.' He turned toward the house. 'That concludes the entertainment, gentlemen, for to-night. I think you can all go to bed.'

'There are two of you watching the car, aren't there?' demanded Lakington.

'Rossiter and Le Grange,' answered a voice.

Peterson paused by the door.

'My dear Lakington, it's quite unnecessary. You underrate that young man. . .'

He disappeared into the house, and the others followed slowly. For the time being Hugh was safe, and with a sigh of relief he stretched his cramped limbs and lay back against the sloping roof. If only he had dared to light a cigarette. . .

III

It was half an hour before Drummond decided that it was safe to start exploring. The moon still shone fitfully through the trees, but since the two car watchers were near the road on the other side of the house, there was but little danger to be apprehended from them. First he took off his shoes, and tying the laces together, he slung them round his neck. Then, as silently as he could, he commenced to scramble upwards.

It was not an easy operation; one slip and nothing could have stopped him slithering down and finally crashing into the garden below, with a broken leg, at the very least, for his pains. In addition, there was the risk of dislodging a slate, an unwise proceeding in a house where most of the occupants slept with one eye open. But at last he got his hands over the ridge of the roof, and in another moment he was sitting straddlewise across it.

The house, he discovered, was built on a peculiar design. The ridge on which he sat continued at the same height all round the top of the roof, and formed, roughly, the four sides of a square. In the middle the roof sloped down to a flat space from which stuck up a glass structure, the top of which was some five or six feet below his level. Around it was a space quite large enough to walk in comfort; in fact, on two sides there was plenty of room for a deck chair. The whole area was completely screened from view, except to anyone in an aeroplane. And what struck him still further was that there was no window that he could see anywhere on the inside of the roof. In fact, it was absolutely concealed and private. Incidentally, the house had originally been built by a gentleman of doubtful sanity, who spent his life observing the spots in Jupiter through a telescope, and having plunged himself and his family into complete penury, sold the house and observatory complete for what he could get. Lakington, struck with its possibilities for his own hobby, bought it on the spot; and from that time Jupiter spotted undisturbed.

With the utmost caution Hugh lowered himself to the full extent of his arms; then he let himself slip the last two or three feet on to the level space around the glass roof. He had no doubt in his mind that he was actually above the secret room, and, on tip-toe, he stole round looking for some spot from which he could get a glimpse below. At the first inspection he thought his time had been wasted; every pane of glass was frosted, and in addition there seemed to be a thick blind of some sort drawn across from underneath, of the same type as is used by photographers for altering the light.

A sudden rattle close to him made him start violently, only to curse himself for a nervous ass the next moment, and lean forward eagerly. One of the blinds had been released from inside the room, and a pale, diffused light came filtering out into the night from the side of the glass roof. He was still craning backwards and forwards to try and find some chink through which he could see, when, with a kind of uncanny deliberation, one of the panes of glass slowly opened. It was worked on a ratchet from inside, and Hugh bowed his thanks to the unseen operator below. Then he leant forward cautiously, and peered in. . .

The whole room was visible to him, and his jaw tightened as he took in the scene. In an armchair, smoking as uncon-cernedly as ever, sat Peterson. He was reading a letter, and occasionally underlining some point with a pencil. Beside him on a table was a big ledger, and every now and then he would turn over a few pages and make an entry. But it was not Peterson on whom the watcher above was concentrating his attention; it was Lakington – and the thing beside him on the sofa.

Lakington was bending over a long bath full of some light-brown liquid from which a faint vapour was rising. He was in his shirt sleeves, and on his hands he wore what looked like rubber gloves, stretching right up to his elbows. After a while he dipped a test-tube into the liquid, and going over to a shelf he selected a bottle and added a few drops to the con-tents of the tube. Apparently satisfied with the result, he returned to the bath and shook in some white powder. Immediately the liquid commenced to froth and bubble, and at the same moment Peterson stood up.

'Are you ready?' he said, taking off his coat and pick-ing up a pair of gloves similar to those the other was wearing.

'Quite,' answered Lakington abruptly. 'We'll get him in.'

They approached the sofa; and Hugh, with a kind of fascinated horror, forced himself to look. For the thing that lay there was the body of the dead Russian, Ivolsky.

The two men picked him up and, having carried the body to the bath, they dropped it into the fuming liquid. Then, as if it was the most normal thing in the world, they peeled off their long gloves and stood watching. For a minute or so nothing happened, and then gradually the body commenced to disappear. A faint, sickly smell came through the open window, and Hugh wiped the sweat off his forehead. It was too horrible, the hideous deliberation of it all. And whatever vile tortures the wretched man had inflicted on others in Russia, yet it was through him that his dead body lay there in the bath, disappearing slowly and relentlessly. . .

Lakington lit a cigarette and strolled over to the fire-place.

'Another five minutes should be enough,' he remarked. 'Damn that cursed soldier!'

Peterson laughed gently, and resumed the study of his ledger.

'To lose one's temper with a man, my dear Henry, is a sign of inferiority. But it certainly is a nuisance that Ivolsky is dead. He could talk more unmitigated drivel to the minute than all the rest of 'em put together. . . I really don't know who to put in the Midland area.'

He leaned back in his chair and blew out a cloud of smoke. The light shone on the calm, impassive face; and with a feeling of wonder that was never far absent from his mind when he was with Peterson, Hugh noted the high, clever forehead, the firmly moulded nose and chin, the sensitive, humorous mouth. The man lying back in the chair watching the blue smoke curling up from his cigar might have been a great lawyer or an eminent divine; some well-known statesman, perhaps, or a Napoleon of finance. There was power in every line of his figure, in every movement of his hands. He might have reached to the top of any profession he had cared to follow. . . Just as he had reached to the top in his present one. . . Some kink in the brain, some little cog wrong in the wonderful mechanism, and a great man had become a great criminal. Hugh looked at the bath: the liquid was almost clear.

'You know my feelings on the subject,' remarked Lakington, taking a red velvet box out of a drawer in the desk. He opened it lovingly, and Hugh saw the flash of diamonds. Lakington let the stones run through his hands, glittering with a thousand flames, while Peterson watched him contemptuously.

'Baubles,' he said scornfully. 'Pretty baubles. What will you get for them?'

'Ten, perhaps fifteen thousand,' returned the other. 'But it's not the money I care about; it's the delight in having them, and the skill required to get them.'

Peterson shrugged his shoulders.

'Skill which would give you hundreds of thousands if you turned it into proper channels.'

Lakington replaced the stones, and threw the end of his cigarette into the grate.

'Possibly, Carl, quite possibly. But it boils down to this, my friend, that you like the big canvas with broad effects, I like the miniature and the well-drawn etching.'

'Which makes us a very happy combination,' said Peterson, rising and walking over to the bath. 'The pearls, don't forget, are your job. The big thing' – he turned to the other, and a trace of excitement came into his voice – 'the big thing is mine.' Then with his hands in his pockets he stood staring at the brown liquid. 'Our friend is nearly cooked, I think.'

'Another two or three minutes,' said Lakington, joining him. 'I must confess I pride myself on the discovery of that mixture. Its only drawback is that it makes murder too easy. . .'

The sound of the door opening made both men swing round instantly; then Peterson stepped forward with a smile.

'Back, my dear. I hardly expected you so soon.'

Irma came a little way into the room, and stopped with a sniff of disgust.

'What a horrible smell!' she remarked. 'What on earth have you been doing?'

'Disposing of a corpse,' said Lakington. 'It's nearly finished.'

The girl threw off her opera cloak, and coming forward, peered over the edge of the bath.

'It's not my ugly soldier?' she cried.

'Unfortunately not,' returned Lakington grimly; and Peterson laughed.

'Henry is most annoyed, Irma. The irrepressible Drummond has scored again.'

In a few words he told the girl what had happened, and she clapped her hands together delightedly.

'Assuredly I shall have to marry that man,' she cried. 'He is quite the least boring individual I have met in this atrocious country.' She sat down and lit a cigarette. 'I saw Walter to-night.'

'Where?' demanded Peterson quickly. 'I thought he was in Paris.'

'He was this morning. He came over especially to see you. They want you there for a meeting at the Ritz.'

Peterson frowned.

'It's most inconvenient,' he remarked with a shade of annoyance in his voice. 'Did he say why?'

'Amongst other things I think they're uneasy about the American,' she answered. 'My dear man, you can easily slip over for a day.'

'Of course I can,' said Peterson irritably; 'but that doesn't alter the fact that it's inconvenient. Things will be shortly coming to a head here, and I want to be on the spot. However—' He started to walk up and down the room, frowning thoughtfully.

'Your fish is hooked, *mon ami*,' continued the girl to Lakington. 'He has already proposed three times; and he has introduced me to a dreadful-looking woman of extreme virtue, who has adopted me as her niece for the great occasion.'

'What great occasion?' asked Lakington, looking up from the bath.

'Why, his coming of age,' cried the girl. 'I am to go to Laidley Towers as an honoured guest of the Duchess of Lampshire.' She threw back her head and laughed. 'What do you think of that, my friend? The old lady will be wearing pearls and all complete, in honour of the great day, and I shall be one of the admiring house party.'

'How do you know she'll have them in the house?' said Lakington.

'Because dear Freddie has told me so,' answered the girl. 'I don't think you're very bright to-night, Henry. When the young Pooh-ba comes of age, naturally his devoted maternal parent will sport her glad rags. Incidentally the tenants are going to present him with a loving cup, or a baby giraffe or something. You might like to annex that, too.' She blew two smoke rings and then laughed.

'Freddie is really rather a dear at times. I don't think I've ever met anyone who is so nearly an idiot without being one. Still,' she repeated thoughtfully, 'he's rather a dear.'

Lakington turned a handle underneath the bath, and the liquid, now clear and still, commenced to sink rapidly. Fascinated, Hugh watched the process; in two minutes the bath was empty – a human body had completely disappeared without leaving a trace. It seemed to him as if he must have been dreaming, as if the events of the whole night had been part of some strange jumbled nightmare. And then, having pinched himself to make sure he was awake, he once more glued his eyes to the open space of the window.

Lakington was swabbing out the bath with some liquid on the end of a mop; Peterson, his chin sunk on his chest, was still pacing slowly up and down; the girl, her neck and shoulders gleaming white in the electric light, was lighting a second cigarette from the stump of the first. After a while

Lakington finished his cleaning operations and put on his coat.

'What,' he asked curiously, 'does he think you are?'

'A charming young girl,' answered Irma, demurely, 'whose father lost his life in the war, and who at present ekes out a precarious existence in a government office. At least, that's what he told Lady Frumpley – she's the woman of unassailable virtue. She was profoundly sentimental and scents a romance in addition to being a snob and scenting a future duke, to say nothing of a future duchess. By the mercy of Allah she's on a committee with his mother for distributing brown-paper underclothes to destitute Belgians, and so Freddie wangled an invite for her. *Voilà tout.*'

'Splendid!' said Lakington slowly. 'Splendid! Young Laidley comes of age in about a week, doesn't he?'

'Monday, to be exact, and so I go down with my dear aunt on Saturday.'

Lakington nodded his head as if satisfied, and then glanced at his watch.'

'What about bed?' he remarked.

'Not yet,' said Peterson, halting suddenly in his walk. 'I must see the Yank before I go to Paris. We'll have him down here now.'

'My dear Carl, at this hour?' Lakington stifled a yawn.

'Yes. Give him an injection, Henry – and, by God, we'll make the fool sign. Then I can actually take it over to the meeting with me.'

He strode to the door, followed by Lakington; and the girl in the chair stood up and stretched her arms above her head. For a moment or two Hugh watched her; then he too stood upright and eased his cramped limbs.

'Make the fool sign.' The words echoed through his brain, and he stared thoughtfully at the grey light which showed the approach of dawn. What was the best thing to do? 'Make' with Peterson generally implied torture if other means failed, and Hugh had no intention of watching any man tortured. At the same time something of the nature of the diabolical plot conceived by Peterson was beginning to take a definite shape in his mind, though many of the most important links were still missing. And with this knowledge had come the realization that he was no longer a free agent. The thing had ceased to be a mere sporting gamble with himself and a few other chosen spirits matched against a gang of criminals; it had become – if his surmise was correct – a national affair. England herself – her very existence – was threatened by one of the vilest plots ever dreamed of in the brain of man. And then, with a sudden rage at his own impotence, he realized that even now he had nothing definite to go on. He *must* know more; somehow or other he must get to Paris; he must attend that meeting at the Ritz. How he was going to do it he hadn't the faintest idea; the farthest he could get as he stood on the roof, watching the first faint streaks of orange in the east, was the definite decision that if Peterson went to Paris, he would go too. And then a sound from the room below brought him back to his vantage point. The American was sitting in a chair, and Lakington, with a hypodermic syringe in his hand, was holding his arm.

He made the injection, and Hugh watched the millionaire. He was still undecided as to how to act, but for the moment, at any rate, there was nothing to be done. And he was very curious to hear what Peterson had to say to the wretched man who, up to date, had figured so largely in every round.

After a while the American ceased staring vacantly in front of him, and passed his hand dazedly over his forehead. Then he half rose from his chair and stared at the two men sitting facing him. His eyes came round to the girl, and with a groan he sank back again, plucking feebly with his hands at his dressing-gown.

'Better, Mr Potts?' said Peterson suavely.

'I – I – ' stammered the other. 'Where am I?'

'At The Elms, Godalming, if you wish to know.'

'I thought – I thought—' He rose swaying.

'What do you want with me? Damn you!'

'Tush, tush,' murmured Peterson. 'There is a lady present, Mr Potts. And our wants are so simple. Just your signature to a little agreement, by which in return for certain services you promise to join us in our – er – labours, in the near future.'

'I remember,' cried the millionaire. 'Now I remember. You swine – you filthy swine, I refuse. . .absolutely.'

'The trouble is, my friend, that you are altogether too big an employer of labour to be allowed to refuse, as I pointed out to you before. You must be in with us, otherwise you might wreck the scheme. Therefore I require your signature. I lost it once, unfortunately – but it wasn't a very good signature; so perhaps it was all for the best.'

'And when you've got it,' cried the American, 'what good will it be to you? I shall repudiate it.' 'Oh, no! Mr Potts,' said Peterson with a thoughtful smile; 'I can assure you, you won't. The distressing malady from which you have recently been suffering will again have you in its grip. My friend Mr Lakington is an expert on that particular illness. It renders you quite unfit for business.

For a while there was silence, and the millionaire stared round the room like a trapped animal.

'I refuse!' he cried at last. 'It's an outrage against humanity. You can do what you like.'

'Then we'll start with a little more thumbscrew,' remarked Peterson, strolling over to the desk and opening a drawer. 'An astonishingly effective implement, as you can see if you look at your thumb.' He stood in front of the quivering man balancing the instrument in his hands. 'It was under its influence you gave us the first signature which we so regrettably lost. I think we'll try it again. . .'

The American gave a strangled cry of terror, and then the unexpected happened. There was a crash as a pane of glass splintered and fell to the floor close beside Lakington; and with an oath he sprang aside and looked up.

'Peep-bo,' came a well-known voice from the skylight. 'Clip him one over the jaw, Potts, my boy, but don't you sign.'

Chapter 8

In Which He Goes to Paris for a Night

I

DRUMMOND had acted on the spur of the moment. It would have been manifestly impossible for any man, certainly one of his calibre, to have watched the American being tortured without doing something to try to help him. At the same time the last thing he had wanted to do was to give away his presence on the roof. The information he had obtained that night was of such vital importance that it was absolutely essential for him to get away with it somehow; and, at the moment, his chances of so doing did not appear particularly bright. It looked as if it was only a question of time before they must get him.

But as usual with Drummond, the tighter the corner, the cooler his head. He watched Lakington dart from the room, followed more slowly by Peterson, and then occurred one of those strokes of luck on which the incorrigible soldier always depended. The girl left the room as well.

She kissed her hand towards him, and then she smiled.

'You intrigue me, ugly one,' she remarked, looking up, 'intrigue me vastly. I am now going out to get a really good view of the kill.'

And the next moment Potts was alone. He was staring up at the skylight, apparently bewildered by the sudden turn of events, and then he heard the voice of the man above speaking clearly and insistently.

'Go out of the room. Turn to the right. Open the front door. You'll see a house through some trees. Go to it. When you get there, stand on the lawn and call "Phyllis." Do you get me?'

The American nodded dazedly; then he made a great effort to pull himself together, as the voice continued:

'Go at once. It's your only chance. Tell her I'm on the roof here.'

With a sigh of relief he saw the millionaire leave the room; then he straightened himself up, and proceeded to reconnoitre his own position. There was a bare chance that the American would get through, and if he did, everything might yet be well. If he didn't – Hugh shrugged his shoulders grimly and laughed.

It had become quite light, and after a moment's indecision Drummond took a running jump and caught the ridge of the sloping roof on the side nearest the road. To stop by the skylight was to be caught like a rat in a trap, and he would have to take his chance of being shot. After all, there was a considerable risk in using firearms so near a main road, where at any time some labourer or other early riser might pass along. Notoriety was the last thing which Peterson desired, and if it got about that one of the pastimes at The Elms was potting stray human beings on the roof, the inquiries might become somewhat embarrassing.

It was as Hugh threw his leg over the top of the roof, and sat straddle-ways, leaning against a chimney-stack, that he got an idea. From where he was he could not see The Larches, and so he did not know what luck the American had had. But he realized that it was long odds against his getting through, and that his chief hope lay in himself. Wherefore, as has just been said, he got an idea – simple and direct; his ideas always were. It occurred to him that far too few unbiased people knew where he was; it further occurred to him that it was a state of affairs which was likely to continue unless he remedied it himself, and so, just as Peterson came strolling round a corner of the house, followed by several men and a long ladder, Hugh commenced to sing. He shouted, he roared at the top of his very powerful voice, and all the time he watched the men below with a wary eye. He saw Peterson look nervously over his shoulder towards the road, and urge the men on to greater efforts, and the gorgeous simplicity of his manoeuvre made Hugh burst out laughing. Then, once again, his voice rose to its full pitch, as he greeted the sun with a bellow which scared every rook in the neighbourhood.

It was just as two labourers came in to investigate the hideous din that Peterson's party discovered the ladder was too short by several yards.

Then with great rapidity the audience grew. A passing milkman; two commercial travellers who had risen with the lark and entrusted themselves and their samples to a Ford car; a gentleman of slightly inebriated aspect, whose trousers left much to the imagination; and finally more farm labourers. Never had such a tit-bit of gossip for the local pub been seen before in the neighbourhood; it would furnish a topic of conversation for weeks to come. And still Hugh sang and Peterson cursed; and still the audience grew. Then, at last, there came the police with notebook all complete, and the singer stopped singing to laugh.

The next moment the laugh froze on his lips. Standing by the skylight, with his revolver raised, was Lakington, and Hugh knew by the expression on his face that his finger was trembling on the trigger. Out of view of the crowd below he did not know of its existence, and, in a flash, Hugh realized his danger. Somehow Lakington had got up on the roof while the soldier's attention had been elsewhere; and now, his face gleaming with an unholy fury, Lakington was advancing step by step towards him with the evident intention of shooting him.

'Good morrow, Henry,' said Hugh quietly. 'I wouldn't fire if I were you. We are observed, as they say in melodrama. If you don't believe me,' his voice grew a little tense, 'just wait while I talk to Peterson, who is at present deep in converse with the village constable and several farm labourers.'

He saw doubt dawn in Lakington's eyes, and instantly followed up his advantage.

'I'm sure you wouldn't like the notoriety attendant upon a funeral, Henry dear; I'm sure Peterson would just hate it. So, to set your mind at rest, I'll tell him you're here.'

It is doubtful whether any action in Hugh Drummond's life ever cost him such an effort of will as the turning of his back on the man standing two yards below him, but he did it apparently without thought. He gave one last glance at the face convulsed with rage, and then with a smile he looked down at the crowd below.

'Peterson,' he called out affably, 'there's a pal of yours up here – dear old Henry. And he's very annoyed at my concert. Would you just speak to him, or would you like me to be more explicit? He is so annoyed that there might be an accident at any moment, and I see that the police have arrived. So – er –'

Even at that distance he could see Peterson's eyes of fury, and he chuckled softly to himself. He had the whole gang absolutely at his mercy, and the situation appealed irresistibly to his sense of humour.

But when the leader spoke, his voice was as suave as ever: the eternal cigar glowed evenly at its normal rate.

'Are you up on the roof, Lakington?' The words came clearly through the still summer air.

'Your turn, Henry,' said Drummond. 'Prompter's voice off – "Yes, dear Peterson, I am here, even upon the roof, with a liver of hideous aspect."'

For one moment he thought he had gone too far, and that Lakington, in his blind fury, would shoot him then and there and chance the consequences. But with a mighty effort the man controlled himself, and his voice, when he answered, was calm.

'Yes, I'm here. What's the matter?'

'Nothing,' cried Peterson, 'but we've got quite a large and appreciative audience down here, attracted by our friend's charming concert, and I've just sent for a large ladder by which he can come down and join us. So there is nothing that you can do – nothing.' He repeated the word with a faint emphasis, and Hugh smiled genially.

'Isn't he wonderful, Henry?' he murmured. 'Thinks of everything; staff work marvellous. But you nearly had a bad lapse then, didn't you? It really would have been embarrassing for you if my corpse had deposited itself with a dull thud on the corns of the police.'

'I'm interested in quite a number of things, Captain Drummond,' said Lakington slowly, 'but they all count as nothing beside one – getting even with you. And when I do. . .' He dropped the revolver into his coat pocket, and stood motionless, staring at the soldier.

'Ah! When!' mocked Drummond. 'There have been so many "whens," Henry dear. Somehow I don't think you can be very clever. Don't go – I'm so enjoying my heart-to-heart talk. Besides, I want to tell you the story about the girl, the soap, and the bath. That's to say, if the question of baths isn't too delicate.'

Lakington paused as he got to the skylight.

'I have a variety of liquids for bathing people in,' he remarked. 'The best are those I use when the patient is alive.'

The next instant he opened a door in the skylight which Hugh had failed to discover during the night, and, climbing down a ladder inside the room, disappeared from view.

'Hullo, old bean!' A cheerful shout from the ground made Hugh look down. There, ranged round Peterson, in an effective group, were Peter Darrell, Algy Longworth, and Jerry Seymour. 'Birds'-nestin'?'

'Peter, old soul,' cried Hugh joyfully, 'I never thought the day would come when I should be pleased to see your face, but it has! For Heaven's sake get a move on with that blinking ladder; I'm getting cramp.'

'Ted and his pal, Hugh, have toddled off in your car,' said Peter, 'so that only leaves us four and Toby.'

For a moment Hugh stared at him blankly, while he did some rapid mental arithmetic. He even neglected to descend at once by the ladder which had at last been placed in position. 'Ted and us four and Toby' made six – and six was the strength of the party as it had arrived. Adding the pal made seven; so who the deuce was the pal?

The matter was settled just as he reached the ground. Lakington, wild-eyed and almost incoherent, rushed from the house, and, drawing Peterson on one side, spoke rapidly in a whisper.

'It's all right,' muttered Algy rapidly. 'They're half-way to London by now, and going like hell if I know Ted.'

It was then that Hugh started to laugh. He laughed till the tears poured down his face, and Peterson's livid face of fury made him laugh still more.

'Oh, you priceless pair!' he sobbed. 'Right under your bally noses. Stole away. Yoicks!' There was another interlude for further hilarity. 'Give it up, you two old dears, and take to knitting. Miss one and purl three, Henry my boy, and Carl in a nightcap can pick up the stitches you drop.' He took out his cigarette case. 'Well, au revoir. Doubtless we shall meet again quite soon. And, above all, Carl, don't do anything in Paris which you would be ashamed of my knowing.'

With a friendly wave he turned on his heel and strolled off, followed by the other three. The humour of the situation was irresistible; the absolute powerlessness of the whole assembled gang to lift a finger to stop them in front of the audience, which as yet showed no sign of departing, tickled him to death. In fact, the last thing Hugh saw, before a corner of the house hid them from sight, was the majesty of the law moistening his indelible pencil in the time-honoured method, and advancing on Peterson with his notebook at the ready.

'One brief interlude, my dear old warriors,' announced Hugh, 'and then we must get gay. Where's Toby?'

'Having his breakfast with your girl,' chuckled Algy. 'We thought we'd better leave someone on guard, and she seemed to love him best.'

'Repulsive hound!' cried Hugh. 'Incidentally, boys, how did you manage to roll up this morning?'

'We all bedded down at your girl's place last night,' said Peter, 'and then this morning, who should come and sing carols outside but our one and only Potts. Then we heard your deafening din on the roof, and blew along.'

'Splendid!' remarked Hugh, rubbing his hands together, 'simply splendid! Though I wish you'd been there to help with that damned gorilla.'

'Help with what?' spluttered Jerry Seymour.

'Gorilla, old dear,' returned Hugh, unmoved. 'A docile little creature I had to kill.'

'The man,' murmured Algy, 'is indubitably mad. I'm going to crank the car.'

II

'Go away,' said Toby, looking up as the door opened and Hugh strolled in. 'Your presence is unnecessary and uncalled for, and we're not pleased. Are we, Miss Benton?'

'Can you bear him, Phyllis?' remarked Hugh with a grin. 'I mean lying about the house all day?'

'What's the notion, old son?' Toby Sinclair stood up, looking slightly puzzled.

'I want you to stop here, Toby,' said Hugh, 'and not let Miss Benton out of your sight. Also keep your eye skinned on The Elms, and let me know by phone to Half Moon Street anything that happens. Do you get me?'

'I get you,' answered the other, 'but I say, Hugh, can't I do something a bit more active? I mean, of course, there's nothing I'd like better than to. . .' He broke off in mild confusion as Phyllis Benton laughed merrily.

'Do something more active!' echoed Hugh. 'You bet your life, old boy. A rapid one-step out of the room. You're far too young for what's coming now.'

With a resigned sigh Toby rose and walked to the door.

'I shall have to listen at the keyhole,' he announced, 'and thereby get earache. You people have no consideration whatever.'

'I've got five minutes, little girl,' whispered Hugh, taking her into his arms as the door closed. 'Five minutes of Heaven. . . By Jove! But you do look great – simply great.'

The girl smiled up at him.

'It strikes me, Master Hugh, that you have failed to remove your beard this morning.'

Hugh grinned.

'Quite right, kid. They omitted to bring me my shaving water on the roof.'

After a considerable interval, in which trifles such as beards mattered not, she smoothed her hair and sat down on the arm of a chair.

'Tell me what's happened, boy,' she said eagerly.

'Quite a crowded night.' With a reminiscent smile he lit a cigarette. And then quite briefly he told her of the events of the past twelve hours, being, as is the manner of a man, more interested in watching the sweet colour which stained her cheeks from time to time, and noticing her quickened breathing when he told her of his fight with the gorilla, and his ascent of the murderous staircase. To him it was all over and now finished, but to the girl who sat listening to the short, half-clipped sentences, each one spoken with a laugh and a jest, there came suddenly the full realization of what this man was doing for her. It was she who had been the cause of his running all these risks; it was her letter that he had answered. Now she felt that if one hair of his head was touched, she would never forgive herself.

And so when he had finished, and pitched the stump of his cigarette into the grate, falteringly she tried to dissuade him.

With her hands on his coat, and her big eyes misty with her fears for him, she begged him to give it all up. And even as she spoke, she gloried in the fact that she knew it was quite useless. Which made her plead all the harder, as is the way of a woman with her man.

And then, after a while, her voice died away, and she fell silent. He was smiling, and so, perforce, she had to smile too. Only their eyes spoke those things which no human being may put into words. And so, for a time, they stood. . .

Then, quite suddenly, he bent and kissed her.

'I must go, little girl,' he whispered. 'I've got to be in Paris to-night. Take care of yourself.'

The next moment he was gone.

'For God's sake take care of her, Toby!' he remarked to that worthy, whom he found sitting disconsolately by the front door. 'Those blighters are the limit.'

'That's all right, old man,' said Sinclair gruffly. 'Good huntin'!'

He watched the tall figure stride rapidly to the waiting car, the occupants of which were simulating sleep as a mild protest at the delay; then, with a smile, he rose and joined the girl.

'Some lad,' he remarked. 'And if you don't mind my saying so, Miss Benton, I wouldn't change him if I was you. Unless, of course,' he added as an afterthought, 'you'd prefer me!'

III

'Have you got him all right, Ted?' Hugh flung the question eagerly at Ted Jerningham, who was lounging in a chair at Half Moon Street, with his feet on the mantelpiece.

'I've got him right enough,' answered that worthy, 'but he don't strike me as being Number One value. He's gone off the boil. Become quite gugga again.' He stood up and stretched himself. 'Your worthy servant is with him, making hoarse noises to comfort him.'

'Hell!' said Hugh. 'I thought we might get something out of him. I'll go and have a look at the bird. Beer in the corner, boys, if you want it.'

He left the room, and went along the passage to inspect the American. Unfortunately Jerningham was only too right: the effects of last night's injection had worn off completely, and the wretched man was sitting motionless in a chair, staring dazedly in front of him.

' 'Opeless, sir,' remarked Denny, rising to his feet as Hugh came into the room. 'He thinks this 'ere meat juice is poison, and he won't touch it.'

'All right, Denny,' said Drummond. 'Leave the poor blighter alone. We've got him back, and that's something. Has your wife told you about her little adventure?'

His servant coughed deprecatingly.

'She has, sir. But, Lor' bless you, she don't bear no malice.'

'Then she's one up on me, Denny, for I bear lots of it towards that gang of swine.' Thoughtfully he stood in front of the millionaire, trying in vain to catch some gleam of sense in the vacant eyes. 'Look at that poor devil; isn't that enough by itself to make one want to kill the whole crowd?' He turned on his heel abruptly, and opened the door. 'Try and get him to eat if you can.'

'What luck?' Jerningham looked up as he came back into the other room.

'Dam' all, as they say in the vernacular. Have you blighters finished the beer?'

'Probably,' remarked Peter Darrell. 'What's the programme now?'

Hugh examined the head on his glass with a professional eye before replying.

'Two things,' he murmured at length, 'fairly leap to the eye. The first is to get Potts away to a place of safety; the second is to get over to Paris.'

'Well, let's get gay over the first, as a kick-off,' said Jerningham, rising. 'There's a car outside the door; there is

England at our disposal. We'll take him away; you pad the hoof to Victoria and catch the boat train.'

'It sounds too easy,' remarked Hugh. 'Have a look out of the window, Ted, and you'll see a man frightfully busy doing nothing not far from the door. You will also see a racing-car just across the street. Put a wet compress on your head, and connect the two.'

A gloomy silence settled on the assembly, to be broken by Jerry Seymour suddenly waking up with a start.

'I've got the stomach ache,' he announced proudly.

His listeners gazed at him unmoved.

'You shouldn't eat so fast,' remarked Algy severely, 'And you certainly oughtn't to drink that beer.'

To avert the disaster he immediately consumed it himself, but Jerry was too engrossed with his brainstorm to notice.

'I've got the stomach ache,' he repeated, 'and she ought to be ready by now. In fact I know she is. My last crash wasn't a bad one. What about it?'

'You mean. . .?' said Hugh, staring at him.

'I mean,' answered Jerry, 'that I'll go off to the aerodrome now, and get her ready. Bring Potts along in half an hour, and I'll take him to the governor's place in Norfolk. Then I'll take you over to Paris.'

'Great! – simply great!' With a report like a gun Hugh hit the speaker on the back, inadvertently knocking him down. Then an idea struck him. 'Not your place, Jerry; they'll draw that at once. Take him to Ted's; Lady Jerningham won't mind, will she, old boy?'

'The mater mind?' Ted laughed. 'Good Lord, no; she gave up minding anything years ago.'

'Right!' said Hugh. 'Off you go, Jerry. By the way, how many will she hold?'

'Two beside me,' spluttered the proud proprietor of the stomach ache. 'And I wish you'd reserve your endearments for people of your own size, you great, fat, hulking monstrosity.'

He reached the door with a moment to spare, and Hugh came back laughing.

'Verily – an upheaval in the grey matter,' he cried, carefully refilling his glass. 'Now, boy, what about Paris?'

'Is it necessary to go at all?' asked Peter.

'It wouldn't have been if the Yank had been sane,' answered Drummond. 'As it is, I guess I've got to. There's something going on, young fellahs, which is big; and I can't help thinking one might get some useful information from the meeting at the Ritz tonight. Why is Peterson hand-in-glove with a wild-eyed, ragged-trousered crowd of revolutionaries? Can you tell me that? If so, I won't go.'

'The great point is whether you'll find out, even if you do,' returned Peter. 'The man's not going to stand in the hall and shout it through a megaphone.'

'Which is where Ted comes in,' said Hugh affably. 'Does not the stomach ache hold two?'

'My dear man,' cried Jerningham, 'I'm dining with a perfectly priceless she to-night!'

'Oh, no, you're not, my lad. You're going to do some amateur acting in Paris. Disguised as a waiter, or a chambermaid, or a coffee machine or something – you will discover secrets.'

'But good Heavens, Hugh!' Jerningham waved both hands in feeble protest.

'Don't worry me,' cried Drummond, 'don't worry me; it's only a vague outline, and you'll look great as a bath-sponge. There's the telephone. . . Hallo!' He picked off the receiver. 'Speaking. Is that you, Toby? Oh! the Rolls has gone, has it? With Peterson inside. Good! So long, old dear.'

He turned to the others.

'There you are, you see. He's left for Paris. That settles it.'

'Conclusively,' murmured Algy mildly. 'Any man who leaves a house in a motor-car always goes to Paris.'

'Dry up!' roared Hugh. 'Was your late military education so utterly lacking that you have forgotten the elementary precept of putting yourself in the enemy's place? If I was Peterson, and I wanted to go to Paris, do you suppose that fifty people knowing about it would prevent me? You're a fool, Algy – and leave me some more beer.'

Resignedly Algy sat down, and after a pause for breath, Drummond continued:

'Now listen – all of you. Ted – off you go, and raise a complete waiter's outfit, dicky and all complete. Peter – you come with me to the aerodrome, and afterwards look up Mullings, at 13, Green Street, Hoxton, and tell him to get in touch with at least fifty demobilized soldiers who are on for a scrap. Algy – you hold the fort here, and don't get drunk on my ale. Peter will join you, when he's finished with Mullings, and he's not to get drunk either. Are you all on?'

'On,' muttered Darrell weakly. 'My head is playing an anthem.'

'It'll play an oratorio before we're through with this job, old son,' laughed Hugh. 'Let's get gay with Potts.'

Ten minutes later he was at the wheel of his car with Darrell and the millionaire behind. Algy, protesting vigorously at being, as he said, left out of it, was endeavouring to console himself by making out how much money he would have won if he'd followed his infallible system of making money on the turf; Jerningham was wandering along Piccadilly anxiously wondering at what shop he could possibly ask for a dicky, and preserve his hitherto blameless reputation. But Hugh seemed in no great hurry to start. A whimsical smile was on his face, as out of the corner of his eye he watched the man who had been busy doing nothing feverishly trying to crank his car, which, after the manner of the brutes, had seized that moment to jib.

'Get away, man – get away,' cried Peter. 'What are you waiting for?'

Hugh laughed.

'Peter,' he remarked, 'the refinements of this game are lost on you.'

Still smiling, he got out and walked up to the perspiring driver.

'A warm day,' he murmured. 'Don't hurry; we'll wait for you.' Then, while the man, utterly taken aback, stared at him speechlessly, he strolled back to his own car.

'Hugh – you're mad, quite mad,' said Peter resignedly, as with a spluttering roar the other car started, but Hugh still smiled. On the way to the aerodrome, he stopped twice after a block in the traffic to make quite sure that the pursuer should have no chance of losing him, and, by the time they were clear of the traffic and spinning towards their destination, the gentleman in the car behind fully agreed with Darrell.

At first he had expected some trick, being a person of tortuous brain; but as time went on, and nothing unexpected happened, he became reassured. His orders were to follow the millionaire, and inform headquarters where he was taken to. And assuredly at the moment it seemed easy money. In fact, he even went so far as to hum gently to himself, after he had put a hand in his pocket to make sure his automatic revolver was still there.

Then, quite suddenly, the humming stopped and he frowned. The car in front had swung off the road, and turned through the entrance of a small aerodrome. It was a complication which had not entered his mind, and with a curse he pulled up his car just short of the gates. What the devil was he to do now? Most assuredly he could not pursue an aeroplane in a motor – even a racer. Blindly, without thinking, he did the first thing that came into his head. He left his car standing where it was, and followed the others into the aerodrome on foot. Perhaps he could find out something from one of the mechanics; someone might be able to tell him where the plane was going.

There she was with the car beside her, and already the millionaire was being strapped into his seat. Drummond was talking to the pilot, and the sleuth, full of eagerness, accosted a passing mechanic.

'Can you tell me where that aeroplane is going to?' he asked ingratiatingly.

It was perhaps unfortunate that the said mechanic had just had a large spanner dropped on his toe, and his answer was not helpful. It was an education in one way, and at any other time the pursuer would have treated it with the respect it deserved. But, as it was, it was not of great value, which made it the more unfortunate that Peter Darrell should have chosen that moment to look round. And all he saw was the mechanic talking earnestly to the sleuth. . . Whereupon he talked earnestly to Drummond. . .

In thinking it over after, that unhappy man, whose job had seemed so easy, found it difficult to say exactly what happened. All of a sudden he found himself surrounded by people – all very affable and most conversational. It took him quite five minutes to get back to his car, and by that time the 'plane was a speck in the west. Drummond was standing by the gates when he got there, with a look of profound surprise on his face.

'One I have seen often,' remarked the soldier; 'two sometimes; three rarely; four never. Fancy four punctures – all at the same time! Dear, dear! I positively insist on giving you a lift.'

He felt himself irresistibly propelled towards Drummond's car, with only time for a fleeting glimpse at his own four flat tyres, and almost before he realized it they were away. After a few minutes, when he had recovered from his surprise, his hand went instinctively to his pocket, to find the revolver had gone. And it was then that the man he had thought mad laughed gently.

'Didn't know I was once a pickpocket, did you?' he remarked affably. 'A handy little gun, too. Is it all right, Peter?'

'All safe,' came a voice from behind.

'Then dot him one.'

The sleuth had a fleeting vision of stars of all colours which danced before his eyes, coupled with a stunning blow on the back of the head. Vaguely he realized the car was pulling up – then blackness. It was not till four hours later that a passing labourer, having pulled him from a not over-dry ditch, laid him out to cool. And, incidentally, with his further sphere of usefulness we are not concerned. . .

IV

'My dear fellow, I told you we'd get here somehow.' Hugh Drummond stretched his legs luxuriously. 'The fact that it was necessary to crash your blinking bus in a stray field in order to avoid their footling passport regulations is absolutely immaterial. The only damage is a dent in Ted's dicky, but all the best waiters have that. They smear it with soup to show their energy. . . My God! Here's another of them.'

A Frenchman was advancing towards them down the stately vestibule of the Ritz waving protesting hands. He addressed himself in a voluble crescendo to Drummond, who rose and bowed deeply. His knowledge of French was microscopic, but such trifles were made to be overcome.

'*Mais oui, Monsieur mon Colonel,*' he remarked affably, when the gendarme paused for lack of breath, '*vous comprenez que notre machine avail crashé dans un field des turnipes. Nous avons lost notre direction. Nous sommes hittés dans l'estomacs. . . Comme ci, comme ca. . . Vous comprenez, n'est-ce-pas, mon Colonel?*' He turned fiercely on Jerry. 'Shut up, you damn fool; don't laugh!'

'*Mais, messieurs, vous n'avez pas des passeports.*' The little man, torn between gratification at his rapid promotion and horror at such an appalling breach of regulations, shot up and down like an agitated semaphore. '*Vous comprenez; c'est defendu d'arriver en Paris sans des passeports?*'

'*Parfaitement, mon Colonel,*' continued Hugh unmoved. '*Mais vous comprenez que nous avons crashé dans un field des turnipes – non; des rognons. . .* What the hell are you laughing at, Jerry?'

'*Oignons,* old boy,' spluttered the latter. '*Rognons* are kidneys.'

'What the dickens does that matter?' demanded Hugh. '*Vous comprenez, mon Colonel, n'est-ce pas? Vive la France! En-bas les Boches! Nous avons crashé.*'

The *gendarme* shrugged his shoulders with a hopeless gesture, and seemed on the point of bursting into tears. Of course this large Englishman was mad; why otherwise should he spit in the kidneys? And that is what he continued to state was his form of amusement. Truly an insane race, and yet he had fought in the brigade next to them near Montauban in July '16 – and he had liked them – those mad Tommies. Moreover, this large, imperturbable man, with the charming smile, showed a proper appreciation of his merits – an appreciation not shared up to the present, regrettable to state, by his own superiors. '*Colonel – parbleu; eh bien! Pourquoi non?*'

At last he produced a notebook; he felt unable to cope further with the situation himself.

'*Votre nom, M'sieur, s'il vous plaît?*'

'Undoubtedly, *mon Colonel,*' remarked Hugh vaguely. '*Nous crashons dans—*'

'*Ah! Mais oui, mais oui, M'sieur.*' The little man danced in his agitation. '*Vous m'avez dejà dit que vous avez craché dans les rognons, mais je désire votre nom.*'

'He wants your name, old dear,' murmured Jerry weakly.

'Oh, does he?' Hugh beamed on the gendarme. 'You priceless little bird! My name is Captain Hugh Drummond.'

And as he spoke, a man sitting close by, who had been an amused onlooker of the whole scene, stiffened suddenly in his chair and stared hard at Hugh. It was only for a second, and then he was once more merely the politely interested spectator. But Hugh had seen that quick look, though he gave no sign; and when at last the Frenchman departed, apparently satisfied, he leaned over and spoke to Jerry.

'See that man with the suit of reach-me-downs and the cigar,' he remarked. 'He's in this game; I'm just wondering on which side.'

He was not left long in doubt, for barely had the swing doors closed behind the *gendarme,* when the man in question rose and came over to him.

'Excuse me, sir,' he said, in a pronounced nasal twang, 'but I heard you say you were Captain Hugh Drummond. I guess you're one of the men I've come across the water to see. My card.'

Hugh glanced at the pasteboard languidly.

'Mr Jerome K. Green,' he murmured. 'What a jolly sort of name.'

'See here, Captain,' went on the other, suddenly displaying a badge hidden under his coat. 'That'll put you wise.'

'Far from it, Mr Green. What's it the prize for – throwing cards into a hat?'

The American laughed.

'I guess I've sort of taken to you,' he remarked. 'You're real fresh. That badge is the badge of the police force of the United States of America; and that same force is humming some at the moment.' He sat down beside Hugh, and bent forward confidentially. 'There's a prominent citizen of New York City been mislaid, Captain; and, from information we've got, we reckon you know quite a lot about his whereabouts.'

Hugh pulled out his cigarette-case.

'Turkish this side – Virginian that. Ah! But I see you're smoking.' With great deliberation he selected one himself, and lit it. 'You were saying, Mr Green?'

The detective stared at him thoughtfully; at the moment he was not quite certain how to tackle this large and self-possessed young man.

'Might I ask why you're over here?' he asked at length, deciding to feel his way.

'The air is free to everyone, Mr Green. As long as you get your share to breathe, you can ask anything you like.'

The American laughed again.

'I guess I'll put my cards down,' he said, with sudden decision. 'What about Hiram C. Potts?'

'What, indeed?' remarked Hugh. 'Sounds like a riddle, don't it?'

'You've heard of him, Captain?'

'Few people have not.'

'Yes – but you've met him recently,' said the detective, leaning forward. 'You know where he is, and' – he tapped Hugh on the knee impressively – 'I want him. I want Hiram C. Potts like a man wants a drink in a dry state. I want to take him back in cottonwool to his wife and daughters. That's why I'm over this side, Captain, just for that one purpose.'

'There seem to me to be a considerable number of people wandering around who share your opinion about Mr Potts,' drawled Hugh. 'He must be a popular sort of cove.'

'Popular ain't the word for it, Captain,' said the other. 'Have you got him now?'

'In a manner of speaking, yes,' answered Hugh, beckoning to a passing waiter. 'Three Martinis.'

'Where is he?' snapped the detective eagerly.

Hugh laughed.

'Being wrapped up in cottonwool by somebody else's wife and daughters. You were a little too quick, Mr Green; you may be all you say – on the other hand, you may not. And these days I trust no one.'

The American nodded his head in approval.

'Quite right,' he remarked. 'My motto – and yet I'm going to trust you. Weeks ago we heard things on the other side, through certain channels, as to a show which was on the rails over here. It was a bit vague, and there were big men in it; but at the time it was no concern of ours. You run your own worries, Captain, over this side.'

Hugh nodded.

'Go on,' he said curtly.

'Then Hiram Potts got mixed up in it; exactly how, we weren't wise to. But it was enough to bring me over here. Two days ago I got this cable.' He produced a bundle of papers, and handed one to Drummond. 'It's in cipher, as you see; I've put the translation underneath.'

Hugh took the cablegram and glanced at it. It was short and to the point:

Captain Hugh Drummond, of Half Moon Street, London, is your man.

He glanced up at the American, who drained his cocktail with the air of a man who is satisfied with life.

'Captain Hugh Drummond, of Half Moon Street, London, is my man,' he chuckled. 'Well, Captain, what about it now? Will you tell me why you've come to Paris? I guess it's something to do with the business I'm on.'

For a few moments Hugh did not reply, and the American seemed in no hurry for an answer. Some early arrivals for dinner sauntered through the lounge, and Drummond watched them idly as they passed. The American detective certainly seemed all right, but. . . Casually, his glance rested on a man sitting just opposite, reading the paper. He took in the short, dark beard – the immaculate, though slightly foreign evening clothes; evidently a wealthy Frenchman giving a dinner party in the restaurant, by the way the head waiter was hovering around. And then suddenly his eyes narrowed, and he sat motionless.

'Are you interested in the psychology of gambling, Mr Green?' he remarked, turning to the somewhat astonished American. 'Some people cannot control their eyes or their mouth if the stakes are big; others cannot control their hands. For instance, the gentleman opposite. Does anything strike you particularly with regard to him?'

The detective glanced across the lounge.

'He seems to like hitting his knee with his left hand,' he said, after a short inspection.

'Precisely,' murmured Hugh. 'That is why I came to Paris.'

Chapter 9

In Which He Has a Near Shave

I

'CAPTAIN, you have me guessing.' The American bit the end off another cigar, and leaned back in his chair. 'You say that swell Frenchman with the waiters hovering about like fleas round a dog's tail is the reason you came to Paris. Is he kind of friendly with Hiram C. Potts?'

Drummond laughed.

'The first time I met Mr Potts,' he remarked, 'that swell Frenchman was just preparing to put a thumbscrew on his second thumb.'

'Second?' The detective looked up quickly.

'The first had been treated earlier in the evening,' answered Drummond quietly. 'It was then that I removed your millionaire pal.'

The other lit his cigar deliberately.

'Say, Captain,' he murmured, 'you ain't pulling my leg by any chance, are you?'

'I am not,' said Drummond shortly. 'I was told, before I met him, that the gentleman over there was one of the boys. . . He is, most distinctly. In fact, though up to date such matters have not been much in my line, I should put him down as a sort of super-criminal. I wonder what name he is passing under here?'

The American ceased pulling at his cigar.

'Do they vary?'

'In England he is clean-shaven, possesses a daughter, and answers to Carl Peterson. As he is at present I should never have known him, but for that little trick of his.'

'Possesses a daughter!' For the first time the detective displayed traces of excitement. 'Holy Smoke! It can't be him!'

'Who?' demanded Drummond.

But the other did not answer. Out of the corner of his eye he was watching three men who had just joined the subject of their talk, and on his face was a dawning amazement. He waited till the whole party had gone into the restaurant, then, throwing aside his caution, he turned excitedly on Drummond.

'Are you certain,' he cried, 'that that's the man who has been monkeying with Potts?'

'Absolutely,' said Hugh. 'He recognized me; whether he thinks I recognized him or not, I don't know.'

'Then what,' remarked the detective, 'is he doing here dining with Hocking, our cotton trust man; with Steinemann, the German coal man; and with that other guy whose face is familiar, but whose name I can't place? Two of 'em, at any rate, Captain, have got more millions than we're ever likely to have thousands.'

Hugh stared at the American.

'Last night,' he said slowly, 'he was foregathering with a crowd of the most atrocious ragged-trousered revolutionaries it's ever been my luck to run up against.'

'We're in it, Captain, right in the middle of it,' cried the detective, slapping his leg. 'I'll eat my hat if that Frenchman isn't Franklyn – or Libstein – or Baron Darott – or any other of the blamed names he calls himself. He's the biggest proposition we've ever been up against on this little old earth, and he's done us every time. He never commits himself, and if he does, he always covers his tracks. He's a genius; he's the goods. Gee!' he whistled gently under his breath. 'If we could only lay him by the heels.'

For a while he stared in front of him, lost in his dream of pleasant anticipation; then, with a short laugh, he pulled himself together.

'Quite a few people have thought the same, Captain,' he remarked,' and there he is – still drinking high-balls. You say he was with a crowd of revolutionaries last night. What do you mean exactly?'

'Bolshevists, Anarchists, members of the Do-no-work-and-have-all-the-money Brigade,' answered Hugh. 'But excuse me a moment. Waiter.'

A man who had been hovering round came up promptly.

'Four of 'em, Ted,' said Hugh in a rapid undertone. 'Frenchman with a beard, a Yank, and two Boches. Do your best.'

'Right-o, old bean!' returned the waiter, 'but don't hope for too much.'

He disappeared unobtrusively into the restaurant, and Hugh turned with a laugh to the American, who was staring at him in amazement.

'Who the devil is that guy?' asked the detective at length.

'Ted Jerningham – son of Sir Patrick Jerningham, Bart., and Lady Jerningham, of Jerningham Hall, Rutland, England,' answered Hugh, still grinning. 'We may be crude in our methods, Mr Green, but you must admit we do our best. Incidentally, if you want to know, your friend Mr Potts is at present tucked away between the sheets at that very house. He went there by aeroplane this morning.' He waved a hand towards Jerry. 'He was the pilot.'

'Travelled like a bird, and sucked up a plate of meat-juice at the end,' announced that worthy, removing his eyes with difficulty from a recently arrived fairy opposite. 'Who says that's nothing, Hugh: the filly across the road there, with that bangle affair round her knee?'

'I must apologize for him, Mr Green,' remarked Hugh. 'He has only recently left school, and knows no better.'

But the American was shaking his head a little dazedly.

'Crude!' he murmured, 'Crude! If you and your pals, Captain, are ever out of a job, the New York police is yours for the asking.' He smoked for a few moments in silence, and then, with a quick hunch of his shoulders, he turned to Drummond. 'I guess there'll be time to throw bouquets after,' he remarked. 'We've got to get busy on what your friend Peterson's little worry is; we've then got to stop it – some old how. Now, does nothing sort of strike you?' He looked keenly at the soldier. 'Revolutionaries, Bolshevists, paid agitators last night: international financiers this evening. Why, the broad outline of the plan is as plain as the nose on your face; and it's just the sort of game that man would love. . .' The detective stared thoughtfully at the end of his cigar, and a look of comprehension began to dawn on Hugh's face.

'Great Scott! Mr Green,' he said, 'I'm beginning to get you. What was defeating me was why two men like Peterson and Lakington should be mixed up with last night's crowd.'

'Lakington! Who's Lakington?' asked the other quickly.

'Number Two in the combine,' answered Hugh, 'and a nasty man.'

'Well, we'll leave him out for the moment,' said the American. 'Doesn't it strike you that there are quite a number of people in this world who would benefit if England became a sort of second Russia? That such a thing would be worth money – big money? That such a thing would be worth paying through the nose for? It would have to be done properly; your small strike here, and your small strike there, ain't no manner of use. One gigantic syndicalist strike all over your country – that's what Peterson's playing for, I'll stake my bottom dollar. How he's doing it is another matter. But he's in with the big financiers: and he's using the tub-thumping Bolshies as tools. Gad! It's a big scheme' – he puffed twice at his cigar – 'a durned big scheme. Your little old country, Captain, is, saving one, the finest on God's earth; but she's in a funny mood. She's sick, like most of us are; maybe she's a little bit sicker than a good many people think. But I reckon Peterson's cure won't do any manner of good, excepting to himself and those blamed capitalists who are putting up the dollars.'

'Then where the devil does Potts come in?' said Hugh, who had listened intently to every word the American had said. 'And the Duchess of Lampshire's pearls?'

'Pearls!' began the American, when the restaurant door opened suddenly and Ted Jerningham emerged. He seemed to be in a hurry, and Hugh half rose in his chair. Then he sat back again, as with miraculous rapidity a crowd of infuriated head waiters and other great ones appeared from nowhere and surrounded Jerningham.

Undoubtedly this was not the way for a waiter to leave the hotel – even if he had just been discovered as an impostor and sacked on the spot. And undoubtedly if he had been a waiter, this large body of scandalized beings would have removed him expeditiously through some secret buttery-hatch, and dropped him on the pavement out of a back entrance.

But not being a waiter, he continued to advance, while his *entourage,* torn between rage at his effrontery and horror at the thought of a scene, followed in his wake.

Just opposite Hugh he halted, and in a clear voice addressed no one in particular:

'You're spotted. Look out. Ledger at Godalming.'

Then, engulfed once more in the crowd, he continued his majestic progress, and finally disappeared a little abruptly from view.

'Cryptic,' murmured the American, 'but some lad. Gee! He had that bunch guessing.'

'The ledger at Godalming,' said Hugh thoughtfully. 'I watched Peterson, through the skylight last night, getting gay with that ledger. I'm thinking we'll have to look inside it, Mr Green.'

He glanced up as one of the chucking-out party came back, and asked what had happened.

'*Mon Dieu, m'sieur,*' cried the waiter despairingly. ''E vas an impostor, *n'est-ce pas – un scélerat;* 'e upset ze fish all over ze shirt-front of Monsieur le Comte.'

'Was that the gentleman with the short beard, dining with three others?' asked Drummond gravely.

'*Mais oui, m'sieur*. He dine here always if 'e is in Paris – does le Comte de Guy. Oh! *Mon Dieu! C'est terrible!*'

Wringing his hands, the waiter went back into the restaurant, and Hugh shook silently.

'Dear old Ted,' he murmured, wiping the tears from his eyes. 'I knew he'd keep his end up.' Then he stood up. 'What about a little dinner at Maxim's? I'm thinking we've found out all we're likely to find, until we can get to that ledger. And thanks to your knowing those birds, Mr Green, our trip to Paris has been of considerable value.'

The American nodded.

'I guess I'm on,' he remarked slowly; 'but, if you take my advice, Captain, you'll look nippy tonight. I wouldn't linger around corners admiring the mud. Things kind o' happen at corners.'

II

But on this particular evening the detective proved wrong. They reached Maxim's without mishap, they enjoyed an excellent dinner, during which the American showed himself to be a born conversationalist, as well as a shrewd man of the world. And over the coffee and liqueurs Hugh gave him a brief outline of what had taken place since he first got mixed up in the affair. The American listened in silence, though amazement shone on his face as the story proceeded. The episode of the disappearing body seemed to tickle his fancy, but even over that he made no remark. Only when Hugh had finished, and early arrivals for supper were beginning to fill the restaurant, did he sum up the matter as he saw it.

'A tough proposition, Captain – damned tough. Potts is our biggest shipping man, but where he comes on the picture at that moment has me beat. As for the old girl's jewels, they don't seem to fit in at all. All we can do is to put our noses inside that ledger, and see the book of the words. It'll sure help some.'

And as Hugh switched off the electric light in his bedroom, having first seen that his torch was ready to hand in case of emergency, he was thinking of the detective's words. Getting hold of the ledger was not going to be easy – far from it; but the excitement of the chase had fairly obsessed him by now. He lay in bed, turning over in his mind every possible and impossible scheme by which he could get into the secret centre room at The Elms. He knew the safe the ledger was kept in: but safes are awkward propositions for the ordinary mortal to tackle. Anyway, it wasn't a thing which could be done in a minute's visit; he would have to manage at least a quarter or half an hour's undisturbed search, the thought of which, with his knowledge of the habits of the household, almost made him laugh out loud. And, at that moment, a fly pinged past his head. . .

He felt singularly wideawake, and, after a while, he gave up attempting to go to sleep. The new development which had come to light that evening was uppermost in his thoughts; and, as he lay there, covered only with a sheet, for the night was hot, the whole vile scheme unfolded itself before his imagination. The American was right in his main idea – of that he had no doubt; and in his mind's eye he saw the great crowds of idle, foolish men led by a few hotheaded visionaries and paid blackguards to their so-called Utopia. Starvation, misery, ruin, utter and complete, lurked in his mental picture; spectres disguised as great ideals, but grinning sardonically under their masks. And once again he seemed to hear the toc-toc of machine-guns, as he had heard them night after night during the years gone by. But this time they were mounted on the pavement of the towns of England, and the swish of the bullets, which had swept like swarms of cockchafers over No Man's Land, now whistled down the streets between rows of squalid houses. . . And once again a fly pinged past his head.

With a gesture of annoyance he waved his arm. It was hot – insufferably hot, and he was beginning to regret that he had followed the earnest advice of the American to sleep with his windows shut and bolted. What on earth could Peterson do to him in a room at the Ritz? But he had promised the detective, and there it was – curtains drawn, window bolted, door locked. Moreover, and he smiled grimly to himself as he remembered it, he had even gone so far as to emulate the hysterical maiden lady of fiction and peer under the bed. . .

The next moment the smile ceased abruptly, and he lay rigid, with every nerve alert. Something had moved in the room. . .

It had only been a tiny movement, more like the sudden creak of a piece of furniture than anything else – but it was not quite like it. A gentle, slithering sound had preceded the creak; the sound such as a man would make who, with infinite precaution against making a noise, was moving in a dark room; a stealthy, uncanny noise. Hugh peered into the blackness tensely. After the first moment of surprise his brain was quite cool. He had looked under the bed, he had hung his coat in the cupboard, and save for those two obvious places there was no cover for a cat. And yet, with the sort of sixth sense that four years of war had given him, he knew that noise had been made by some human agency. Human! The thought of the cobra at The Elms flashed into his mind, and his mouth set more grimly. What if Peterson had introduced some of his abominable menagerie into the room? . . . Then, once more, the thing like a fly sounded loud in his ear. And was it his imagination, or had he heard a faint sibilant hiss just before?

Suddenly it struck him that he was at a terrible disadvantage. The thing, whatever it was, knew at any rate approximately his position: he had not the slightest notion where it was. And a blind man boxing a man who could see would have felt just about as safe. With Hugh, such a conclusion meant instant action. It might be dangerous on the floor: it most certainly was far more so in bed. He felt for his torch, and then, with one convulsive bound, he was standing by the door, with his hand on the electric-light switch.

Then he paused and listened intently. Not a sound could he hear; the thing, whatever it was, had become motionless at his sudden movement. For an appreciable time he stood there, his eyes searching the darkness – but even he could see nothing, and he cursed the American comprehensively under his breath. He would have given anything for even the faintest grey light, so that he could have some idea of what it was and where it was. Now he felt utterly helpless, while every moment he imagined some slimy, crawling brute touching his bare feet – creeping up him. . .

He pulled himself together sharply. Light was essential, and at once. But, if he switched it on there would be a moment when the thing would see him before he could see the thing – and such moments are not helpful. There only remained his torch; and on the Ancre, on one occasion, he had saved his life by judicious use. The man behind one of those useful implements is in blackness far more impenetrable than the blackest night, for the man in front is dazzled. He can only shoot at the torch: therefore, hold it to one side and in front of you. . .

The light flashed out, darting round the room. Ping! Something hit the sleeve of his pyjamas, but still he could see nothing. The bed, with the clothes thrown back; the washstand; the chair with his trousers and shirt – everything was as it had been when he turned in. And then he heard a second sound – distinct and clear. It came from high up, near the ceiling, and the beam caught the big cupboard and travelled up. It reached the top, and rested there, fixed and steady. Framed in the middle of it, peering over the edge, was a little hairless, brown face, holding what looked like a tube in its mouth. Hugh had one glimpse of a dark, skinny hand putting something in the tube, and then he switched off the torch and ducked, just as another fly pinged over his head and hit the wall behind.

One thing, at any rate, was certain: the other occupant of the room was human, and with that realization all his nerve returned. There would be time enough later on to find out how he got there, and what those strange pinging noises had been caused by. Just at that moment only one thing was on the programme; and without a sound he crept round the bed towards the cupboard, to put that one thing into effect in his usual direct manner.

Twice did he hear the little whistling hiss from above, but nothing sang past his head. Evidently the man had lost him, and was probably still aiming at the door. And then, with hands that barely touched it, he felt the outlines of the cupboard.

It was standing an inch or two from the wall, and he slipped his fingers behind the back on one side. He listened for a moment, but no movement came from above; then, half facing the wall, he put one leg against it. There was one quick, tremendous heave; a crash which sounded deafening; then silence. And once again he switched on his torch. . .

Lying on the floor by the window was one of the smallest men he had ever seen. He was a native of sorts, and Hugh turned him over with his foot. He was quite unconscious, and the bump on his head where it had hit the floor was rapidly swelling to the size of a large orange. In his hand he still clutched the little tube, and Hugh gingerly removed it. Placed in position at one end was a long splinter of wood, with a sharpened point: and by the light of his torch Hugh saw that it was faintly discoloured with some brown stain.

He was still examining it with interest when a thunderous knock came on the door. He strolled over and switched on the electric light; then he opened the door.

An excited night-porter rushed in, followed by two or three other people in varying stages of undress, and stopped in amazement at the scene. The heavy cupboard, with a great crack across the back, lay face downwards on the floor; the native still lay curled up and motionless.

'One of the hotel pets?' queried Hugh pleasantly, lighting a cigarette. 'If it's all the same to you, I wish you'd remove him. He was – ah – finding it uncomfortable on the top of the cupboard.'

It appeared that the night-porter could speak English; it also appeared that the lady occupying the room below had rushed forth demanding to be led to the basement, under the misapprehension that war had again been declared and the Germans were bombing Paris. It still further appeared that there was something most irregular about the whole proceeding – the best people at the Ritz did not do these things. And then, to crown everything, while the uproar was at its height, the native on the floor, opening one beady and somewhat dazed eye, realized that things looked unhealthy. Unnoticed, he lay 'doggo' for a while; then, like a rabbit which has almost been trodden on, he dodged between the legs of the men in the room, and vanished through the open door. Taken by surprise, for a moment no one moved: then, simultaneously, they dashed into the passage. It was empty, save for one scandalized old gentleman in a nightcap, who was peering out of a room opposite angrily demanding the cause of the hideous din.

Had he seen a native – a black man? He had seen no native, and if other people only drank water, they wouldn't, either. In fact, the whole affair was scandalous, and he should write to the papers about it. Still muttering, he withdrew, banging his door, and Hugh, glancing up, saw the American detective advancing towards them along the corridor.

'What's the trouble, Captain?' he asked as he joined the group.

'A friend of the management elected to spend the night on the top of my cupboard, Mr Green,' answered Drummond, 'and got cramp halfway through.'

The American gazed at the wreckage in silence. Then he looked at Hugh, and what he saw on that worthy's face apparently decided him to maintain that policy. In fact, it was not till the night-porter and his attendant minions had at last, and very dubiously, withdrawn, that he again opened his mouth.

'Looks like a hectic night,' he murmured. 'What happened?' Briefly Hugh told him what had occurred, and the detective whistled softly.

'Blowpipe and poisoned darts,' he said shortly, returning the tube to Drummond. 'Narrow escape – damned narrow! Look at your pillow.'

Hugh looked: embedded in the linen were four pointed splinters similar to the one he held in his hand; by the door were three more, lying on the floor.

'An engaging little bird,' he laughed; 'but nasty to look at.'

He extracted the little pieces of wood and carefully placed them in an empty matchbox: the tube he put into his cigarette-case.

'Might come in handy: you never know,' he remarked casually.

'They might if you stand quite still,' said the American, with a sudden, sharp command in his voice. 'Don't move.'

Hugh stood motionless, staring at the speaker who, with eyes fixed on his right forearm, had stepped forward. From the loose sleeve of his pyjama coat the detective gently pulled another dart and dropped it into the matchbox.

'Not far off getting you that time, Captain,' he cried cheerfully. 'Now you've got the whole blamed outfit.'

III

It was the Comte de Guy who boarded the boat express at the Gare du Nord the next day; it was Carl Peterson who stepped off the boat express at Boulogne. And it was only Drummond's positive assurance which convinced the American that the two characters were the same man.

He was leaning over the side of the boat reading a telegram when he first saw Hugh ten minutes after the boat had left the harbour; and if he had hoped for a different result to the incident of the night before, no sign of it showed on his face. Instead he waved cheerily to Drummond.

'This is a pleasant surprise,' he remarked affably. 'Have you been to Paris, too?'

For a moment Drummond looked at him narrowly. Was it a stupid bluff, or was the man so sure of his power of disguise that he assumed with certainty he had not been recognized? And it suddenly struck Hugh that, save for that one tell-tale habit – a habit which, in all probability, Peterson himself was unconscious of – he would *not* have recognized him.

'Yes,' he answered lightly. 'I came over to see how you behaved yourself!'

'What a pity I didn't know!' said Peterson, with a good-humoured chuckle. He seemed in excellent spirits, as he carefully tore the telegram into tiny pieces and dropped them overboard. 'We might have had another of our homely little chats over some supper. Where did you stay?'

'At the Ritz. And you?'

'I always stop at the Bristol,' answered Peterson. 'Quieter than the Ritz, I think.'

'Yes, it was quite dreadful last night,' murmured Hugh. 'A pal of mine – quite incorrigible – that bird over there' – he pointed to Ted Jerningham, who was strolling up and down the deck with the American – 'insisted on dressing up as a waiter.' He laughed shortly at the sudden gleam in the other's eye, as he watched Jerningham go past. 'Not content with that, he went and dropped the fish over some warrior's boiled shirt, and had to leave in disgrace.' He carefully selected a cigarette. 'No accountin' for this dressing-up craze, is there, Carl? You'd never be anything but your own sweet self, would you, little one? Always the girls' own friend – tender and true.' He laughed softly; from previous experience he knew that this particular form of baiting invariably infuriated Peterson. 'Some day, my Carl, you must tell me of your life, and your early struggles, amidst all the bitter temptation of this wicked world.'

'Some day,' snarled Peterson, 'I'll—'

'Stop' Drummond held up a protesting hand. 'Not that, my Carl – anything but that.'

'Anything but what?' said the other savagely.

'I felt it in my bones,' answered Drummond, 'that you were once more on the point of mentioning my decease. I couldn't bear it, Carl: on this beautiful morning I should burst into tears. It would be the seventeenth time that that sad event has been alluded to either by you or our Henry; and I'm reluctantly beginning to think that you'll have to hire an assassin, and take lessons from him.' He looked thoughtfully at the other, and an unholy joy began to dawn on his face. 'I see you have thrown away your cigar, Carl. May I offer you a cigarette? No? But why so brusque? Can it be – oh no! surely not – can it be that my little pet is feeling icky-boo? Face going green – slight perspiration – collar tight – only the yawning stage between him and his break-fast! Some people have all the fun of the fair. And I thought of asking you to join me below at lunch. There's some excellent fat pork. . .'

A few minutes later, Jerningham and the American found him leaning by himself against the rail, still laughing weakly.

'I ask no more of life,' he remarked when he could speak. 'Anything else that may come will be an anti-climax.'

'What's happened?' asked Jerningham.

'It's happening,' said Drummond joyfully. 'It couldn't pos-sibly be over yet. Peterson, our one and only Carl, has been overcome by the waves. And when he's feeling a little better I'll take him a bit of crackling. . .' Once again he gave way to unrestrained mirth, which finally subsided sufficiently to allow him to stagger below and feed.

At the top of the stairs leading to the luncheon saloon, he paused, and glanced into the secret place reserved for those who have from early childhood voted for a Channel tunnel.

'There he is,' he whispered ecstatically, 'our little Carl, busy recalling his past. It may be vulgar, Ted: doubtless it is. I don't care. Such trifles matter not in the supreme moments of one's life; and I can imagine of only one more supreme than this.'

'What's that?' asked Ted, firmly piloting him down the stairs.

'The moment when he and Henry sit side by side and recall their pasts together,' murmured Hugh solemnly. 'Think of it, man – think of it! Each cursin' the other between spasms. My hat! What a wonderful, lovely dream to treasure through the weary years!' He gazed abstractedly at the waiter. 'Roast beef – underdone,' he remarked, 'and take a plate of cold fat up to the silence room above. The third gentleman from the door would like to look at it.'

But the third gentleman from the door, even in the midst of his agony, was consoled by one reflection.

'Should it be necessary, letter awaits him.' So had run the telegram, which he had scattered to the winds right under Drummond's nose. And it *was* necessary. The mutton-headed young sweep had managed to escape once again: though Petro had assured him that the wretched native had never yet failed. And he personally had seen the man clamber on to the top of the cupboard. . .

For a moment his furious rage overcame his sufferings. . . Next time. . .next time. . . And then the seventh wave of several seventh waves arrived. He had a fleeting glimpse of the scoundrel Drummond, apparently on the other end of a see-saw, watching him delightedly from outside; then, with a dreadful groan, he snatched his new basin, just supplied by a phlegmatic steward, from the scoundrel next him, who had endeavoured to appropriate it.

IV

'Walk right in, Mr Green,' said Hugh, as, three hours later, they got out of a taxi in Half Moon Street. 'This is my little rabbit-hutch.'

He followed the American up the stairs, and produced his latchkey. But before he could even insert it in the hole the door was flung open, and Peter Darrell stood facing him with evident relief in his face.

'Thank the Lord you've come, old son,' he cried, with a brief look at the detective. 'There's something doing down at Godalming I don't like.'

He followed Hugh into the sitting-room.

'At twelve o'clock to-day Toby rang up. He was talking quite ordinarily – you know the sort of rot he usually gets off his chest – when suddenly he stopped quite short and said, "My God! What do you want?" I could tell he'd looked up, because his voice was muffled. Then there was the sound of a scuffle, I heard Toby curse, then nothing more. I rang and rang and rang – no answer.'

'What did you do?' Drummond, with a letter in his hand which he had taken off the mantelpiece, was listening grimly.

'Algy was here. He motored straight off to see if he could find out what was wrong. I stopped here to tell you.'

'Anything through from him?'

'Not a word. There's foul play, or I'll eat my hat.'

But Hugh did not answer. With a look on his face which even Peter had never seen before, he was reading the letter. It was short and to the point, but he read it three times before he spoke.

'When did this come?' he asked.

'An hour ago,' answered the other. 'I very nearly opened it.'

'Read it,' said Hugh. He handed it to Peter and went to the door.

'Denny,' he shouted, 'I want my car round at once.' Then he came back into the room. 'If they've hurt one hair of her head,' he said, his voice full of a smouldering fury, 'I'll murder that gang one by one with my bare hands.'

'Say, Captain, may I see this letter?' said the American; and Hugh nodded.

'"*For pity's sake, come at once,*"' read the detective aloud. '"*The bearer of this is trustworthy.*"' He thoughtfully picked his teeth. 'Girl's writing. Do you know her?'

'My fiancée,' said Hugh shortly.

'Certain?' snapped the American.

'Certain!' cried Hugh. 'Of course I am. I know every curl of every letter.'

'There is such a thing as forgery,' remarked the detective dispassionately.

'Damn it, man!' exploded Hugh; 'do you imagine I don't know my own girl's writing?'

'A good many bank cashiers have mistaken their customers' writing before now,' said the other, unmoved. 'I don't like it, Captain. A girl in *real* trouble wouldn't put in that bit about the bearer.'

'You go to hell,' remarked Hugh briefly. 'I'm going to Godalming.'

'Well,' drawled the American, 'not knowing Godalming, I don't know who scores. But, if you go there – I come, too.'

'And me,' said Peter, brightening up.

Hugh grinned.

'Not you, old son. If Mr Green will come, I'll be delighted; but I want you here at headquarters.'

He turned round as his servant put his head in at the door.

'Car here, sir. Do you want a bag packed?'

'No – only my revolver. Are you ready, Mr Green?'

'Sure thing,' said the American. 'I always am.'

'Then we'll move.' And Peter, watching the car resignedly from the window, saw the American grip his seat with both hands, and then raise them suddenly in silent prayer, while an elderly charlady fled with a scream to the safety of the area below.

They did the trip in well under the hour, and the detective got out of the car with a faint sigh of relief.

'You've missed your vocation, Captain,' he murmured. 'If you pushed a bath-chair it would be safer for all parties. I bolted two bits of gum in that excursion.'

But Drummond was already out of earshot, dodging rapidly through the bushes on his way to The Larches; and when the American finally overtook him, he was standing by a side-door knocking hard on the panels.

'Seems kind of empty,' said the detective thoughtfully, as the minutes went by and no one came. 'Why not try the front door?'

'Because it's in sight of the other house,' said Hugh briefly. 'I'm going to break in.'

He retreated a yard from the door, then, bracing his shoulder, he charged it once. And the door, as a door, was not. . . Rapidly the two men went from room to room – bedrooms, servants' quarters, even the bathroom. Every one was empty: not a sound could be heard in the house. Finally, only the dining-room remained, and as they stood by the door looking round, the American shifted his third piece of gum to a new point of vantage.

'Somebody has been rough-housing by the look of things,' he remarked judicially. 'Looks like a boozing den after a thick night.'

'It does,' remarked Hugh grimly, taking in the disorder of the room. The tablecloth was pulled off, the telephone lay on the floor. China and glass, smashed to pieces, littered the carpet; but what caught his eye, and caused him suddenly to step forward and pick it up, was a plain circle of glass with a black cord attached to it through a small hole.

'Algy Longworth's eyeglass,' he muttered. 'So he's been caught, too.'

And it was at that moment that, clear and distinct through the still evening air, they heard a woman's agonized scream. It came from the house next door, and the American, for a brief space, even forgot to chew his gum.

The next instant he darted forward.

'Stop, you young fool!' he shouted, but he was too late.

He watched Drummond, running like a stag, cross the lawn and disappear in the trees. For a second he hesitated; then, with a shrug of square shoulders, he rapidly left the house by the way they had entered. And a few minutes later, Drummond's car was skimming back towards London, with a grim-faced man at the wheel, who had apparently felt the seriousness of the occasion so acutely as to deposit his third piece of spearmint on the underneath side of the steering-wheel for greater safety.

But, seeing that the owner of the car was lying in blissful unconsciousness in the hall of The Elms, surrounded by half a dozen men, this hideous vandalism hurt him not.

Chapter 10

In Which the Hun Nation
Decreases by One

I

DRUMMOND had yielded to impulse – the blind, all-powerful impulse of any man who is a man to get to the woman he loves if she wants him. As he had dashed across the lawn to The Elms, with the American's warning cry echoing in his ears, he had been incapable of serious thought. Subconsciously he had known that, from every point of view, it was the act of a madman; that he was deliberately putting his head into what, in all probability, was a carefully prepared noose: that, from every point of view, he could help Phyllis better by remaining a free agent outside. But when a girl shrieks, and the man who loves her hears it, arguments begin to look tired. And what little caution might have remained to Hugh completely vanished as he saw the girl watching him with agonized terror in her face, from an upstairs window, as he dashed up to the house. It was only for a brief second that he saw her; then she disappeared suddenly, as if snatched away by some invisible person.

'I'm coming, darling.' He had given one wild shout, and hurled himself through the door which led into the house from the garden. A dazzling light of intense brilliance had shone in his face, momentarily blinding him; then had come a crushing blow on the back of his head. One groping, wild step forward, and Hugh Drummond, dimly conscious of men all round him, had pitched forward on his face into utter oblivion.

'It's too easy.' Lakington's sneering voice broke the silence, as he looked vindictively at the unconscious man.

'So you have thought before, Henry,' chuckled Peterson, whose complete recovery from his recent unfortunate indisposition was shown by the steady glow of the inevitable cigar. 'And he always bobs up somehow. If you take my advice you'll finish him off here and now, and run no further risks.'

'Kill him while he's unconscious?' Lakington laughed evilly. 'No, Carl, not under any circumstances whatever. He has quite a lengthy score to pay and, by God! he's going to pay it this time.' He stepped forward and kicked Drummond twice in the ribs with a cold, animal fury.

'Well, don't kick him when he's down, guv'nor. You'll 'ave plenty o' time after.' A hoarse voice from the circle of men made Lakington look up.

'You cut it out, Jem Smith,' he snarled, 'or I might find plenty of time after for others besides this young swine.' The ex-pugilist muttered uneasily under his breath, but said no more, and it was Peterson who broke the silence.

'What are you going to do with him?'

'Lash him up like the other two,' returned Lakington, 'and leave him to cool until I get back to-morrow. But I'll bring him round before I go, and just talk to him for a little. I wouldn't like him not to know what was going to happen to him. Anticipation is always delightful.' He turned to two of the men standing near. 'Carry him into my room,' he ordered, 'and another of you get the rope.'

And so it was that Algy Longworth and Toby Sinclair, with black rage and fury in their hearts, watched the limp form of their leader being carried into the central room. Swathed in rope, they sat motionless and impotent, in their respective chairs, while they watched the same process being performed on Drummond. He was no amateur at the game, was the rope-winder, and by the time he had finished, Hugh resembled nothing so much as a lifeless brown mummy. Only his head was free, and that lolled forward helplessly.

Lakington watched the performance for a time; then, wearying of it, he strolled over to Algy's chair.

'Well, you puppy,' he remarked, 'are you going to try shouting again?' He picked up the rhinoceros-hide riding-whip lying on the floor, and bent it between his hands. 'That weal on your face greatly improves your beauty, and next time you'll get two, and a gag as well.'

'How's the jaw, you horrible bit of dreg?' remarked Algy insultingly, and Toby laughed.

'Don't shake his nerve, Algy,' he implored. 'For the first time in his filthy life he feels safe in the same room as Hugh.'

The taunt seemed to madden Lakington, who sprang across the room and lashed Sinclair over the face. But even after the sixth cut no sound came from the helpless man, though the blood was streaming down inside his collar. His eyes, calm and sneering, met those of the raving man in front of him without a quiver, and, at last, Peterson himself intervened.

'Stop it, Lakington.' His voice was stern as he caught the other's upraised arm. 'That's enough for the time.'

For a moment it seemed as if Lakington would have struck Peterson himself; then he controlled himself, and, with an ugly laugh, flung the whip into a corner.

'I forgot,' he said slowly. 'It's the leading dog we want – not the puppies that run after him yapping.' He spun round on his heel. 'Have you finished?'

The rope-artist bestowed a final touch to the last knot, and surveyed his handiwork with justifiable pride.

'Cold mutton,' he remarked tersely, 'would be lively compared to him when he wakes up.'

'Good! Then we'll bring him to.'

Lakington took some crystals from a jar on one of the shelves, and placed them in a tumbler. Then he added a few drops of liquid and held the glass directly under the unconscious man's nose. Almost at once the liquid began to effervesce, and in less than a minute Drummond opened his eyes and stared dazedly round the room. He blinked foolishly as he saw Longworth and Sinclair; then he looked down and found he was similarly bound himself. Finally he glanced up at the man bending over him, and full realization returned.

'Feeling better, my friend?' With a mocking smile, Lakington laid the tumbler on a table close by.

'Much, thank you, Henry,' murmured Hugh. 'Ah! And there's Carl. How's the tummy, Carl? I hope for your sake that it's feeling stronger than the back of my head.'

He grinned cheerfully, and Lakington struck him on the mouth.

'You can stop that style of conversation, Captain Drummond,' he remarked. 'I dislike it.'

Hugh stared at the striker in silence.

'Accept my congratulations,' he said at length, in a low voice which, despite himself, shook a little. 'You are the first man who has ever done that, and I shall treasure the memory of that blow.'

'I'd hate it to be a lonely memory,' remarked Lakington. 'So here's another, to keep it company.' Again he struck him, then with a laugh he turned on his heel. 'My compliments to Miss Benton,' he said to a man standing near the door, 'and ask her to be good enough to come down for a few minutes.'

The veins stood out on Drummond's forehead at the mention of the girl, but otherwise he gave no sign; and, in silence, they waited for her arrival.

She came almost at once, a villainous-looking blackguard with her, and as she saw Hugh she gave a pitiful little moan and held out her hand to him.

'Why did you come, boy?' she cried. 'Didn't you know it was only a forgery – that note?'

'Ah! was it?' said Hugh softly. 'Was it, indeed?'

'An interesting point,' murmured Lakington. 'Surely if a charming girl is unable – or unwilling – to write herself to her fiancé, her father is a very suitable person to supply the deficiency. Especially if he has been kindly endowed by Nature with a special aptitude for – er – imitating writing.'

Mr Benton, who had been standing outside the door, came lurching into the room.

'Quite ri', Laking – Laking – ton,' he announced solemnly. 'Dreadful thing to sep – separate two young people.' Then he saw Drummond, and paused, blinking foolishly. 'Whash he all tied up for li' that?'

Lakington smiled evilly.

'It would be a pity to lose him, now he's come, wouldn't it?'

The drunken man nodded two or three times; then a thought seemed to strike him, and he advanced slowly towards Hugh, wagging a finger foolishly.

'Thash reminds me, young fellah,' he hiccoughed gravely, 'you never asked my consent. You should have asked father's consent. Mosh incon – inconshiderate. Don't you agree with me, Mishter Peterson?'

'You will find the tantalus in the dining-room,' said Peterson coldly. 'I should say you require one more drink to produce complete insensibility, and the sooner you have it the better.'

'Inshensibility!' With outraged dignity the wretched man appealed to his daughter. 'Phyllis, did you hear? Thish man says I'sh in – inebri. . . Says I'sh drunk. Gratui. . .tous inshult. . .'

'Oh, father, father,' cried the girl, covering her face with her hands. 'For pity's sake go away! You've done enough harm as it is.'

Mr Benton tacked towards the door, where he paused, swaying.

'Disgraceful,' he remarked solemnly. 'Rising generation no reshpect for elders and bettersh! Teach 'em lesson, Lakington. Do 'em all good. One – two – three, all ranged in a – in a row. Do 'em good—' His voice tailed off, and, after a valiant attempt to lean against a door which was not there, he collapsed gracefully in a heap on the floor.

'You vile hound,' said Phyllis, turning like a young tigress on Lakington. 'It's your doing entirely, that he's in that condition.'

But Lakington merely laughed.

'When we're married,' he answered lightly, 'we'll put him into a really good home for inebriates.'

'Married!' she whispered tensely. 'Married! Why, you loathsome reptile, I'd kill myself before I married you.'

'An excellent curtain,' remarked Lakington suavely, 'for the third act of a melodrama. Doubtless we can elaborate it later. In the meantime, however – he glanced at his watch—' time presses. And I don't want to go without telling you a little about the programme, Captain Drummond. Unfortunately both Mr Peterson and I have to leave you for to-night; but we shall be returning to-morrow morning – or, at any rate, I shall. You will be left in charge of Heinrich – you remember the filthy Boche? – with whom you had words the other night. As you may expect, he entertains feelings of great friendship and affection for you, so you should not lack for any bodily comforts, such as may be possible in your present somewhat cramped position. Then to-morrow, when I return, I propose to try a few experiments on you, and, though I fear you will find them painful, it's a great thing to suffer in the cause of science. . . You will always have the satisfaction of knowing that dear little Phyllis will be well cared for.' With a sudden quick movement, he seized the girl and kissed her before she realized his intention. The rope round Drummond creaked as he struggled impotently, and Lakington's sneering face seemed to swim in a red glow.

'That is quite in keeping, is it not?' he snarled, 'to kiss the lady, and to strike the man like this – and this – and this? . . .' A rain of blows came down on Drummond's face, till, with a gasping sigh, the girl slipped fainting to the floor.

'That'll do, Lakington,' said Peterson, intervening once more. 'Have the girl carried upstairs, and send for Heinrich. It's time we were off.'

With an effort Lakington let his hand fall to his side, and stood back from his victim.

'Perhaps for the present, it will,' he said slowly. 'But to-morrow – to-morrow, Captain Drummond, you shall scream to Heaven for mercy, until I take out your tongue and you can scream no more.' He turned as the German came into the room. 'I leave them to you, Heinrich,' he remarked shortly. 'Use the dog-whip if they shout, and gag them.'

The German's eyes were fixed on Hugh gloatingly.

'They will not shout twice,' he said in his gutteral voice. 'The dirty Boche to it himself will see.'

II

'We appear,' remarked Hugh quietly, a few minutes later, 'to be in for a cheery night.'

For a moment the German had left the room, and the three motionless, bound figures, sitting grotesquely in their chairs, were alone.

'How did they get you, Toby?'

'Half a dozen of 'em suddenly appeared,' answered Sinclair shortly, 'knocked me on the head, and the next thing I knew I was here in this damned chair.'

'Is that where you got your face?' asked Hugh.

'No,' said Toby, and his voice was grim. 'We share in the matter of faces, old man.'

'Lakington again, was it?' said Hugh softly. 'Dear Heavens! if I could get one hand on that. . .' He broke off and laughed. 'What about you, Algy?'

'I went blundering in over the way, old bean,' returned that worthy, 'and some dam' fellow knocked my eye-glass off. So, as I couldn't see to kill him, I had to join the picnic here.'

Hugh laughed, and then suddenly grew serious.

'By the way, you didn't see a man chewing gum on the horizon, did you, when I made my entrance? Dog-robber suit, and face like a motor-mascot.'

'Thank God, I was spared that!' remarked Algy.

'Good!' returned Hugh. 'He's probably away with it by now, and he's no fool. For I'm thinking it's only Peter and him between us and—' He left his remark unfinished, and for a while there was silence. 'Jerry is over in France still, putting stamp-paper on his machine; Ted's gone up to see that Potts is taking nourishment.'

'And here we sit like three well-preserved specimens in a bally museum,' broke in Algy, with a rueful laugh. 'What'll they do to us, Hugh?'

But Drummond did not answer, and the speaker, seeing the look on his face, did not press the question.

Slowly the hours dragged on, until the last gleams of daylight had faded from the skylight above, and a solitary electric light, hung centrally, gave the only illumination. Periodically Heinrich had come in to see that they were still secure; but from the sounds of the hoarse laughter which came at frequent intervals through the half-open door, it was evident that the German had found other and more congenial company. At length he appeared carrying a tray with bread and water on it, which he placed on a table near Hugh.

'Food for you, you English swine,' he remarked, looking gloatingly at each in turn. 'Herr Lakington the order gave, so that you will be fit to-morrow morning. Fit for the torture.' He thrust his flushed face close to Drummond's, and then deliberately spat at him.

Algy Longworth gave a strangled grunt, but Drummond took no notice. For the past half-hour he had been sunk in thought, so much so that the others had believed him asleep. Now, with a quiet smile, he looked up at the German.

'How much, my friend,' he remarked, 'are you getting for this?'

The German leered at him.

'Enough to see that you to-morrow are here,' he said.

'And I always believed that yours was a business nation,' laughed Hugh. 'Why, you poor fool, I've got a thousand pounds in notes in my cigarette-case.' For a moment the German stared at him; then a look of greed came into his pig-eyes.

'You hof, hof you?' he grunted. 'Then the filthy Boche will for you of them take care.'

Hugh looked at him angrily.

'If you do,' he cried, 'you must let me go.'

The German leered still more.

'*Natürlich*. You shall out of the house at once walk.'

He stepped up to Drummond and ran his hands over his coat, while the others stared at one another in amazement. Surely Hugh didn't imagine the swine would really let him go; he would merely take the money and probably spit in his face again. Then they heard him speaking, and a sudden gleam of comprehension dawned on their faces.

'You'll have to undo one of the ropes, my friend, before you can get at it,' said Hugh quietly.

For a moment the German hesitated. He looked at the ropes carefully; the one that bound the arms and the upper part of the body was separate from the rope round the legs. Even if he did undo it the fool Englishman was still helpless, and he knew that he was unarmed. Had he not himself removed his revolver, as he lay unconscious in the hall? What risk was there, after all? Besides, if he called someone else in he would have to share the money.

And, as he watched the German's indecision, Hugh's forehead grew damp with sweat. . . Would he undo the rope? Would greed conquer caution?

At last the Boche made up his mind, and went behind the chair. Hugh felt him fumbling with the rope, and flashed an urgent look of caution at the other two.

'You'd better be careful, Heinrich,' he remarked, 'that none of the others see, or you might have to share.'

The German ceased undoing the knot, and grunted. The English swine had moments of brightness, and he went over and closed the door. Then he resumed the operation of untying the rope; and, since it was performed behind the chair, he was in no position to see the look on Drummond's face. Only the two spectators could see that, and they had almost ceased breathing in their excitement. That he had a plan they knew; what it was they could not even guess.

At last the rope fell clear, and the German sprang back.

'Put the case on the table,' he cried, having not the slightest intention of coming within range of those formidable arms.

'Certainly not,' said Hugh, 'until you undo my legs. Then you shall have it.'

Quite loosely he was holding the case in one hand; but the others, watching his face, saw that it was strained and tense.

'First I the notes must have.' The German strove to speak conversationally, but all the time he was creeping nearer and nearer to the back of the chair. 'Then I your legs undo, and you may go.'

Algy's warning cry rang out simultaneously with the lightning dart of the Boche's hand as he snatched at the cigarette-case over Drummond's shoulder. And then Drummond laughed a low, triumphant laugh. It was the move he had been hoping for, and the German's wrist was held fast in his vice-like grip. His plan had succeeded.

And Longworth and Sinclair, who had seen many things in their lives, the remembrance of which will be with them till their dying day, had never seen and are never likely to see anything within measurable distance of what they saw in the next few minutes. Slowly, inexorably, the German's arm was being twisted, while he uttered hoarse, gasping cries, and beat impotently at Drummond's head with his free hand. Then at last there was a dull crack as the arm broke, and a scream of pain, as he lurched round the chair and stood helpless in front of the soldier, who still held the cigarette-case in his left hand.

They saw Drummond open the cigarette-case and take from it what looked like a tube of wood. Then he felt in his pocket and took out a match-box, containing a number of long thin splinters. And having fitted one of the splinters into the tube, he put the other end in his mouth.

With a quick heave they saw him jerk the German round and catch his unbroken arm with his free left hand. And the two bound watchers looked at Hugh's eyes as he stared at the moaning Boche, and saw that they were hard and merciless.

There was a sharp, whistling hiss, and the splinter flew from the tube into the German's face. It hung from his cheek, and even the ceaseless movement of his head failed to dislodge it.

'I have broken your arm, Boche,' said Drummond at length, 'and now I have killed you. I'm sorry about it; I wasn't particularly anxious to end your life. But it had to be done.'

The German, hardly conscious of what he had said owing to the pain in his arm, was frantically kicking the Englishman's legs, still bound to the chair; but the iron grip on his wrists never slackened. And then quite suddenly came the end. With one dreadful, convulsive heave the German jerked himself free, and fell doubled up on the floor. Fascinated, they watched him writhing and twisting, until, at last, he lay still. . . The Boche was dead. . .

'My God!' muttered Hugh, wiping his forehead. 'Poor brute.'

'What was that blow-pipe affair?' cried Sinclair hoarsely.

'The thing they tried to finish me with in Paris last night,' answered Hugh grimly, taking a knife out of his waistcoat pocket. 'Let us trust that none of his pals come in to look for him.'

A minute later he stood up, only to sit down again abruptly, as his legs gave way. They were numbed and stiff with the hours he had spent in the same position, and for a while he could do nothing but rub them with his hands, till the blood returned and he could feel once more.

Then, slowly and painfully, he tottered across to the others and set them free as well. They were in an even worse condition than he had been; and it seemed as if Algy would never be able to stand again, so completely dead was his body from the waist downwards. But, at length, after what seemed an eternity to Drummond, who realized only too well that should the gang come in they were almost as helpless in their present condition as if they were still bound in their chairs, the other two recovered. They were still stiff and cramped – all three of them – but at any rate they could move; which was more than could be said of the German, who lay twisted and rigid on the floor, with his eyes staring up at them – a glassy, horrible stare.

'Poor brute!' said Hugh again, looking at him with a certain amount of compunction. 'He was a miserable specimen – but still. . .' He shrugged his shoulders. 'And the contents of my cigarette-case are half a dozen gaspers, and a ten-bob Bradbury patched together with stamp-paper!'

He swung round on his heel as if dismissing the matter, and looked at the other two.

'All fit now? Good! We've got to think what we're going to do, for we're not out of the wood yet by two or three miles.'

'Let's get the door open,' remarked Algy, 'and explore.'

Cautiously they swung it open, and stood motionless. The house was in absolute silence; the hall was deserted.

'Switch out the light,' whispered Hugh. 'We'll wander round.'

They crept forward stealthily in the darkness, stopping every now and then to listen. But no sound came to their ears; it might have been a house of the dead.

Suddenly Drummond, who was in front of the other two, stopped with a warning hiss. A light was streaming out from under a door at the end of a passage, and, as they stood watching it, they heard a man's voice coming from the same room. Someone else answered him, and then there was silence once more.

At length Hugh moved forward again, and the others followed. And it was not until they got quite close to the door that a strange, continuous noise began to be noticeable – a noise which came most distinctly from the lighted room. It rose and fell with monotonous regularity; at times it resembled a brass band – at others it died away to a gentle murmur. And occasionally it was punctuated with a strangled snort. . .

'Great Scott!' muttered Hugh excitedly, 'the whole boiling bunch are asleep, or I'll eat my hat.'

'Then who was it who spoke?' said Algy. 'At least two of 'em are awake right enough.'

And, as if in answer to his question, there came the voice again from inside the room.

'Wal, Mr Darrell, I guess we can pass on, and leave this bunch.'

With one laugh of joyful amazement Hugh flung open the door, and found himself looking from the range of a yard into two revolvers.

'I don't know how you've done it, boys,' he remarked, 'but you can put those guns away. I hate looking at them from that end.'

'What the devil have they done to all your dials?' said Darrell, slowly lowering his arm.

'We'll leave that for the time,' returned Hugh grimly, as he shut the door. 'There are other more pressing matters to be discussed.'

He glanced round the room, and a slow grin spread over his face. There were some twenty of the gang, all of them fast asleep. They sprawled grotesquely over the table, they lolled in chairs; they lay on the floor, they huddled in corners. And, without exception, they snored and snorted.

'A dandy bunch,' remarked the American, gazing at them with satisfaction. 'That fat one in the corner took enough dope to kill a bull, but he seems quite happy.' Then he turned to Drummond. 'Say now, Captain, we've got a lorry load of the boys outside; your friend here thought we'd better bring 'em along. So it's up to you to get busy.'

'Mullings and his crowd,' said Darrell, seeing the look of mystification on Hugh's face. 'When Mr Green got back and told me you'd shoved your great mutton-head in it again, I thought I'd better bring the whole outfit.'

'Oh, you daisy!' cried Hugh, rubbing his hands together, 'you pair of priceless beans! The Philistines are delivered into our hands, even up to the neck.' For a few moments he stood, deep in thought; then once again the grin spread slowly over his face. 'Right up to their necks,' he repeated, 'so that it washes round their back teeth. Get the boys in, Peter; and get these lumps of meat carted out to the lorry. And, while you do that, we'll go upstairs and mop up.'

III

Even in his wildest dreams Hugh had never imagined such a wonderful opportunity. To be in complete possession of the house, with strong forces at his beck and call, was a state of affairs which rendered him almost speechless.

'Up the stairs on your hands and knees,' he ordered, as they stood in the hall. 'There are peculiarities about this staircase which require elucidation at a later date.'

But the murderous implement which acted in conjunction with the fifth step was not in use, and they passed up the stairs in safety.

'Keep your guns handy,' whispered Hugh. 'We'll draw each room in turn till we find the girl.'

But they were not to be put to so much trouble. Suddenly a door opposite opened, and the man who had been guarding Phyllis Benton peered out suspiciously. His jaw fell, and a look of aghast surprise spread over his face as he saw the four men in front of him. Then he made a quick movement as if to shut the door, but before he realized what had happened the American's foot was against it, and the American's revolver was within an inch of his head.

'Keep quite still, son,' he drawled, 'or I guess it might sort of go off.'

But Hugh had stepped past him, and was smiling at the girl who, with a little cry of joyful wonder, had risen from her chair.

'Your face, boy,' she whispered, as he took her in his arms, regardless of the other, 'your poor old face! Oh! that brute, Lakington!'

Hugh grinned.

'It's something to know, old thing,' he remarked cheerily, 'that anything could damage it. Personally I have always thought that any change on it must be for the better.'

He laughed gently, and for a moment she clung to him, unmindful of how he had got to her, glorying only in the fact that he had. It seemed to her that there was nothing which this wonderful man of hers couldn't manage; and now, blindly trusting, she waited to be told what to do. The nightmare was over; Hugh was with her. . .

'Where's your father, dear?' he asked her after a little pause.

'In the dining-room, I think,' she answered with a shiver, and Hugh nodded gravely.

'Are there any cars outside?' He turned to the American.

'Yours,' answered that worthy, still keeping his eyes fixed on his prisoner's face, which had now turned a sickly green.

'And mine is hidden behind Miss Benton's greenhouse unless they've moved it,' remarked Algy.

'Good,' said Hugh. 'Algy, take Miss Benton and her father up to Half Moon Street – at once. Then come back here.'

'But Hugh—' began the girl appealingly.

'At once, dear, please.' He smiled at her tenderly, but his tone was decided. 'This is going to be no place for you in the near future.' He turned to Longworth and drew him aside. 'You'll have a bit of a job with the old man,' he whispered. 'He's probably paralytic by now. But get on with it, will you? Get a couple of the boys to give you a hand.'

With no further word of protest the girl followed Algy, and Hugh drew a breath of relief.

'Now, you ugly-looking blighter,' he remarked to the cowering ruffian, who was by this time shaking with fright, 'we come to you. How many of these rooms up here are occupied – and which?

It appeared that only one was occupied – everyone else was below. . . The one opposite. . . In his anxiety to please, he moved towards it; and with a quickness that would have done even Hugh credit, the American tripped him up.

'Not so blamed fast, you son of a gun,' he snapped, 'or there sure will be an accident.'

But the noise he made as he fell served a good purpose. The door of the occupied room was flung open, and a thin, weedy object clad in a flannel night-gown stood on the threshold blinking foolishly.

'Holy smoke!' spluttered the detective, after he had gazed at the apparition in stunned silence for a time. 'What, under the sun, is it?'

Hugh laughed.

'Why, it's the onion-eater; the intimidated rabbit,' he said delightedly. 'How are you, little man?'

He extended an arm, and pulled him into the passage, where he stood spluttering indignantly.

'This is an outrage, sir,' he remarked; a positive outrage.'

'Your legs undoubtedly are,' remarked Hugh, gazing at them dispassionately. 'Put on some trousers – and get a move on. Now you' – he jerked the other man to his feet – 'when does Lakington return?'

'Termorrow, sir,' stammered the other.

'Where is he now?'

The man hesitated for a moment, but the look in Hugh's eyes galvanized him into speech.

'He's after the old woman's pearls, sir – the Duchess of Lampshire's.'

'Ah!' returned Hugh softly. 'Of course he is. I forgot.'

'Strike me dead, guv'nor,' cringed the man. 'I never meant no 'arm – I didn't really. I'll tell you all I know, sir. I will, strife.'

'I'm quite certain you will,' said Hugh. 'And if you don't, you swine, I'll make you. When does Peterson come back?'

'Termorrow, too, sir, as far as I knows,' answered the man, and at that moment the intimidated rabbit shot rapidly out of his room, propelled by an accurate and forcible kick from Toby, who had followed him in to ensure rapidity of toilet.

'And what's he doing?' demanded Drummond.

'On the level, guvnor, I can't tell yer. Strife, I can't; 'e can.' The man pointed to the latest arrival, who, with his night-dress tucked into his trousers, stood gasping painfully after the manner of a recently landed fish.

'I repeat, sir,' he sputtered angrily, 'that this is an outrage. By what right. . .'

'Dry up,' remarked Hugh briefly. Then he turned to the American. 'This is one of the ragged-trousered brigade I spoke to you about.'

For a while the three men studied him in silence; then the American thoughtfully transferred his chewing-gum to a fresh place.

'Wal,' he said, 'he looks like some kind o' disease; but I guess he's got a tongue. Say, flop-ears, what are you, anyway?'

'I am the secretary of a social organization which aims at the amelioration of the conditions under which the workers of the world slave,' returned the other with dignity.

'You don't say,' remarked the American, unmoved. 'Do the workers of the world know about it?'

'And again I demand to know,' said the other, turning on Drummond, 'the reason for this monstrous indignity.'

'What do you know about Peterson, little man?' said Hugh, paying not the slighest attention to his protests.

'Nothing, save that he is the man whom we have been looking for, for years,' cried the other. 'The man of stupendous organizing power, who has brought together and welded into one the hundreds of societies similar to mine, who before this have each, on their own, been feebly struggling towards the light. Now we are combined, and our strength is due to him.'

Hugh exchanged glances with the American.

'Things become clearer,' he murmured. 'Tell me, little man,' he continued, 'now that you're all welded together, what do you propose to do?'

'That you shall see in good time,' cried the other triumphantly. 'Constitutional methods have failed and, besides, we've got no time to wait for them. Millions are groaning under the intolerable bonds of the capitalist; those millions we shall free, to a life that is worthy of a man. And it will all be due to our leader – Carl Peterson.'

A look of rapt adoration came into his face, and the American laughed in genuine delight.

'Didn't I tell you, Captain, that that guy was the goods?' But there was no answering smile on Hugh's face.

'He's the goods right enough,' he answered grimly. 'But what worries me is how to stop their devilry.'

At that moment Darrell's voice came up from the hall.

'The whole bunch are stowed away, Hugh. What's the next item?'

Hugh walked to the top of the stairs.

'Bring 'em both below,' he cried over his shoulder, as he went down. A grin spread over his face as he saw half a dozen familiar faces in the hall, and he hailed them cheerily.

'Like old times, boys,' he laughed. 'Where's the driver of the lorry?'

'That's me, sir.' One of the men stepped forward. 'My mate's outside.'

'Good,' said Hugh. 'Take your bus ten miles from here: then drop that crowd one by one on the road as you go along. You can take it from me that none of 'em will say anything about it, even when they wake up. Then take her back to your garage; I'll see you later.'

'Now,' went on Hugh, as they heard the sound of the departing lorry, 'we've got to set the scene for to-morrow morning.' He glanced at his watch. 'Just eleven. How long will it take me to get the old buzz-box to Laidley Towers?'

'Laidley Towers,' echoed Darrell. 'What the devil are you going there for?'

'I just can't bear to be parted from Henry for one moment longer than necessary,' said Hugh quietly. 'And Henry is there, in a praiseworthy endeavour to lift the Duchess's pearls. . . Dear Henry!' His two fists clenched, and the American looking at his face, laughed softly.

But it was only for a moment that Drummond indulged in the pleasures of anticipation; all that could come after. And just now there were other things to be done – many others, if events next morning were to go as they should.

'Take those two into the centre room,' he cried. 'Incidentally there's a dead Boche on the floor, but he'll come in very handy in my little scheme.'

'A dead Boche!' The intimidated rabbit gave a frightened squeak. 'Good heavens! you ruffian, this is beyond a joke.'

Hugh looked at him coldly.

'You'll find it beyond a joke, you miserable little rat,' he said quietly, 'if you speak to me like that.' He laughed as the other shrank past him. 'Three of you boys in there,' he ordered briskly, 'and if either of them gives the slightest trouble clip him over the head. Now let's have the rest of the crowd in here, Peter.'

They came filing in, and Hugh waved a cheery hand in greeting.

'How goes it, you fellows,' he cried with his infectious grin. 'Like a company pow-wow before popping the parapet. What! And it's a bigger show this time, boys, than any you've had over the water.' His face set grimly for a moment; then he grinned again, as he sat down on the foot of the stairs. 'Gather round, and listen to me.'

For five minutes he spoke, and his audience nodded delightedly. Apart from their love for Drummond – and three out of every four of them knew him personally – it was a scheme which tickled them to death. And he was careful to tell them just enough of the sinister design of the master-criminal to make them realize the bigness of the issue.

'That's all clear, then,' said Drummond, rising. 'Now I'm off. Toby, I want you to come too. We ought to be there by midnight.'

'There's only one point, Captain,' remarked the American, as the group began to disperse. 'That safe – and the ledger.' He fumbled in his pocket, and produced a small india-rubber bottle. 'I've got the soup here – gelignite,' he explained, as he saw the mystified look on the other's face. 'I reckoned it might come in handy. Also a fuse and detonator.'

'Splendid!' said Hugh, 'Splendid! You're an acquisition, Mr Green, to any gathering. But I think – I *think* – Lakington first. Oh! yes – most undoubtedly – Henry first!'

And once again the American laughed softly at the look on his face.

Chapter 11

In Which Lakington Plays His Last 'Coup'

I

'TOBY, I've got a sort of horrid feeling that the hunt is nearly over.'

With a regretful sigh Hugh swung the car out of the sleeping town of Godalming in the direction of Laidley Towers. Mile after mile dropped smoothly behind the powerful two-seater, and still Drummond's eyes wore a look of resigned sadness.

'Very nearly over,' he remarked again. 'And then once more the tedium of respectability positively stares us in the face.'

'You'll be getting married, old bean,' murmured Toby Sinclair hopefully.

For a moment his companion brightened up.

'True, O King,' he answered. 'It will ease the situation somewhat; at least, I suppose so. But think of it, Toby, no Lakington, no Peterson – nothing at all to play about with and keep one amused.'

'You're very certain, Hugh.' With a feeling almost of wonder Sinclair glanced at the square-jawed, ugly profile beside him. 'There's many a slip. . .'

'My dear old man,' interrupted Drummond, 'there's only one cure for the proverb-quoting disease – a dose of salts in the morning.' For a while they raced on through the warm summer's night in silence, and it was not till they were within a mile of their destination that Sinclair spoke again.

'What are you going to do with them, Hugh?'

'Who – our Carl and little Henry?' Drummond grinned gently. 'Why, I think that Carl and I will part amicably – unless, of course, he gives me any trouble. And as for Lakington – we'll have to see about Lakington.' The grin faded from his face as he spoke. 'We'll have to see about our little Henry,' he repeated softly. 'And I can't help feeling, Toby, that between us we shall find a method of ridding the earth of such a thoroughly unpleasing fellow.'

'You mean to kill him?' grunted the other non-committally.

'Just that and no more,' responded Hugh. 'To-morrow morning as ever is. But he's going to get the shock of his young life before it happens.'

He pulled the car up silently in the deep shadows of some trees, and the two men got out.

'Now, old boy, you take her back to The Elms. The ducal abode is close to – I remember in my extreme youth being worse than passing sick by those bushes over there after a juvenile bun-worry. . .'

'But confound it all,' spluttered Toby Sinclair. 'Don't you want me to help you?'

'I do: by taking the buzz-box back. This little show is my shout.'

Grumbling disconsolately, Sinclair stepped back into the car.

'You make me tired,' he remarked peevishly. 'I'll be damned if you get any wedding present out of me. In fact,' and he fired a Parthian shot at his leader, 'you won't have any wedding. I shall marry her myself!'

For a moment or two Hugh stood watching the car as it disappeared down the road along which they had just come, while his thoughts turned to the girl now safely asleep in his flat in London. Another week – perhaps a fortnight – but no more. Not a day more. . . And he had a pleasant conviction that Phyllis would not require much persuasion to come round to his way of thinking – even if she hadn't arrived there already. . . And so delightful was the train of thought thus conjured up, that for a while Peterson and Lakington were forgotten. The roseate dreams of the young about to wed have been known to act similarly before.

Wherefore to the soldier's instinctive second nature, trained in the war and sharpened by his grim duel with the gang, must be given the credit of preventing the ringing of the wedding-bells being postponed for good. The sudden snap of a twig close by, the sharp hiss of a compressed-air-rifle, seemed simultaneous with Hugh hurling himself flat on his face behind a sheltering bush. In reality there was that fraction of a second between the actions which allowed the bullet to pass harmlessly over his body instead of finishing his career there and then. He heard it go zipping through the undergrowth as he lay motionless on the ground; then very cautiously he turned his head and peered about. A man with an ordinary revolver is at a disadvantage against someone armed with a silent gun, especially when he is not desirous of alarming the neighbourhood.

A shrub was shaking a few yards away, and on it Hugh fixed his half-closed eyes. If he lay quite still the man, who-ever he was, would probably assume the shot had taken effect, and come and investigate. Then things would be eas-ier, as two or three Boches had discovered to their cost in days gone by.

For two minutes he saw no one; then very slowly the branches parted and the white face of a man peered through. It was the chauffeur who usually drove the Rolls-Royce, and he seemed unduly anxious to satisfy himself that all was well before coming nearer. The fame of Hugh Drummond had spread abroad amongst the satellites of Peterson.

At last he seemed to make up his mind, and came out into the open. Step by step he advanced towards the motionless figure, his weapon held in readiness to shoot at the faintest movement. But the soldier lay sprawling and inert, and by the time the chauffeur had reached him there was no doubt in that worthy's mind that, at last, this wretched meddler with things that concerned him not had been laid by the heels. Which was as unfortunate for the chauffeur as it had been for unwary Huns in the past.

Contemptuously he rolled Drummond over; then, noting the relaxed muscles and inert limbs, he laid his gun on the ground preparatory to running through his victim's pockets. And the fact that such an action was a little more foolish than offering a man-eating tiger a peppermint lozenge did not trouble the chauffeur. In fact, nothing troubled him again.

He got out one gasping cry of terror as he realized his mistake; then he had a blurred consciousness of the world upside down, and everything was over. It was Olaki's most dangerous throw, carried out by gripping the victim's wrists and hurling his body over by a heave of the legs. And nine times out of ten the result was a broken neck. This was one of the nine.

For a while the soldier stared at the body, frowning thoughtfully. To have killed the chauffeur was inconvenient, but since it had happened it necessitated a little rearrangement of his plans. The moon was setting and the night would become darker, so there was a good chance that Lakington would not recognize that the driver of his car had changed. And if he did – well, it would be necessary to forgo the somewhat theatrical entertainment he had staged for his benefit at The Elms. Bending over the dead man, he removed his long grey driving-coat and cap; then, without a sound, he threaded his way through the bushes in search of the car.

He found it about a hundred yards nearer the house, so well hidden in a small space off the road that he was almost on top of it before he realized the fact. To his relief it was empty, and placing his own cap in a pocket under the seat he put on the driving-coat of his predecessor. Then, with a quick glance round to ensure that everything was in readiness for the immediate and rapid departure such as he imagined

Lakington would desire, he turned and crept stealthily towards the house.

II

Laidley Towers was *en fête*. The Duchess, determined that every conceivable stunt should be carried out which would make for the entertainment of her guests, had spared no pains to make the evening a success. The Duke, bored to extinction, had been five times routed out of his study by his indefatigable spouse, and was now, at the moment Hugh first came in sight of the house, engaged in shaking hands with a tall, aristocratic-looking Indian. . .

'How-d'ye-do,' he murmured vacantly. 'What did you say the dam' fellah's name was, my dear?' he whispered in a hoarse undertone to the Duchess, who stood beside him welcoming the distinguished foreigner.

'We're so glad you could come, Mr Ram Dar,' remarked the Duchess affably. 'Everyone is so looking forward to your wonderful entertainment.' Round her neck were the historic pearls, and as the Indian bowed low over her outstretched hand, his eyes gleamed for a second.

'Your Grace is too kind.' His voice was low and deep, and he glanced thoughtfully around the circle of faces near him. 'Maybe the sands that come from the mountains that lie beyond the everlasting snows will speak the truth; maybe the gods will be silent. Who knows. . .who knows?'

As if unconsciously his gaze rested on the Duke, who manfully rose to the occasion.

'Precisely, Mr Rum Rum,' he murmured helpfully; 'who indeed? If they let you down, don't you know, perhaps you could show us a card trick?'

He retired in confusion, abashed by the baleful stare of the Duchess, and the rest of the guests drew closer. The jazz band was having supper; the last of the perspiring tenants had departed, and now the bonne-bouche of the evening was about to begin.

It had been the Marquis of Laidley himself who had suggested getting hold of this most celebrated performer, who had apparently never been in England before. And since the Marquis of Laidley's coming-of-age was the cause of the whole evening's entertainment, his suggestion had been hailed with acclamation. How he had heard about the Indian, and from whom, were points about which he was very vague; but since he was a very vague young man, the fact elicited no comment. The main thing was that here, in the flesh, was a dark, mysterious performer of the occult, and what more could a house party require? And in the general excitement Hugh Drummond crept closer to the open window. It was the Duchess he was concerned with and her pearls, and the arrival of the Indian was not going to put him off his guard. . . Then suddenly his jaw tightened: Irma Peterson had entered the room with young Laidley.

'Do you want anything done, Mr Ram Dar?' asked the Duchess – 'the lights down or the window shut?'

'No, I thank you,' returned the Indian. 'The night is still; there is no wind. And the night is dark – dark with strange thoughts, that thronged upon me as I drew nigh to the house – whispering through the trees.' Again he fixed his eyes on the Duke. 'What is your pleasure, Protector of the Poor?'

'Mine?' cried that pillar of the House of Lords, hurriedly stifling a yawn. 'Any old thing, my dear fellow. . . You'd much better ask one of the ladies.'

'As you will,' returned the other gravely; 'but if the gods speak the truth, and the sand does not lie, I can but say what is written.'

From a pocket in his robe he took a bag and two small bronze dishes, and placing them on a table, stood waiting.

'I am ready,' he announced. 'Who first will learn of things that are written on the scroll of Fate?'

'I say, hadn't you better do it in private, Mr Rum?' murmured the Duke apprehensively. 'I mean, don't you know, it might be a little embarrassing if the jolly old gods really do give tongue; and I don't see anybody getting killed in the rush.'

'Is there so much to conceal?' demanded the Indian, glancing round the group, contempt in his brooding eyes. 'In the lands that lie beyond the snows we have nothing to conceal. There is nothing that can be concealed, because all is known.'

And it was at that moment that the intent watcher outside the window began to shake with silent mirth. For the face was the face of the Indian, Ram Dar, but the voice was the voice of Lakington. It struck him that the next ten minutes or so might be well worth while. The problem of removing the pearls from the Duchess's neck before such an assembly seemed to present a certain amount of difficulty even to such an expert as Henry. And Hugh crept a little nearer the window, so as to miss nothing. He crept near enough, in fact, to steal a look at Irma, and in doing so saw something which made him rub his eyes and then grin once more. She was standing on the outskirts of the group, an evening wrap thrown loosely over her arm. She edged a step or two towards a table containing bric-à-brac, the centre of which was occupied, as the place of honour, by a small inlaid Chinese cabinet – a box standing on four grotesquely carved legs. It was a beautiful ornament, and he dimly remembered having heard its history – a story which reflected considerable glory on the predatory nature of a previous Duke. At the moment, however, he was not concerned with its past history, but with its present fate; and it was the consummate quickness of the girl that made him rub his eyes.

She took one lightning glance at the other guests who were craning eagerly forward round the Indian; then she half dropped her wrap on the table and picked it up again. It was done so rapidly, so naturally, that for a while Hugh thought he had made a mistake. And then a slight rearrangement of her wrap to conceal a hard outline beneath, as she joined the others, dispelled any doubts. The small inlaid Chinese cabinet now standing on the table was not the one that had been here previously. The original was under Irma Peterson's cloak. . .

Evidently the scene was now set – the necessary props were in position – and Hugh waited with growing impatience for the principal event. But the principal performer seemed in no hurry. In fact, in his dry way Lakington was thoroughly enjoying himself. An intimate inside knowledge of the skeletons that rattled their bones in the cupboards of most of those present enabled the gods to speak with disconcerting accuracy; and as each victim insisted on somebody new facing the sands that came from beyond the mountains, the performance seemed likely to last indefinitely.

At last a sudden delighted burst of applause came from the group, announcing the discomfiture of yet another guest, and with it Lakington seemed to tire of the amusement. Engrossed though he was in the anticipation of the main item which was still to be staged, Drummond could not but admire the extraordinary accuracy of the character study. Not a detail had been overlooked; not a single flaw in Lakington's acting could he notice. It *was* an Indian who stood there, and when a few days later Hugh returned her pearls to the Duchess, for a long time neither she nor her husband would believe that Ram Dar had been an Englishman disguised. And when they had at last been persuaded of that fact, and had been shown the two cabinets side by side, it was the consummate boldness of the crime, coupled with its extreme simplicity, that staggered them. For it was only in the reconstruction of it that the principal beauty of the scheme became apparent. The element of luck was reduced to a minimum, and at no stage of the proceedings was it impossible, should things go amiss, for Lakington to go as he had come, a mere Indian entertainer. Without the necklace, true, in such an event; but unsuspected, and free to try again. As befitted his last, it was perhaps his greatest effort. . . And this was what happened as seen by the fascinated onlooker crouching near the window outside.

Superbly disdainful, the Indian tipped back his sand into the little bag, and replacing it in his pocket, stalked to the open window. With arms outstretched he stared into the darkness, seeming to gather strength from the gods whom he served.

'Do your ears not hear the whisperings of the night?' he demanded. 'Life rustling in the leaves; death moaning through the grasses.' And suddenly he threw back his head and laughed, a fierce, mocking laugh; then he swung round and faced the room. For a while he stood motionless, and Hugh, from the shelter of the bushes, wondered whether the two quick flashes that had come from his robe as he spoke – flashes such as a small electric torch will give, and which were unseen by anyone else – were a signal to the defunct chauffeur.

Then a peculiar look came over the Indian's face, as his eyes fell on the Chinese cabinet.

'Where did the Protector of the Poor obtain the sacred cabinet of the Chow Kings?' He peered at it reverently, and the Duke coughed.

'One of my ancestors picked it up somewhere,' he answered apologetically.

'Fashioned with the blood of men, guarded with their lives, and one of your ancestors picked it up!' The Duke withered completely under the biting scorn of the words, and seemed about to say something, but the Indian had turned away, and his long, delicate fingers were hovering over the box. 'There is power in this box,' he continued, and his voice was low and thoughtful. 'Years ago a man who came from the land where dwells the Great Brooding Spirit told me of this thing. I wonder. . . I wonder. . .'

With gleaming eyes he stared in front of him, and a woman shuddered audibly.

'What is it supposed to do?' she ventured timidly.

'In that box lies the power unknown to mortal man, though the priests of the Temple City have sometimes discovered it before they pass beyond. Length you know, and height, and breadth – but in that box lies more.'

'You don't mean the fourth dimension, do you?' demanded a man incredulously.

'I know not what you call it, sahib,' said the Indian quietly. 'But it is the power which renders visible or invisible at will.'

For a moment Hugh felt an irresistible temptation to shout the truth through the window, and give Lakington away; then his curiosity to see the next move in the game conquered the wish, and he remained silent. So perfect was the man's acting that, in spite of having seen the substitution of the boxes, in spite of knowing the whole thing was bunkum, he felt he could almost believe it himself. And as for the others – without exception – they were craning forward eagerly, staring first at the Indian and then at the box.

'I say, that's a bit of a tall order, isn't it, Mr Rum Bar?' protested the Duke a little feebly. 'Do you mean to say you can put something into that box, and it disappears?'

'From mortal eye, Protector of the Poor, though it is still there,' answered the Indian. 'And that only, too, for a time. Then it reappears again. So runs the legend.'

'Well, stuff something in and let's see,' cried young Laidley, starting forward, only to pause before the Indian's outstretched arm.

'Stop, sahib,' he ordered sternly. 'To you that box is nothing; to others – of whom I am one of the least – it is sacred beyond words.' He stalked away from the table, and the guests' disappointment showed on their faces.

'Oh, but Mr Ram Dar,' pleaded the Duchess, 'can't you satisfy our curiosity after all you've said?' For a moment he seemed on the point of refusing outright; then he bowed, a deep Oriental bow.

'Your Grace,' he said with dignity, 'for centuries that box contained the jewels – precious beyond words – of the reigning Queens of the Chow Dynasty. They were wrapped in silver and gold tissue – of which this is a feeble, modern substitute.'

From a cummerbund under his robe he drew a piece of shining material, the appearance of which was greeted with cries of feminine delight.

'You would not ask me to commit sacrilege?' Quietly he replaced the material in his belt and turned away, and Hugh's eyes glistened at the cleverness with which the man was acting. Whether they believed it or not, there was not a soul in the room by this time who was not consumed with eagerness to put the Chinese cabinet to the test.

'Supposing you took my pearls, Mr Ram Dar,' said the Duchess diffidently. 'I know that compared to such historic jewels they are poor, but perhaps it would not be sacrilege.'

Not a muscle on Lakington's face twitched, though it was the thing he had been playing for. Instead he seemed to be sunk in thought, while the Duchess continued pleading, and the rest of the party added their entreaties. At length she undid the fastening and held the necklace out, but he only shook his head.

'You ask a great thing of me, your Grace,' he said. 'Only by the exercise of my power can I show you this secret – even if I can show you at all. And you are unbelievers.' He paced slowly to the window, ostensibly to commune with the gods on the subject; more materially to flash once again the signal into the darkness. Then, as if he had decided suddenly, he swung round.

'I will try,' he announced briefly, and the Duchess headed the chorus of delight. 'Will the Presences stand back, and you, your Grace, take that?' He handed her the piece of material. 'No hand but yours must touch the pearls. Wrap them up inside the silver and gold.' Aloofly he watched the process. 'Now advance alone, and open the box. Place the pearls inside. Now shut and lock it.' Obediently the Duchess did as she was bid; then she stood waiting for further instructions.

But apparently by this time the Great Brooding Spirit was beginning to take effect. Singing a monotonous, harsh chant, the Indian knelt on the floor, and poured some powder into a little brazier. He was still close to the open window, and finally he sat down with his elbows on his knees, and his head rocking to and fro in his hands.

'Less light – less light!' The words seemed to come from a great distance – ventriloquism in a mild way was one of Lakington's accomplishments; and as the lights went out a greenish, spluttering flame rose from the brazier. A heavy, odorous smoke filled the room, but framed and motionless in the eerie light sat the Indian, staring fixedly in front of him. After a time the chant began again; it grew and swelled in volume till the singer grew frenzied and beat his head with his hands. Then abruptly it stopped.

'Place the box upon the floor,' he ordered, 'in the light of the Sacred Fire.' Hugh saw the Duchess kneel down on the opposite side of the brazier, and place the box on the floor, while the faces of the guests – strange and ghostly in the green light – peered like spectres out of the heavy smoke. This was undoubtedly a show worth watching.

'Open the box!' Harshly the words ran through the silent room, and with fingers that trembled a little the Duchess turned the key and threw back the lid.

'Why, it's empty!' she cried in amazement, and the guests craned forward to look.

'Put not your hand inside,' cried the Indian in sudden warning, 'or perchance it will remain empty.'

The Duchess rapidly withdrew her hand, and stared incredulously through the smoke at his impassive face.

'Did I not say that there was power in the box?' he said dreamily. 'The power to render invisible – the power to render visible. Thus came protection to the jewels of the Chow Queens.'

'That's all right, Mr Ram Dar,' said the Duchess a little apprehensively. 'There may be power in the box, but my pearls don't seem to be.'

The Indian laughed.

'None but you has touched the cabinet, your Grace; none but you must touch it till the pearls return. They are there now; but not for mortal eyes to see.'

Which, incidentally, was no more than the truth.

'Look, oh! sahibs, look; but do not touch. See that to your vision the box is empty. . .' He waited motionless, while the guests thronged round, with expressions of amazement; and Hugh, safe from view in the thick, sweet-smelling smoke, came even nearer in his excitement.

'It is enough,' cried the Indian suddenly. 'Shut the box, your Grace, and lock it as before. Now place it on the table whence it came. Is it there?'

'Yes.' The Duchess's voice came out of the green fog.

'Go not too near,' he continued warningly. 'The gods must have space – the gods must have space.'

Again the harsh chant began, at times swelling to a shout, at times dying away to a whisper. And it was during one of these latter periods that a low laugh, instantly checked, disturbed the room. It was plainly audible, and someone irritably said, 'Be quiet!' It was not repeated, which afforded Hugh, at any rate, no surprise. For it had been Irma Peterson who had laughed, and it might have been hilarity or it might have been a signal.

The chanting grew frenzied and more frenzied; more and more powder was thrown on the brazier till dense clouds of the thick vapour were rolling through the room, completely obscuring everything save the small space round the brazier, and the Indian's tense face poised above it.

'Bring the box, your Grace,' he cried harshly, and once more the Duchess knelt in the circle of light, with a row of dimly seen faces above her.

'Open; but as you value your pearls – touch them not.' Excitedly she threw back the lid, and a chorus of cries greeted the appearance of the gold and silver tissue at the bottom of the box.

'They're here, Mr Ram Dar.'

In the green light the Indian's sombre eyes stared round the group of dim faces.

'Did I not say,' he answered, 'that there was power in the box? But in the name of that power – unknown to you – I warn you: Do not touch those pearls till the light has burned low in the brazier. If you do they will disappear – never to return. Watch, but do not touch!'

Slowly he backed towards the window, unperceived in the general excitement; and Hugh dodged rapidly towards the car. It struck him that the seance was over, and he just had time to see Lakington snatch something which appeared to have been let down by a string from above, before turning into the bushes and racing for the car. As it was he was only a second or two in front of the other, and the last vision he had through a break in the trees, before they were spinning smoothly down the deserted road, was an open window in Laidley Towers from which dense volumes of vapour poured steadily out. Of the house party behind, waiting for the light to burn low in the brazier, he could see no sign through the opaque wall of green fog.

It took five minutes, so he gathered afterwards from a member of the house party, before the light had burned sufficiently low for the Duchess to consider it safe to touch the pearls. In various stages of asphyxiation the assembled guests had peered at the box, while the cynical comments of the men were rightly treated by the ladies with the contempt they deserved. Was the necklace not there, wrapped in its gold and silver tissue, where a few minutes before there had been nothing?

'Some trick of that beastly light,' remarked the Duke peevishly. 'For heaven's sake throw the dam' thing out of the window.'

'Don't be a fool, John,' retorted his spouse. 'If you could do this sort of thing, the House of Lords might be of some use to somebody.'

And when two minutes later they stared horror-struck at a row of ordinary marbles laboriously unwrapped from a piece of gold and silver tissue, the Duke's pungent agreement with his wife's sentiment passed uncontradicted. In fact, it is to be understood that over the scene which followed it was best to draw a decent veil.

III

Drummond, hunched low over the wheel, in his endeavour to conceal his identity from the man behind, knew nothing of that at the time. Every nerve was centred on eluding the pursuit he thought was a certainty; for the thought of Lakington, when everything was prepared for his reception, being snatched from his clutches even by the majesty of the law was more than he could bear. And for much the same reason he did not want to have to deal with him until The Elms was reached; the staging there was so much more effective.

But Lakington was far too busy to bother with the chauffeur.

One snarling curse as they had entered, for not having done as he had been told, was the total of their conversation during the trip. During the rest of the time the transformation to the normal kept Lakington busy, and Hugh could see him reflected in the windscreen removing the make-up from his face, and changing his clothes.

Even now he was not quite clear how the trick had been worked. That there had been two cabinets, that was clear – one false, the other the real one. That they had been changed at the crucial moment by the girl Irma was also obvious. But how had the pearls disappeared in the first case, and then apparently reappeared again? For of one thing he was quite certain. Whatever was inside the parcel of gold and silver tissue which, for all he knew, they might be still staring at, it was not the historic necklace.

And he was still puzzling it over in his mind when the car swung into the drive at The Elms.

'Change the wheels as usual,' snapped Lakington as he got out, and Hugh bent forward to conceal his face. 'Then report to me in the central room.'

And out of the corner of his eye Hugh watched him enter the house with one of the Chinese cabinets clasped in his hand. . .

'Toby,' he remarked to that worthy, whom he found mournfully eating a ham sandwich in the garage, 'I feel sort of sorry for our Henry. He's just had the whole complete ducal outfit guessing, dressed up as an Indian; he's come back here with a box containing the Duchess's pearls or I'll eat my hat, and feeling real good with himself; and now instead of enjoying life he's got to have a little chat with me.'

'Did you drive him back?' demanded Sinclair, producing a bottle of Bass.

'Owing to the sudden decease of his chauffeur I had to,' murmured Hugh. 'And he's very angry over something. Let's go on the roof.'

Silently they both climbed the ladder which had been placed in readiness, to find Peter Darrell and the American detective already in position. A brilliant light streamed out through the glass dome, and the inside of the central room was clearly visible.

'He's already talked to what he thinks is you,' whispered Peter ecstatically, 'and he is not in the best of tempers.'

Hugh glanced down, and a grim smile flickered round his lips. In the three chairs sat the motionless, bound figures, so swathed in rope that only the tops of their heads were visible, just as Lakington had left him and Toby and Algy earlier in the evening. The only moving thing in the room was the criminal himself, and at the moment he was seated at the table with the Chinese cabinet in front of him. He seemed to be doing something inside with a penknife, and all the time he kept up a running commentary to the three bound figures.

'Well, you young swine, have you enjoyed your night?' A feeble moan came from one of the chairs. 'Spirit broken at last, is it?' With a quick turn of his wrist he prised open two flaps of wood, and folded them back against the side.

Then he lifted out a parcel of gold and silver tissue from underneath.

'My hat!' muttered Hugh, 'what a fool I was not to think of it! Just a false bottom actuated by closing the lid. And a similar parcel in the other cabinet.'

But the American, whistling gently to himself, had his eyes fixed on the rope of wonderful pearls which Lakington was holding lovingly in his hands.

'So easy, you scum,' continued Lakington, 'and you thought to pit yourselves against me. Though if it hadn't been for Irma' – he rose and stood in front of the chair where he had last left Drummond – 'it might have been awkward. She was quick, Captain Drummond, and that fool of a chauffeur failed to carry out my orders and create a diversion. You will see what happens to people who fail to carry out my orders in a minute. And after that you'll never see anything again.'

'Say, he's a dream – that guy,' muttered the American. 'What pearls are those he's got?'

'The Duchess of Lampshire's,' whispered Hugh. 'Lifted right under the noses of the whole bally house party.'

With a grunt the detective rearranged his chewing-gum; then once more the four watchers on the roof glued their eyes to the glass. And the sight they saw a moment or two afterwards stirred even the phlegmatic Mr Green.

A heavy door was swinging slowly open, apparently of its own volition, though Hugh, stealing a quick glance at Lakington, saw that he was pressing some small studs in a niche in one of the walls. Then he looked back at the door, and stared dumbfounded. It was the mysterious cupboard of which Phyllis had spoken to him, but nothing he had imagined from her words had prepared him for the reality. It seemed to be literally crammed to overflowing with the most priceless loot. Gold vessels of fantastic and beautiful shapes littered the floor; while on the shelves were arranged the most wonderful collection of precious stones, which shone and scintillated in the electric light till their glitter almost blinded the watchers.

'Shades of Chu Chin Chow, Ali Baba and the forty pundits!' muttered Toby. 'The dam' man's a genius.'

The pearls were carefully placed in a position of honour, and for a few moments Lakington stood gloating over his collection.

'Do you see them, Captain Drummond?' he asked quietly. 'Each thing obtained by my brain – my hands. All mine – mine!' His voice rose to a shout. 'And you pit your puny wits against me.' With a laugh he crossed the room, and once more pressed the studs. The door swung slowly to and closed without a sound, while Lakington still shook with silent mirth.

'And now,' he resumed, rubbing his hands, 'we will prepare your bath, Captain Drummond.' He walked over to the shelves where the bottles were ranged, and busied himself with some preparations. 'And while it is getting ready, we will just deal with the chauffeur who neglected his orders.'

For a few minutes he bent over the chemicals, and then he poured the mixture into the water which half filled the long bath at the end of the room. A faintly acid smell rose to the four men above, and the liquid turned a pale green.

'I told you I had all sorts of baths, didn't I?' continued Lakington; 'some for those who are dead, and some for those who are alive. This is the latter sort, and has the great advantage of making the bather wish it was one of the former. He stirred the liquid gently with a long glass rod. 'About five minutes before we're quite ready,' he announced. 'Just time for the chauffeur.'

He went to a speaking-tube, down which he blew. Somewhat naturally there was no answer, and Lakington frowned.

'A stupid fellow,' he remarked softly. 'But there is no hurry; I will deal with him later.'

'You certainly will,' muttered Hugh on the roof. 'And perhaps not quite so much later as you think, friend Henry.'

But Lakington had returned to the chair which contained, as he thought, his chief enemy, and was standing beside it with an unholy joy shining on his face.

'And since I have to deal with him later, Captain Drummond, D.S.O., M.C., I may as well deal with you now. Then it will be your friend's turn. I am going to cut the ropes, and carry you, while you're so numbed that you can't move, to the bath. Then I shall drop you in, Captain Drummond, and when, afterwards, you pray for death, I shall mercifully spare your life – for a while.'

He slashed at the ropes behind the chair, and the four men craned forward expectantly.

'There,' snarled Lakington. 'I'm ready for you, you young swine.'

And even as he spoke, the words died away on his lips, and with a dreadful cry he sprang back. For with a dull, heavy thud the body of the dead German Heinrich rolled off the chair and sprawled at his feet.

'My God!' screamed Lakington. 'What has happened? I—I—'

He rushed to the bell and pealed it frantically, and with a smile of joy Hugh watched his frenzied terror. No one came in answer to the ring, and Lakington dashed to the door, only to recoil into the room with a choking noise in his throat. Outside in the hall stood four masked men, each with a revolver pointing at his heart.

'My cue,' muttered Hugh. 'And you understand, fellows, don't you? He's my meat.'

The next moment he had disappeared down the ladder, and the three remaining watchers stared motionless at the grim scene. For Lakington had shut the door and was crouching by the table, his nerve utterly gone. And all the while the puffed, bloated body of the German sprawled on the floor. . .

Slowly the door into the hall opened, and with a scream of fear Lakington sprang back. Standing in the doorway was Hugh Drummond, and his face was grim and merciless.

'You sent for your chauffeur, Henry Lakington,' he remarked quietly. 'I am here.'

'What do you mean?' muttered Lakington thickly.

'I drove you back from Laidley Towers to-night,' said Hugh with a slight smile. 'The proper man was foolish and had to be killed.' He advanced a few steps into the room, and the other shrank back. 'You look frightened, Henry. Can it be that the young swine's wits are, after all, better than yours?'

'What do you want?' gasped Lakington, through dry lips.

'I want you, Henry – just you. Hitherto you've always used gangs of your ruffians against me. Now my gang occupies this house. But I'm not going to use them. It's going to be just – you and I. Stand, up, Henry, stand up – as I have always stood up to you.' He crossed the room and stood in front of the cowering man.

'Take half – take half,' he screamed. 'I've got treasure – I've. . .'

And Drummond hit him a fearful blow on the mouth.

'I shall take all, Henry, to return to their rightful owners. Boys' – he raised his voice – 'carry out these other two, and undo them.'

The four masked men came in, and carried out the two chairs.

'The intimidated rabbit, Henry, and the kindly gentleman you put to guard Miss Benton,' he remarked as the door closed. 'So now we may regard ourselves as being alone. Just you and I. And one of us, Lakington – you devil in human form – is going into that bath.'

'But the bath means death,' shrieked Lakington – 'death in agony.'

'That will be unfortunate for the one who goes in,' said Drummond, taking a step towards him.

'You would murder me?' half sobbed the terrified man.

'No, Lakington; I'm not going to murder you.' A gleam of hope came into the other's eyes. 'But I'm going to fight you in order to decide which of us two ceases to adorn the earth; that is, if your diagnosis of the contents of the bath is correct. What little gleam of pity I might have possessed for you has been completely extinguished by your present exhibition of nauseating cowardice. Fight, you worm, fight; or I'll throw you in!'

And Lakington fought. The sudden complete turning of the tables had for the moment destroyed his nerve; now, at Drummond's words, he recovered himself. There was no mercy on the soldier's face, and in his inmost heart Lakington knew that the end had come. For strong and wiry though he was, he was no match for the other.

Relentlessly he felt himself being forced towards the deadly liquid he had prepared for Drummond, and as the irony of the thing struck him, the sweat broke out on his forehead and he cursed aloud. At last he backed into the edge of the bath and his struggles redoubled. But still there was no mercy on the soldier's face, and he felt himself being forced farther and farther over the liquid until he was only held from falling into it by Drummond's grip on his throat.

Then, just before the grip relaxed and he went under, the soldier spoke once more:

'Henry Lakington,' he said, 'the retribution is just.'

Drummond sprang back, and the liquid closed over the wretched man's head. But only for a second. With a dreadful cry, Lakington leapt out, and even Drummond felt a momentary qualm of pity. For the criminal's clothes were already burnt through to the skin, and his face – or what was left of it – was a shining copper colour. Mad with agony, he dashed to the door, and flung it open. The four men outside, aghast at the spectacle, recoiled and let him through. And the kindly mercy which Lakington had never shown to anyone in his life was given to him at the last.

Blindly he groped his way up the stairs, and as Drummond got to the door the end came. Someone must have put in gear the machinery which worked on the fifth step, or perhaps it was automatic. For suddenly a heavy steel weight revolving on an arm whizzed out from the wall and struck Lakington behind the neck. Without a sound he fell forward and the weight, unchecked, clanged sullenly home. And thus did the invention of which he was proudest break the inventor's own neck. Truly, the retribution was just. . .

'That only leaves Peterson,' remarked the American, coming into the hall at that moment, and lighting a cigar.

'That only leaves Peterson,' agreed Drummond. 'And the girl,' he added as an afterthought.

Chapter 12

In Which the Last Round
Takes Place

I

IT was during the next hour or two that the full value of
Mr Jerome K. Green as an acquisition to the party became
apparent. Certain other preparations in honour of Peterson's
arrival were duly carried out, and then arose the question of
the safe in which the all-important ledger was kept.

'There it is,' said Drummond, pointing to a heavy steel door
flush with the wall, on the opposite side of the room to the
big one containing Lakington's ill-gotten treasure. 'And it
doesn't seem to me that you're going to open that one by
pressing any buttons in the wall.'

'Then, Captain,' drawled the American, 'I guess we'll open
it otherwise. It's sure plumb easy. I've been getting gay with
some of the household effects, and this bar of soap sort of
caught my eye.'

From his pocket he produced some ordinary yellow soap,
and the others glanced at him curiously.

'I'll just give you a little demonstration,' he continued,
'of how our swell cracksmen over the water open safes
when the owners have been so tactless as to remove the keys.'

Dexterously he proceeded to seal up every crack in the safe
door with the soap, leaving a small gap at the top unsealed.
Then round that gap he built what was to all intents and purposes a soap dam.

'If any of you boys,' he remarked to the intent group
around him, 'think of taking this up as a means of livelihood,

be careful of this stuff.' From another pocket he produced an india-rubber bottle. 'Don't drop it on the floor if you want to be measured for your coffin. There'll just be a boot and some bits to bury.'

The group faded away, and the American laughed.

'Might I ask what it is?' murmured Hugh politely from the neighbourhood of the door.

'Sure thing, Captain,' returned the detective, carefully pouring some of the liquid into the soap dam. 'This is what I told you I'd got – gelignite; or, as the boys call it, the oil. It runs right round the cracks of the door inside the soap.' He added a little more, and carefully replaced the stopper in the bottle. 'Now a detonator and a bit of fuse, and I guess we'll leave the room.'

'It reminds one of those dreadful barbarians the Sappers, trying to blow up things,' remarked Toby, stepping with some agility into the garden; and a moment or two later the American joined them.

'It may be necessary to do it again,' he announced, and as he spoke the sound of a dull explosion came from inside the house. 'On the other hand,' he continued, going back into the room and quietly pulling the safe door open, 'it may not. There's your book, Captain.'

He calmly relit his cigar as if safe opening was the most normal undertaking, and Drummond lifted out the heavy ledger and placed it on the table.

'Go out in relays, boys,' he said to the group of men by the door, 'and get your breakfasts. I'm going to be busy for a bit.'

He sat down at the table and began to turn the pages. The American was amusing himself with the faked Chinese cabinet; Toby and Peter sprawled in two chairs, unashamedly snoring. And after a while the detective put down the cabinet, and coming over, sat at Drummond's side.

Every page contained an entry – sometimes half a dozen – of the same type, and as the immensity of the project dawned on the two men their faces grew serious.

'I told you he was a big man, Captain,' remarked the American, leaning back in his chair and looking at the open book through half-closed eyes.

'One can only hope to Heaven that we're in time,' returned Hugh. 'Damn it, man,' he exploded, 'surely the police must know of this!'

The American closed his eyes still more.

'Your English police know most things,' he drawled, 'but you've sort of got some peculiar laws in your country. With us, if we don't like a man – something happens. He kind o' ceases to sit up and take nourishment. But over here, the more scurrilous he is, the more he talks bloodshed and riot, the more constables does he get to guard him from catching cold.'

The soldier frowned.

'Look at this entry here,' he grunted. 'That blighter is a Member of Parliament. What's he getting four payments of a thousand pounds for?'

'Why, surely, to buy some nice warm underclothes with,' grinned the detective. Then he leaned forward and glanced at the name. 'But isn't he some pot in one of your big trade unions?'

'Heaven knows,' grunted Hugh. 'I only saw the blighter once, and then his shirt was dirty.' He turned over a few more pages thoughtfully. 'Why, if these are the sums of money Peterson has blown, the man must have spent a fortune. Two thousand pounds to Ivolsky. Incidentally, that's the bloke who had words with the whatnot on the stairs.'

In silence they continued their study of the book. The whole of England and Scotland had been split up into districts, regulated by population rather than area, and each district appeared to be in charge of one director. A varying number of sub-districts in every main division had each their sub-director and staff, and at some of the names Drummond rubbed his eyes in amazement. Briefly, the duties of every man were outlined: the locality in which his work lay, his

233

exact responsibilities, so that overlapping was reduced to a minimum. In each case the staff was small, the work largely that of organization. But in each district there appeared ten or a dozen names of men who were euphemistically described as lecturers; while at the end of the book there appeared nearly fifty names – both of men and women – who were proudly denoted as first-class general lecturers. And if Drummond had rubbed his eyes at some of the names on the organizing staffs, the first-class general lecturers deprived him of speech.

'Why,' he spluttered after a moment, 'a lot of these people's names are absolute household words in the country. They may be swine – they probably are. Thank God! I've very rarely met any; but they ain't criminals.'

'No more is Peterson,' grinned the American; 'at least not on that book. See here, Captain, it's pretty clear what's happening. In any country today you've got all sorts and conditions of people with more wind than brain. They just can't stop talking, and as yet it's not a criminal offence. Some of 'em believe what they say, like Spindleshanks upstairs; some of 'em don't. And if they don't, it makes 'em worse: they start writing as well. You've got clever men, intellectual men – look at some of those guys in the first-class general lecturers – and they're the worst of the lot. Then you've got another class – the men with the business brain, who think they're getting the sticky end of it, and use the talkers to pull the chestnuts out of the fire for them. And the chestnuts, who are the poor blamed decent working-men, are promptly dropped in the ash-pit to keep 'em quiet. They all want something for nothing, and I guess it can't be done. They all think they're fooling one another, and what's really going on at the moment is that Peterson is fooling the whole bunch. He wants all the strings in his hands, and it looks to me as if he'd got 'em there. He's got the money – and we know where he got it from; he's got the organization – all either red-hot revolutionaries, or intellectual wind-storms, or calculating knaves. He's amalgamated 'em, Captain; and the whole blamed lot, whatever they may think, are really working for him.'

Drummond, thoughtfully, lit a cigarette.

'Working towards a revolution in this country,' he remarked quietly.

'Sure thing,' answered the American. 'And when he brings it off, I guess you won't catch Peterson for dust. He'll pocket the boodle, and the boobs will stew in their own juice. I guessed it in Paris; that book makes it a certainty. But it ain't criminal. In a Court of Law he could swear it was an organization for selling bird-seed.'

For a while Drummond smoked in silence, while the two sleepers shifted uneasily in their chairs. It all seemed so simple in spite of the immensity of the scheme. Like most normal Englishmen, politics and labour disputes had left him cold in the past; but no one who ever glanced at a newspaper could be ignorant of the volcano that had been simmering just beneath the surface for years past.

'Not one in a hundred' – the American's voice broke into his train of thought – 'of the so-called revolutionary leaders in this country are disinterested, Captain. They're out for Number One, and when they've talked the boys into bloody murder, and your existing social system is down-and-out, they'll be the leaders in the new one. That's what they're playing for – power; and when they've got it, God help the men who gave it to 'em.'

Drummond nodded, and lit another cigarette. Odd things he had read recurred to him: trade unions refusing to allow discharged soldiers to join them; the reiterated threats of direct action. And to what end?

A passage in a part of a ledger evidently devoted to extracts from the speeches of the first-class general lecturers caught his eye:

'To me, the big fact of modern life is the war between classes. . . People declare that the method of direct action inside a country will produce a revolution. I agree. . .it involves the creation of an army.'

And beside the cutting was a note by Peterson in red ink: 'An excellent man! Send for protracted tour.'

The note of exclamation appealed to Hugh; he could see the writer's tongue in his cheek as he put it in.

'It involves the creation of an army. . .' The words of an intimidated rabbit came back to his mind. 'The man of stupendous organizing power, who has brought together and welded into one the hundreds of societies similar to mine, who before this have each, on their own, been feebly struggling towards the light. Now we are combined, and our strength is due to him.' In other words, the army was on the road to completion, an army where ninety per cent of the fighters – duped by the remaining ten – would struggle blindly towards a dim, half-understood goal, only to find out too late that the whip of Solomon had been exchanged for the scorpion of his son. . .

'Why can't they be made to understand, Mr Green?' he cried bitterly. 'The working-man – the decent fellow—'

The American thoughtfully picked his teeth.

'Has anyone tried to make 'em understand, Captain? I guess I'm no intellectual guy, but there was a French writer fellow – Victor Hugo – who wrote something that sure hit the nail on the head. I copied it out, for it seemed good to me.' From his pocket-book he produced a slip of paper. '"*The faults of women, children, servants, the weak, the indigent, and the ignorant are the faults of husbands, father, masters, the strong, the rich, and the learned.*" Wal!' he leaned back in his chair, 'there you are. Their proper leaders have sure failed them, so they're running after that bunch of cross-eyed skaters. And sitting here, watching 'em run, and laughing fit to beat the band, is your pal Peterson!'

It was at that moment that the telephone bell rang, and after a slight hesitation Hugh picked up the receiver.

'Very well,' he grunted, after listening for a while, 'I will tell him.'

He replaced the receiver and turned to the American.

'Mr Ditchling will be here for the meeting at two, and Peterson will be late,' he announced slowly.

'What's Ditchling when he's at home?' asked the other.

'One of the so-called leaders,' answered Hugh briefly, turning over the pages of the ledger. 'Here's his dossier, according to Peterson. 'Ditchling, Charles. Good speaker; clever; unscrupulous. Requires big money; worth it. Drinks.'

For a while they stared at the brief summary, and then the American burst into a guffaw of laughter.

'The mistake you've made, Captain, in this country is not giving Peterson a seat in your Cabinet. He'd have the whole caboose eating out of his hand; and if you paid him a few hundred thousand a year, he might run straight and grow pigs as a hobby. . .'

II

It was a couple of hours later that Hugh rang up his rooms in Half Moon Street. From Algy, who spoke to him, he gathered that Phyllis and her father were quite safe, though the latter was suffering in the manner common to the morning after. But he also found out another thing – that Ted Jerningham had just arrived with the hapless Potts in tow, who was apparently sufficiently recovered to talk sense. He was weak still and dazed, but no longer imbecile.

'Tell Ted to bring him down to The Elms at once,' ordered Hugh. 'There's a compatriot of his here, waiting to welcome him with open arms.'

'Potts is coming, Mr Green,' he said, putting down the receiver. 'Our Hiram C. And he's talking sense. It seems to me that we may get a little light thrown on the activities of Mr Hocking and Herr Steinemann, and the other bloke.'

The American nodded slowly.

'Von Gratz,' he said. 'I remember his name now. Steel man. Maybe you're right, Captain, and that he knows something; anyway, I guess Hiram C. Potts and I stick closer than brothers till I restore him to the bosom of his family.'

But Mr Potts, when he did arrive, exhibited no great inclination to stick close to the detective; in fact, he showed the greatest reluctance to enter the house at all. As Algy had said, he was still weak and dazed, and the sight of the place where he had suffered so much produced such an effect on him that for a while Hugh feared he was going to have a relapse. At length, however, he seemed to get back his confidence, and was persuaded to come into the central room.

'It's all right, Mr Potts,' Drummond assured him over and over again. 'Their gang is dispersed, and Lakington is dead. We're all friends here now. You're quite safe. This is Mr Green, who has come over from New York especially to find you and take you back to your family.'

The millionaire stared in silence at the detective, who rolled his cigar round in his mouth.

'That's right, Mr Potts. There's the little old sign.' He threw back his coat, showing the police badge, and the millionaire nodded. 'I guess you've had things humming on the other side, and if it hadn't been for the Captain here and his friends they'd be humming still.'

'I am obliged to you, sir,' said the American, speaking for the first time to Hugh. The words were slow and hesitating, as if he was not quite sure of his speech. 'I seem to remember your face,' he continued, 'as part of the awful nightmare I've suffered the last few days – or is it weeks? I seem to remember having seen you, and you were always kind.'

'That's all over now, Mr Potts,' said Hugh gently. 'You got into the clutches of the most infernal gang of swine, and we've been trying to get you out again.' He looked at him quietly. 'Do you think you can remember enough to tell us what happened at the beginning? Take your time,' he urged. 'There's no hurry.'

The others drew nearer eagerly, and the millionaire passed his hand dazedly over his forehead.

'I was stopping at the Carlton,' he began, 'with Granger, my secretary. I sent him over to Belfast on a shipping deal and—' He paused and looked round the group. 'Where is Granger?' he asked.

'Mr Granger was murdered in Belfast, Mr Potts,' said Drummond quietly, 'by a member of the gang that kidnapped you.'

'Murdered! Jimmy Granger murdered!' He almost cried in his weakness. 'What did the swine want to murder him for?'

'Because they wanted you alone,' explained Hugh. 'Private secretaries ask awkward questions.'

After a while the millionaire recovered his composure, and with many breaks and pauses the slow, disjointed story continued.

'Lakington! That was the name of the man I met at the Carlton. And then there was another. . . Peter. . . Peterson. That's it. We all dined together, I remember, and it was after dinner, in my private sitting-room, that Peterson put up his proposition to me. . . It was a suggestion that he thought would appeal to me as a business man. He said – what was it? – that he could produce a gigantic syndicalist strike in England – revolution, in fact; and that as one of the biggest shipowners – the biggest, in fact – outside this country, I should be able to capture a lot of the British carrying trade. He wanted two hundred and fifty thousand pounds to do it, paid one month after the result was obtained. . . Said there were others in it. . .'

'On that valuation,' interrupted the detective thoughtfully, 'it makes one million pounds sterling,' and Drummond nodded. 'Yes, Mr Potts; and then?'

'I told him,' said the millionaire, 'that he was an infernal scoundrel, and that I'd have nothing whatever to do with such a villianous scheme. And then – almost the last thing I

239

can remember – I saw Peterson look at Lakington. Then they both sprang on me, and I felt something prick my arm. And after that I can't remember anything clearly. Your face, sir' – he turned to Drummond – 'comes to me out of a kind of dream; and yours, too,' he added to Darrell. 'But it was like a long, dreadful nightmare, in which vague things, over which I had no power, kept happening, until I woke up late last night in this gentleman's house.' He bowed to Ted Jerningham, who grinned cheerfully.

'And mighty glad I was to hear you talking sense again, sir,' he remarked. 'Do you mean to say you have no recollection of how you got there?'

'None, sir; none,' answered the millionaire. 'It was just part of the dream.'

'It shows the strength of the drug those swine used on you,' said Drummond grimly. 'You went there in an aeroplane, Mr Potts.'

'An aeroplane!' cried the other in amazement. 'I don't remember it. I've got no recollection of it whatever. There's only one other thing that I can lay hold of, and that's all dim and muzzy. . . Pearls. . . A great rope of pearls. . . I was to sign a paper; and I wouldn't. . . I did once, and then there was a shot, and the light went out, and the paper disappeared. . .'

'It's at my bank at this moment, Mr Potts,' said Hugh; 'I took that paper, or part of it, that night.'

'Did you?' The millionaire looked at him vaguely. 'It was to promise them a million dollars when they had done what they said. . . I remember that. . . And the pearl necklace. . . The Duchess of. . .' He paused and shook his head wearily.

'The Duchess of Lampshire's?' prompted Hugh.

'That's it,' said the other. 'The Duchess of Lampshire's. It was saying that I wanted her pearls, I think, and would ask no questions as to how they were got.'

The detective grunted.

'Wanted to incriminate you properly, did they? Though it seems to me that it was a blamed risky game. There should have been enough money from the other three to run the show without worrying you, when they found you weren't for it.'

'Wait,' said the millionaire, 'that reminds me. Before they assaulted me at the Carlton, they told me the others wouldn't come in unless I did.'

For a while there was silence, broken at length by Hugh.

'Well, Mr Potts, you've had a mouldy time, and I'm very glad it's over. But the person you've got to thank for putting us fellows on to your track is a girl. If it hadn't been for her, I'm afraid you'd still be having nightmares.'

'I would like to see her and thank her,' said the millionaire quickly.

'You shall,' grinned Hugh. 'Come to the wedding; it will be in a fortnight or thereabouts.'

'Wedding!' Mr Potts looked a little vague.

'Yes! Mine and hers. Ghastly proposition, isn't it?'

'The last straw,' remarked Ted Jerningham. 'A more impossible man as a bridegroom would be hard to think of. But in the meantime I pinched half a dozen of the old man's Perrier Jouet 1911 and put 'em in the car. What say you?'

'Say!' snorted Hugh. 'Idiot boy! Does one speak on such occasions?'

And it was so. . . .

III

'What's troubling me,' remarked Hugh later, 'is what to do with Carl and that sweet girl Irma.'

The hour for the meeting was drawing near, and though no one had any idea as to what sort of a meeting it was going to be, it was obvious that Peterson would be one of the happy throng.

'I should say the police might now be allowed a look in,' murmured Darrell mildly. 'You can't have the man lying about the place after you're married.'

'I suppose not,' answered Drummond regretfully. 'And yet it's a dreadful thing to finish a little show like this with the police – if you'll forgive my saying so, Mr Green.'

'Sure thing,' drawled the American. 'But we have our uses, Captain, and I'm inclined to agree with your friend's suggestion. Hand him over along with his book, and they'll sweep up the mess.'

'It would be an outrage to let the scoundrel go,' said the millionaire fiercely. 'The man Lakington you say is dead; there's enough evidence to hang this brute as well. What about my secretary in Belfast?'

But Drummond shook his head.

'I have my doubts, Mr Potts, if you'd be able to bring that home to him. Still, I can quite understand your feeling rattled with the bird.' He rose and stretched himself; then he glanced at his watch. 'It's time you all retired, boys; the party ought to be starting soon. Drift in again with the lads, the instant I ring the bell.'

Left alone Hugh made certain once again that he knew the right combination of studs on the wall to open the big door which concealed the stolen store of treasure – and other things as well; then, lighting a cigarette, he sat down and waited.

The end of the chase was in sight, and he had determined it should be a fitting end, worthy of the chase itself – theatrical, perhaps, but at the same time impressive. Something for the Ditchlings of the party to ponder on in the silent watches of the night. . . Then the police – it would have to be the police, he admitted sorrowfully – and after that, Phyllis.

And he was just on the point of ringing up his flat to tell her that he loved her, when the door opened and a man came in. Hugh recognized him at once as Vallance Nestor, an author of great brilliance – in his own eyes – who had lately devoted himself to the advancement of revolutionary labour.

'Good afternoon,' murmured Drummond affably. 'Mr Peterson will be a little late. I am his private secretary.'

The other nodded and sat down languidly.

'What did you think of my last little effort in the Midlands?' he asked, drawing off his gloves.

'Quite wonderful,' said Hugh. 'A marvellous help to the great Cause.'

Vallance Nestor yawned slightly and closed his eyes, only to open them again as Hugh turned the pages of the ledger on the table.

'What's that?' he demanded.

'This is the book,' replied Drummond carelessly, 'where Mr Peterson records his opinions of the immense value of all his fellow-workers. Most interesting reading.'

'Am I in it?' Vallance Nestor rose with alacrity.

'Why, of course,' answered Drummond. 'Are you not one of the leaders? Here you are.' He pointed with his finger, and then drew back in dismay. 'Dear, dear! There must be some mistake.'

But Vallance Nestor, with a frozen and glassy eye, was staring fascinated at the following choice description of himself:

'Nestor, Vallance. Author – so-called. Hot-air factory, but useful up to a point. Inordinately conceited and a monumental ass. Not fit to be trusted far.'

'What,' he spluttered at length, 'is the meaning of this abominable insult?'

But Hugh, his shoulders shaking slightly, was welcoming the next arrival – a rugged, beetle-browed man, whose face seemed vaguely familiar, but whose name he was unable to place.

'Crofter,' shouted the infuriated author, 'look at this as a description of me.'

And Hugh watched the man, whom he now knew to be one of the extremist members of Parliament, walk over and glance at the book. He saw him conceal a smile, and then Vallance Nestor carried the good work on.

'We'll see what he says about you – impertinent blackguard.'

Rapidly he turned the pages, and Hugh glanced over Crofter's shoulder at the dossier.

He just had time to read: 'Crofter, John. A consummate blackguard. Playing entirely for his own hand. Needs careful watching,' when the subject of the remarks, his face convulsed with fury, spun round and faced him.

'Who wrote that?' he snarled.

'Must have been Mr Peterson,' answered Hugh placidly. 'I see you had five thousand out of him, so perhaps he considers himself privileged. A wonderful judge of character, too,' he murmured, turning away to greet Mr Ditchling, who arrived somewhat opportunely, in company with a thin, pale man – little more than a youth – whose identity completely defeated Drummond.

'My God!' Crofter was livid with rage. 'Me and Peterson will have words this afternoon. Look at this, Ditchling.' On second thoughts he turned over some pages. 'We'll see what this insolent devil has to say about you.'

'Drinks!' Ditchling thumped the table with a heavy fist. 'What the hell does he mean? Say you, Mr Secretary – what's the meaning of this?'

'They represent Mr Peterson's considered opinions of you all,' said Hugh genially. 'Perhaps this other gentleman. . .'

He turned to the pale youth, who stepped forward with a surprised look. He seemed to be not quite clear what had upset the others, but already Nestor had turned up his name.

'Terrance, Victor. A wonderful speaker. Appears really to believe that what he says will benefit the working-man. Consequently very valuable; but indubitably mad.'

'Does he mean to insult us deliberately?' demanded Crofter, his voice still shaking with passion.

'But I don't understand,' said Victor Terrance dazedly. 'Does Mr Peterson not believe in our teachings, too?' He turned slowly and looked at Hugh who shrugged his shoulders.

'He should be here at any moment,' he answered, and as he spoke the door opened and Carl Peterson came in.

'Good afternoon, gentlemen,' he began, and then he saw Hugh. With a look of speechless amazement he stared at the soldier, and for the first time since Hugh had known him his face blanched. Then his eyes fell on the open ledger, and with a dreadful curse he sprang forward. A glance at the faces of the men who stood watching him told him what he wanted to know, and with another oath his hand went to his pocket.

'Take your hand out, Carl Peterson.' Drummond's voice rang through the room, and the archcriminal, looking sullenly up, found himself staring into the muzzle of a revolver. 'Now, sit down at the table – all of you. The meeting is about to commence.'

'Look here,' blustered Crofter, 'I'll have the law on you. . .'

'By all manner of means, Mr John Crofter, consumate blackguard,' answered Hugh calmly. 'But that comes afterwards. Just now – sit down.'

'I'm damned if I will,' roared the other, springing at the soldier. And Peterson, sitting sullenly at the table trying to readjust his thoughts to the sudden blinding certainty that through some extraordinary accident everything had miscarried, never stirred as a half-stunned Member of Parliament crashed to the floor beside him.

'Sit down, I said,' remarked Drummond affably. 'But if you prefer to lie down, it's all the same to me. Are there any more to come, Peterson?'

'No, damn you. Get it over!'

'Right. Throw your gun on the floor.' Drummond picked the weapon up and put it in his pocket; then he rang the bell. 'I had hoped,' he murmured, 'for a larger gathering, but one cannot have everything, can one, Mr Monumental Ass?'

But Vallance Nestor was far too frightened to resent the insult; he could only stare foolishly at the soldier, while he plucked at his collar with a shaking hand. Save to Peterson, who understood, if only dimly, what had happened, the thing had come as such a complete surprise that even the sudden entrance of twenty masked men, who ranged themselves in single rank behind their chairs, failed to stir the meeting. It seemed merely in keeping with what had gone before.

'I shall not detain you long, gentlemen,' began Hugh suavely. 'Your general appearance and the warmth of the weather have combined to produce in me a desire for sleep. But before I hand you over to the care of the sportsmen who stand so patiently behind you, there are one or two remarks I wish to make. Let me say at once that on the subject of Capital and Labour I am supremely ignorant. You will therefore be spared any dissertation on the subject. But from an exhaustive study of the ledger which now lies upon the table, and a fairly intimate knowledge of its author's movements, I and my friends have been put to the inconvenience of treading on you.

'There are many things, we know, which are wrong in this jolly old country of ours; but given time and the right methods I am sufficiently optimistic to believe that they could be put right. That, however, would not suit your book. You dislike the right method, because it leaves all of you much where you were before. Every single one of you – with the sole possible exception of you, Mr Terrance, and you're mad – is playing with revolution for his own ends: to make money out of it – to gain power. . .

'Let us start with Peterson – your leader. How much did you say he demanded, Mr Potts, as the price of revolution?'

With a strangled cry Peterson sprang up as the American millionaire, removing his mask, stepped forward.

'Two hundred and fifty thousand pounds, you swine, was what you asked me.' The millionaire stood confronting his tormentor, who dropped back in his chair with a groan. 'And when I refused, you tortured me. Look at my thumb.'

With a cry of horror the others sitting at the table looked at the mangled flesh, and then at the man who had done it. This, even to their mind, was going too far.

'Then there was the same sum,' continued Drummond, 'to come from Hocking, the American cotton man – half German by birth; Steinemann, the German coal man; von Gratz, the German steel man. Is that not so, Peterson?' It was an arrow at a venture, but it hit the mark, and Peterson nodded.

'So one million pounds was the stake this benefactor of humanity was playing for,' sneered Drummond. 'One million pounds, as the mere price of a nation's life-blood. . . But at any rate he had the merit of playing big, whereas the rest of you scum, and the other beauties so ably catalogued in that book, messed about at his beck and call for packets of bull's-eyes. Perhaps you laboured under the delusion that you were fooling him, but the whole lot of you are so damned crooked that you probably thought of nothing but your own filthy skins.

'Listen to me.' Hugh Drummond's voice took on a deep, commanding ring, and against their will the four men looked at the broad, powerful soldier, whose sincerity shone clear in his face. 'Not by revolutions and direct action will you make this island of ours right – though I am fully aware that that is the last thing you would wish to see happen. But with your brains, and for your own unscrupulous ends, you gull the working-man into believing it. And he, because you can talk with your tongues in your cheeks, is led away. He believes you will give him Utopia; whereas, in reality, you are leading him to hell. And you know it. Evolution is our only chance – not revolution; but you, and others like you, stand to gain more by the latter. . .'

His hand dropped to his side, and he grinned.

'Quite a break for me,' he remarked. 'I'm getting hoarse. I'm now going to hand you four over to the boys. There's an admirable, but somewhat muddy pond outside, and I'm sure you'd like to look for newts. If any of you want to summon me for assault and battery, my name is Drummond – Captain Drummond, of Half Moon Street. But I warn you that that book will be handed in to Scotland Yard to-night. Out with 'em, boys, and give 'em hell. . .'

'And now, Carl Peterson,' he remarked, as the door closed behind the last of the struggling prophets of a new world, 'it's time that you and I settled our little account, isn't it?'

The master-criminal rose and stood facing him. Apparently he had completely recovered himself; the hand with which he lit his cigar was as steady as a rock.

'I congratulate you, Captain Drummond,' he remarked suavely. 'I confess I have no idea how you managed to escape from the somewhat cramped position I left you in last night, or how you have managed to install your own men in this house. But I have even less idea how you discovered about Hocking and the other two.'

Hugh laughed shortly.

'Another time, when you disguise yourself as the Comte de Guy, remember one thing, Carl. For effective concealment it is necessary to change other things beside your face and figure. You must change your mannerisms and unconscious little tricks. No – I won't tell you what it is that gave you away. You can ponder over it in prison.'

'So you mean to hand me over to the police, do you?' said Peterson slowly.

'I see no other course open to me,' replied Drummond. 'It will be quite a *cause célèbre,* and ought to do a lot to edify the public.'

The sudden opening of the door made both men look round. Then Drummond bowed, to conceal a smile.

'Just in time, Miss Irma,' he remarked, 'for settling day.'

The girl swept past him and confronted Peterson.

'What has happened?' she panted. 'The garden is full of people whom I've never seen. And there were two men running down the drive covered with weeds and dripping with water.'

Peterson smiled grimly.

'A slight setback has occurred, my dear. I have made a big mistake – a mistake which has proved fatal. I have under-estimated the ability of Captain Drummond; and as long as I live I shall always regret that I did not kill him the night he went exploring in this house.'

Fearfully the girl faced Drummond; then she turned again to Peterson.

'Where's Henry?' she demanded.

'That again is a point upon which I am profoundly ignorant,' answered Peterson. 'Perhaps Captain Drummond can enlighten us on that also?'

'Yes,' remarked Drummond, 'I can. Henry has had an accident. After I drove him back from the Duchess's last night' – the girl gave a cry, and Peterson steadied her with his arm – 'we had words – dreadful words. And for a long time, Carl, I thought it would be better if you and I had similar words. In fact, I'm not sure even now that it wouldn't be safer in the long run. . .'

'But where is he?' said the girl, through dry lips.

'Where you ought to be, Carl,' answered Hugh grimly. 'Where, sooner or later, you will be.'

He pressed the studs in the niche of the wall, and the door of the big safe swung open slowly. With a scream of terror the girl sank half-fainting on the floor, and even Peterson's cigar dropped on the floor from his nerveless lips. For, hung from the ceiling by two ropes attached to his arms, was the dead body of Henry Lakington. And even as they watched it, it sagged lower, and one of the feet hit sullenly against a beautiful old gold vase. . .

'My God!' muttered Peterson. 'Did you murder him?'

'Oh, no! 'answered Drummond. 'He inadvertently fell into the bath he got ready for me, and then when he ran up the stairs in considerable pain, that interesting mechanical device broke his neck.'

'Shut the door,' screamed the girl; 'I can't stand it.'

She covered her face with her hands, shuddering, while the door swung slowly to again.

'Yes,' remarked Drummond thoughtfully, 'it should be an interesting trial. I shall have such a lot to tell them about the little entertainments here, and all your endearing ways.'

With the big ledger under his arm he crossed the room, and called to some men who were standing outside in the hall; and as the detectives, thoughtfully supplied by Mr Green, entered the central room, he glanced for the last time at Carl Peterson and his daughter. Never had the cigar glowed more evenly between the master-criminal's lips; never had the girl Irma selected a cigarette from her gold and tortoiseshell case with more supreme indifference.

'Goodbye, my ugly one!' she cried, with a charming smile, as two of the men stepped up to her.

'Goodbye,' Hugh bowed, and a tinge of regret showed for a moment in his eyes.

'Not goodbye, Irma.' Carl Peterson removed his cigar, and stared at Drummond steadily. 'Only *au revoir,* my friend; only *au revoir.*'

Epilogue

'I SIMPLY can't believe it, Hugh.' In the lengthening shadows Phyllis moved a little nearer to her husband, who, quite regardless of the publicity of their position, slipped an arm round her waist.

'Can't believe what, darling?' he demanded lazily.

'Why, that all that awful nightmare is over. Lakington dead, and the other two in prison, and us married.'

'They're not actually in jug yet, old thing,' said Hugh. 'And somehow. . .' he broke off and stared thoughtfully at a man sauntering past them. To all appearances he was a casual visitor taking his evening walk along the front of the well-known seaside resort so largely addicted to honeymoon couples. And yet. . .was he? Hugh laughed softly; he'd got suspicion on the brain.

'Don't you think they'll be sent to prison?' cried the girl.

'They may be sent right enough, but whether they arrive or not is a different matter. I don't somehow see Carl picking oakum. It's not his form.'

For a while they were silent, occupied with matters quite foreign to such trifles as Peterson and his daughter.

'Are you glad I answered your advertisement?' inquired Phyllis at length.

'The question is too frivolous to deserve an answer,' remarked her husband severely.

'But you aren't sorry it's over?' she demanded.

'It isn't over, kid; it's just begun.' He smiled at her tenderly. 'Your life and mine. . .isn't it just wonderful?'

And once again the man sauntered past them. But this time he dropped a piece of paper on the path, just at Hugh's feet, and the soldier, with a quick movement which he hardly stopped to analyse, covered it with his shoe. The girl hadn't seen the action; but then, as girls will do after such remarks, she was thinking of other things. Idly Hugh watched the saunterer disappear in the more crowded part of the esplanade, and for a moment there came on to his face a look which, happily for his wife's peace of mind, she failed to notice.

'No,' he said, *à propos* of nothing, 'I don't see the gentleman picking oakum. Let's go and eat, and after dinner I'll run you up to the top of the headland. . .'

With a happy sigh she rose. It *was* just wonderful! and together they strolled back to their hotel. In his pocket was the piece of paper; and who could be sending him messages in such a manner save one man – a man now awaiting his trial?

In the hall he stayed behind to inquire for letters, and a man nodded to him.

'Heard the news?' he inquired.

'No,' said Hugh. 'What's happened?'

'That man Peterson and the girl have got away. No trace of 'em.' Then he looked at Drummond curiously. 'By the way, you had something to do with that show, didn't you?'

'A little,' smiled Hugh. 'Just a little.'

'Police bound to catch 'em again,' continued the other. 'Can't hide yourself these days.'

And once again Hugh smiled, as he drew from his pocket the piece of paper:

'Only *au revoir*, my friend; only *au revoir*.'

He glanced at the words written in Peterson's neat writing, and the smile broadened. Assuredly life was still good; assuredly. . .

'Are you ready for dinner, darling?' Quickly he swung round, and looked at the sweet face of his wife.

'Sure thing, kid,' he grinned. 'Dead sure; I've had the best appetiser the old pot-house can produce.'

'Well, you're very greedy. Where's mine?'

'Effects of bachelordom, old thing. For the moment I forgot you. I'll have another. Waiter – two Martinis.'

And into an ash-tray near by, he dropped a piece of paper torn into a hundred tiny fragments.

'Was that a love-letter?' she demanded with assumed jealousy.

'Not exactly, sweetheart,' he laughed back. 'Not exactly.' And over the glasses their eyes met. 'Here's to hoping, kid; here's to hoping.'

Case Notes

Professor Robert Giddings

Bulldog Drummond – the first, and arguably the best of Sapper's ten Bulldog Drummond thrillers – was published in 1920 to instant acclaim. Subtitled *The Adventures of a Demobilised Officer Who Found Peace Dull*, it had more of an impact than any of the sequels. Nevertheless, Sapper (the pen name of Herman Cyril McNeile) was one of the most successful popular novelists of the period between the two World Wars, and the Bulldog Drummond books brought him public recognition and considerable financial rewards.

Bulldog Drummond launched itself on the crest of a wave of crime thrillers, initiated in England by Edgar Wallace. They broke away from the more gentlemanly detective sleuthing, popular at the turn of the century, to make way for a tougher, more square-jawed hero figure (often with transatlantic overtones), frequently battling against sinister foreigners and unravelling fiendish international conspiracies. Sapper's thrillers were part of a Golden Age of English detective fiction. Alongside the books of writers like John Buchan and Dornford Yates, they fed into the political and social climate of the interwar years.

Like thousands of ex-servicemen returning home in 1918, Captain Hugh 'Bulldog' Drummond, who had served his country so loyally during the First World War, finds civilian life lacking in zest and excitement. He misses the companionship and action of those terrible years of conflict. He longs not simply for adventure, but also to put his life at the service of the country he so dearly loves. When he places the advertisement that begins: 'Demobilised officer, finding peace incredibly tedious, would welcome diversion', we know we are in for something very different. His first assignment initially appears to be a straightforward case of blackmail but develops into something much more complex and dangerous. Having found and rescued a kidnapped millionaire, he begins to unravel an extensive political conspiracy under the criminal mastermind of arch-villain Carl Peterson, against whom he is to pit his wits (and strength) for the next three books.

Drummond, true to type, is well-built, a keen sportsman and inevitably good at boxing. He believes in justice and fair play, is proud to drive a British Bentley and prefers British beer to anything too fancy or exotic. As Colin Watson – who wrote an insightful study of English crime writers, *Snobbery With Violence* – says, the consistency with which Drummond is referred to by his military rank, 'Captain', is more than significant. The rank suggests experience and authority, but is not as Blimpish as Colonel or General would have been, nor so professional and diplomatic as Major. 'In Captain Drummond', Watson says, 'we have a man with exactly the right status to appeal to a generation with a constitutional respect for titles and with minds in which the word 'ex-Service' had attained special emotional lustre to compensate for the drab realties of demobilisation'.

There are those who consider it was only the untimely death in a motorcycle accident of national hero and man of action T. E. Lawrence that prevented his eventually being used as a plenipotentiary envoy to Hitler's Germany. And it has to be acknowledged that the fairly wide appeal of Oswald Mosley's British Union of Fascists dates from the same period and has common cause in the feeling that strong individual action was the way to solve complex political matters.

Bulldog Drummond predated James Bond by thirty-three years, which Ian Fleming gratefully acknowledged. He is part of that quintessential interwar public school elite – patriotic at heart and bordering on the xenophobic, as well as a sophisticated man about town who enjoys London's 'Clubland' and the privileges it bestows. In some ways, he ploughs the familiar field of other Clubland heroes of the time, like Raffles, Nayland Smith, Richard Hannay and several of Agatha Christie's characters, but the added drama comes from the fact that Drummond's antagonists are very much nastier and his pursuit and often violent persecution of them appealed to British xenophobia and anti-Semitism. The hatred the super-villain Carl Peterson generated is not located in any particular nationality. What makes him vile is the fact that he is nasty, sinister and *foreign*. His loyal girl-friend, Irma, is not just a girl who likes to have fun. She is a lubricious vamp.

Drummond frequently finds himself up against evil characters of varying nationalities. Although typical for the period, McNeile's books are, to a modern reader, riddled with jingoism and racism, featuring disparaging references to foreigners (Bolsheviks, Dagos) and in particular to Jews. For McNeile, the Englishman, by virtue of his race and homeland, was simply superior to any other. He was, after all, the bulldog breed. In Richard Usborne's study of neglected English thrillers, *Clubland Heroes*, he notes that Bulldog Drummond: 'favoured straight, rode straight, played straight, lit cigarettes all the time, spoke in jovial "old boy" slang. . . when relaxed, curtly when speaking to cads. His foreigners fought dirty, carried knives, emitted guttural snarls, used thumb screws and little known Asiatic poisons; and their eyes were full of malignant hate.'

Appropriate to the myth that McNeile draws on to make Bulldog Drummond a modern Arthurian knight, the villains Drummond continually has to take on are cunning and formidably clever. In this first adventure, the twisted, intellectual criminal Henry Lakington's supreme brilliance accidentally causes his own death, while the fiendish Peterson escapes from police custody to surface in the next three books.

The historian A. J. P. Taylor considered the great vogue for thrillers of this type was curious though he was reluctant to consider it enlightening, in spite of the new twist:

'The less literate classes had always read thrillers when they read anything. Sexton Blake continued his fortnightly adventures until the outbreak of the Second World War – read by boys in the more educated classes and by adults lower down. Sapper, Dornford Yates and John Buchan provided thrillers at a slightly more sophisticated level, with fine old-fashioned codes of morality merging into dislike of foreigners and Jews. . .'

These xenophobic stereotypes were delineated by Orwell in his essay 'Boys' Weeklies' (1940) and he suggests that in such fiction, foreigners can be classified in much the same way as insects:

'As a rule it is assumed that foreigners of any one race are all alike and will conform more or less exactly to the following patterns:

Frenchman: Excitable. Wears beard, gesticulates wildly.
Spaniard, Mexican, etc.: Sinister, treacherous.
Arab, Afghan, etc.: Sinister, treacherous.
Chinese: Sinister, treacherous. Wears pigtail.
Italian: Excitable. Grinds barrel-organ or carries stiletto.
Swede, Dane, etc.: Kind-hearted, stupid.
Negro: Comic, very faithful.'

Echoes of his world still reverberate. As Ian Fleming himself confided, his James Bond was Sapper from the waist up but Mickey Spillane from below.

'Sapper' was the pseudonym Herman Cyril McNeile adopted while serving as an officer in the Royal Engineers (popularly known as 'sappers') during the First World War. McNeile was born in 1888 in Bodmin, Cornwall. His father was an officer in the Royal Navy and later governor of the Royal Naval Prison at Lewes in East Sussex. McNeile was educated at Cheltenham College and the Royal Military Academy at Woolwich before joining the Royal Engineers in 1907. He served with distinction in the Great War and saw action at both the first and second battle of Ypres. He was awarded the Military Cross and mentioned in dispatches.

Serving officers were not allowed to publish under their own names, so using the pen name 'Sapper' he wrote his first stories, about life in the trenches, for the *Daily Mail*. These vivid and racy wartime action stories, such as *The Lieutenant and Others* (1915); *Sergeant Michael Cassidy R. E.* (1915); *Men, Women and Guns* (1916) and *No Man's Land* (1917), managed to convey all the excitement and exhilaration of war without the boredom and slaughter of life at the front.

Within a year of publication in book form, these stories achieved sales of 200,000 copies. *Daily Mail* proprietor Lord Northcliffe was so impressed by the vividness of the writing that he moved heaven and earth to try and have McNeile released from military service so that he could employ him as a war correspondent. He failed and McNeile continued to serve in the army until 1919 when he resigned, with the rank of lieutenant colonel, and became a full-time writer. The extraordinary success of *Bulldog Drummond* far exceeded that of his previous works and he went on to write – among other things – ten novels featuring his hero.

In 1914, the same year he was promoted to the rank of captain, he had married Violet Baird Douglas, daughter of Lieutenant Colonel Arthur Sholto Douglas of the Cameron Highlanders. They had two sons and lived quietly at King's and Princes' Farm, West Chiltington, near Pulborough, Sussex, where Sapper died in August 1937 at the age of forty-eight.

At the time of his death, he had been working on a stage play, *Bulldog Drummond Again*, with his friend Gerard Fairlie (1899–1983). Fairlie is thought to have been the model for Bulldog Drummond. He was a prolific author and scriptwriter and, like Sapper, was educated at the Royal Military Academy. He was commissioned in the Scots Guards. There was much of Bulldog Drummond about him. He was both an Army boxing champion and member of the British bobsleigh team in France in 1924. After McNeile's death, Fairlie continued the Bulldog Drummond series, and produced seven more books under the Sapper name.

Bulldog Drummond enjoyed an exhilarating afterlife beyond the pages of his books. The first book was adapted for the stage in 1921 and produced, to great acclaim, at the Wyndham's Theatre with Sir Gerald Du Maurier in the lead. The play enjoyed equal success in New York. On the screen (notably in the thirties), Drummond has been played by Jack Buchanan, Ralph Richardson, Ray Milland, John Howard, Ronald Colman and – in the sixties, hot on the heels of Sean Connery's Bond – by Richard Johnson.

A Bulldog Drummond radio serial ran from 1941 to 1954 starring George Coulouris and the Drummond legacy surfaced again in Kim Newman's 1991 short story, *Pitbull Brittan*. The story is a parody of Bulldog Drummond and Britain during the Thatcher years, in which our hero battles against a group of international conspirators responsible for the 1984 miners' strike. Drummond also has a cameo role in Newman's novel *The Bloody Red Baron*. Possibly one of the greatest tributes of all is the fact that in John le Carré's *Tinker Tailor Soldier Spy*, Bulldog (Drummond) is one of the nicknames proposed by Jumbo for former British spy turned teacher Jim Prideaux.

Ian Fleming may have been a world away from Herman Cyril McNeile, but Bond's debt to Drummond is incalculable. As Anthony Lejeune wrote in *The Times* on 18 October 1986:

'Ian Fleming, himself entitled to an Old Etonian tie, knew the reality of secret intelligence, but James Bond, as he said, was an updated version of Bulldog Drummond. Bond's opponents, to begin with, were secret agents of Smersh, an all too real organization for killing enemies of the Soviet Union; but later, on the rather odd grounds that 'one can't go on teasing the Russians', Ian Fleming changed the villains to Spectre, a fantastic body of worldwide criminals. This suited the film-makers, who eschew political villains unless defunct, like the Nazis, or maniacally right-wing.'

That is why, in Sapper's 1920 *Bulldog Drummond*, when we meet the conspirators – le Comte de Guy, Hocking,

Steinemann and von Gratz – dining together at the Hotel Nationale in Berne at the end of December 1918, we seem to have met them before. And perhaps we have, in the world of James Bond. *Spectre* by any other name.

References

Wesley Britton, *Beyond Bond: Spies in Fiction and Film* (2005)
Otto Penzler et al., *Detectionary* (1977)
Richard Usborne, *Clubland Heroes* (1953, rev. edn, 1974)
Colin Watson, *Snobbery With Violence: English Crime Stories and their Audience* (rev. edn, 1979)